More Black People

Kyle Powell

SRL PUBLISHING

More Black People

People

Kyle Powell

SRL Publishing Ltd
London
www.srlpublishing.co.uk

First published worldwide by SRL Publishing in 2024

ISBN: 978-1-915073-33-4

1 3 5 7 9 10 8 6 4 2

A CIP catalogue record for this book is available from the
British Library

SRL Publishing is a Climate Positive publisher offsetting more
carbon emissions than it emits.

To all of my brothers and sisters who are striving to make their way in a system designed to prevent us from flourishing.

Keep going – we are but a step on a long journey.

iv

Preface

'More Black People!' is a satirical look at Diversity and Inclusion (D&I) in the corporate world of today. Following the events of 2020 - George Floyd's murder and the rise of the Black Lives Matter (BLM) movement - race was (temporarily) brought to the forefront of Western consciousness, and, for the first time, fully embraced and engaged with by many White people, including large corporations.

However, despite many well-meaning individuals, there are more selfish and less altruistic motives for some organisations and corporations who have 'taken on' the fight against racism. Many companies view D&I as an opportunity to be perceived in a more positive light; virtue signalling to the world they are an 'ethical' and 'moral' organisation, a 'good place to work', and/or a 'good' place from which to buy goods or services. In reality, there is often little to no genuine care nor commitment to these issues. From a personal perspective, I have worked on multiple D&I teams, across different blue-chip companies, and have seen first-hand how superficial the level of commitment can be. When it comes to putting up dollars to support D&I work, more often than not, they mysteriously cannot be found - despite billions in turnover.

Lack of follow-through

Taking a look at some of the statistics from companies that had made commitments in 2020, to where we are now, we can see there has been an issue with follow through. Companies that would have all benefited from the initial positive traditional and social media attention have not honoured their commitments.

The Creative Investment Research (CIR) conducted a report into resources promised by US companies following George Floyd's death. These resources would be used for everything from transforming their own internal recruiting and inclusion programmes to investing into communities of colour. 67 billion dollars from 271 companies were committed, but only 652 million dollars been disbursed at the start of 2022 (Financial Times).

(Bloomberg) America's top 50 biggest companies had promised to contribute $49.5 billion dollars. It is thought 90% of that amount is allocated as loans or investments that the companies may end up profiting from, with only $4.2 billion dollars pledged as direct grants. Only a small fraction ($70 million) went to organisations dedicated to criminal justice reforms – one of the areas in greatest need of change, considering its impact on the black community.

CIR's Chief Executive has compared businesses making unfulfilled racial equity pledges to companies that market a revolutionary new product to investors, enjoy a rising share price as a result, but never actually deliver the goods.

It's not all bad

While it is true we have a long way to go, there are some examples of companies that appear to be on the right track. Microsoft has shown signs of sustained commitment following their 2020 commitment to racial equality. Microsoft claims it is increasing the amount of business it does with black-owned financial institutions and suppliers.

PayPal has promised to support underserved communities and close the racial wealth gap with $535 million. PayPal claims that, to date, about $500 million of its commitment has been put into action, including $15 million in grants, in partnership with the Association for Enterprise Opportunity, to around 1,400 Black-owned small businesses.

Intel claims to have surpassed its $1 million pledge to support non-profits and community organisations addressing social injustice and promoting anti-racism, by giving $1.2 million in anti-racism and social equity grants to organizations including UNESCO, the Obama Foundation, and the Greater Houston Community Foundation.

Since 2021 Netflix has committed $70 million of its $100 million commitment in deposits into financial institutions that support the Black community.

Back To The Story

I believe we need to have more full and frank discussions about this important issue. We are striving to evolve as a society, but too often progress is impeded by greed, discrimination, and fear. My hope is that this book will prompt people to properly consider the changes they want to see in the world, and how they are honouring the commitments they have made.

Prologue

Opportunity In Misery

The dust had barely settled on the scandalous revelation that senior-level politicians had been involved in the orchestration of the assault on teenager Damon Adebola, and the subsequent riots led by pan-African organisation, African Descent. Pressure for a General Election had been steadily growing across all political parties.

"I'd like to ask the Right Honourable Gentleman, how can we trust those in power to govern with integrity after all that has transpired? The people need to have their voices heard," called a senior Opposition politician.

Jonathan ducked and weaved as he tried to make his way through the crowd of protestors that had congregated outside of the Tube station. "No justice, no peace!" shouted someone with a megaphone. "We need change, we need change!" called the crowd in response. He was unaware why there was so much uproar and commotion. He just wanted to get to his gran's and was already late. By the time he arrived she was sitting comfortably sipping on a tea and looking at a newspaper.

"Sorry I'm late," he said as he leaned in for a kiss. "There were all these protestors outside the station from the Damon Adebola inquest. They've caused delays on the Tube, too."

"Mi know, mi know, it in the paper, too. All dis stress and summin over the African Descent ting. The riots and protest is dangerous. People fi get hurt."

"I know. I don't get it, if I'm honest. Sometimes I feel like I should be closer to this stuff," Jonathan admitted.

"You need to stay away from trouble. It don't concern you, ya hear?"

Jonathan wanted to challenge, but accepted the tone, a tone he was used to hearing growing up, a tone that said this was not a discussion. "How are you, Gran?" he said, changing the topic.

"You know, mi good," she replied with a small cough.

"Good. As long as they're looking after my favourite person. So we getting the cards out, some Black Jack?"

"You want a beating so early?" she laughed. "But wait, tell mi first, you find someone yet?"

"Gran, you know I work hard. There isn't much time for that stuff."

"How you mean 'that stuff'? Love? Love is life. It is why we are here, not those games and cartoons."

"Gran," he pleaded, hoping for a reprieve, but he knew she was right: what was more important than love? The truth was he had been trying, a bit at least. Jonathan was self-aware enough to know he wasn't the archetypal attractive male. His qualities were more subtle and nuanced. He wasn't the type to be in the bar on a Friday night, but the digital approach wasn't bearing much fruit either. After some coercion, he'd downloaded pretty much all the apps, uploaded his *best* pics, but failed to generate much interest. It seemed the Jourdan Dunns of the world didn't have much interest or time for a man of his disposition. "So, Black Jack time?"

"Ok, get di cards dem."

***

The results from the Inertia internal survey were in and, to Deborah's relief, they were marginally better than the previous year. She had her tea ready, calendar blocked and was ready to interrogate the findings. The annual anonymous questionnaire gave staff the opportunity to share their thoughts and feelings about the company's environment and performance. Were people clear about and happy with the strategic direction of the organisation? Did they feel heard and valued? Did they believe they had appropriate opportunities for development and career fulfilment? And did the company provide a culturally progressive environment? Most of the questions were on a scale of 1 to 10, but there were a few which had free text options for more detailed feedback. The real reason Deborah was so happy with the results was because she would be able to share the outcome with the executive committee and hopefully use it as leverage for her own promotion to the committee. She played around with the Power Point, trying to figure out the best way to present the findings. *Do I need to highlight the year-on-year improvement?* As she fiddled, she took a look at some of the more detailed feedback provided. She noticed a couple of comments that she had not registered in prior years: "It would be good to see more diversity throughout the organisation. We need to recognise and educate on issues of D&I." *What is D&I?*. She sipped her tea.

***

"Sir, we have the report for you."

"Just leave it on the desk," he said as he scrolled

through the evening news updates. The growing public discontent and political in-fighting was becoming more vehement. He opened the report and flicked through the detailed profiles, each accompanied by a photo. He read and re-read the profiles before stopping on one for closer inspection. He studied this image. There was a level of charisma that could be detected from the photo alone; his academics were stellar, upbringing well-suited and choice of partner perfect. "This is our man," he said to himself, rewarding himself with a sip of whisky.

Part 1

Chapter 1

Media Mayhem

Calvin James, CJ to some, sat back in his chair and turned his head to the ceiling, away from his flash cards, an aid to learning his speech. "Opportunity for the people... long overdue change... for far too long..." he said in a mumble, focusing on his key words, trying his best to get his story straight.

The door burst open. "Mr James, they're ready for you," Colleen the short, spotty, party aide spat out in exhausted fashion.

She must have sprinted all the way here. The ministerial support seemed to be getting younger and younger by the day.

It was time. This speech could change his life forever; perhaps even change the country. He took a deep breath, brought himself to his feet, and checked his phone one last time. It was filled with alerts, messages and reminders, but still no message from her. The aide held the door open as Calvin slowly left the room. He knew he should have been excited; he'd worked his entire career for this moment, but for some reason, it felt more like he was walking to his own execution.

In the auditorium the crowd bustled with enthusiasm. He made his way up a short staircase that led onto the stage and to a lectern covered in microphones. Calvin adjusted his suit jacket one last time before turning to look out towards the audience; he found it hard to see much past the first couple of rows as bright lights. He was able make out some friendly faces up front, all giving him warm and encouraging smiles, but there was a noticeable spare seat – his wife had stayed true to her word and not attended.

***

A few rows back, just beyond the harsh façade of the cameras' lights, Andy Dewsberry and Dale Cummings lay in wait. Andy was five foot eight and a half, nine on a good day, with thinning mousey brown hair. He had a slim build with a pot belly, which he'd noticed was growing at a worrying rate in recent years. Dale stood slightly shorter at five foot six, naturally more portly than his compatriot, with a similar hair issue but a balding crown. They sat with itchy feet awaiting their moment.

"What's the signal again?" Dale whispered eagerly to Andy.

Andy rolled his eyes in frustration. They'd been over this at least a dozen times in the last twenty-four hours alone. "When he says it's time for questions, I throw the eggs and you run up there and show your t-shirt, right?" Andy explained tersely.

Dale considered the steps carefully, going through the plan *again*. "So we ask questions, then you throw the eggs and I show the t-shirt?"

Andy's temper was rising. Things were risky enough already, and Dale's incompetence wasn't any help. "Why would we ask?!" He paused, trying to compose himself with some deep breaths, index finger massaging the tension from his forehead. "When I tell you, you go and

10

show the shirt, okay?"

"Ok, Andy, relax. I'm nervous, you know."

"We're all bloody nerv-!" He stopped himself again. "Alright, Dale, it'll be fine."

***

"Thank you for making the time today, everyone. I'll try my best to keep this short and sweet… the way my grandmother used to describe me," Calvin began, garnering some chuckles from the audience. Shadow Chancellor James was naturally charismatic, funny without trying, coupled with a keen intellect. It was evident why he was tipped for public office at an early age. Some went even further, earmarking him as a leadership candidate.

"I know there have been rumours. Many may have expected this announcement sooner. I apologise for making my supporters wait. But I would like to take this opportunity to formally announce my challenge for party leadership – better late than never, I guess – as my wife said to me in Santorini in response to my apparently tardy proposal." The announcement was met with thunderous applause from the crowd, along with hearty laughter. Calvin continued to lay out his plan for the party, outlining the key changes he hoped to make, and how they would benefit not only the party, but also the country.

Before long it was time for questions. Andy stooped to unzip his backpack, retrieving the eggs. He looked at Dale, who was staring blankly back at him. Andy mouthed the words 'Go now' as he stood and began to hurl the eggs at the stage. Dale quickly made his way down the side of the crowd and up towards the stage. The first couple of eggs barely made it to their target but generated enough commotion to throw Calvin off his responses.

People looked around as murmurs and questioning erupted. "What's going on?" someone shouted. Security were whispering into their collars when an egg crashed against Calvin's chest, yolk dripping down his royal blue suit. Seconds later he was rushed off stage.

Almost at the same time, Dale made it to the front of the stage, ready to unveil his t-shirt and shout the slogan, when he was harshly spiked by one of the larger members of the security team. The rugby tackle sent him flying like a child's stuffed toy. The wind was completely taken from him. He gasped dramatically, unsure if he would ever breathe again. He'd never felt anything like this. Andy had also been accosted by security. The pair were ushered out of sight backstage as Andy shouted, "Not in our country! Not while the NBF is here!"

Dale could barely walk, let alone contribute to the shouting.

***

Backstage, Calvin was in a state of shock, "What the fuck was that?" he asked Colleen, the only other member of his team present. She stayed silent, unsure of the exact words to convey her mix of frustration and sympathy. "I thought the audience was supposed to be vetted. I get enough of this shit online. I don't need it at my own leadership announcement." Calvin was not naïve to the state of play. This type of backlash was par for the course for a person of colour in the political sphere; however, despite his ever-thickening skin, he still experienced moments of fragility.

"Is there anything I can do, Sir?" she offered.

"No, no, I'll be fine," he replied, regaining his

composure. Colleen quietly exited the room, reading that some privacy would be appreciated.

He searched his phone, still no messages. His frustration grew again. *I need a drink.* "Colleen!" he called, ready to request some whisky. But to no avail: he was alone.

***

Jonathan was having his now customary late lunch; swept up again in perfecting a set of logo design options for his new account. He reached for his all-terrain zip-up fleece, knowing the air-conditioning in the cafeteria would be on its usual high setting. He studied his frayed cuffs, reluctantly acknowledging it was probably time for a replacement. Shuffling quickly to the lift, he hoped he wouldn't have to wait too long. As he approached the lift door, he saw Jenna and Charlotte from Research and Insights engaged in a deep and passionate conversation; well, passionate from Charlotte's side at least, as she tended to be. From what he could hear, they were talking about Charlotte's latest failed dating experience.

Jonathan tried to stop himself from staring at Jenna, a skill he was yet to master. Something told him he was at little risk of getting caught; someone like her would never register someone like him. Despite having worked at the same company for several years, he was transfixed once again by her beauty, seeing her as if it was the first time. He could never understand why she was such good friends with Charlotte. They seemed to be so different - at least, different to the version of Jenna he'd dreamt up.

The lift arrived. Charlotte pushed past Jonathan as if he wasn't there: treatment he was used to by now. Jenna held back, allowing him to go first. Jonathan of course returned the offer, insisting she went ahead. The pair continued their conversation, leaving Jonathan to return to his thoughts. He looked down at his shoes, suddenly self-conscious about his appearance in such close proximity to someone like her who was not only beautiful, but also polite.

"I said: no way darlin. You want to get my goodies, you gotta take me somewhere that is at least £100 a head, right?" Charlotte said vigorously. "These boys these days, I don't know what to tell ya."

Jenna nodded in passive agreement, clearly not sharing Charlotte's passion for the princess treatment.

***

It was late by the time Jonathan arrived home, at least late for him as someone who rarely rushed back, comfortable with the consistent glow of his workstation. He put a couple of ready meals in the fridge and made his way to his bedroom desk to fire up his computer for the evening. Most people would not regard Jonathan as someone who was living life to the fullest, but for him it was plenty. The majority of his friends were digital, and he was at peace in his own company… as long as he had access to a computer or his sketch pad, sometimes even the happy medium of both that his tablet afforded him.

He thought about his to do list for the coming day as the computer's processor whirred into life, itself unknowingly preparing for another evening of Medi-evil Quest. Medi-evil Quest was a popular online Role Player Game for those in the know. Jonathan was an avid player, having worked his way up to a Level 26 Grand Wizard. His phone buzzed to life as the game booted up. He'd received a text from Kevin, letting him know the rest of the group were ready to start the game. As he joined, he could see the group chat had been bustling with activity for about fifteen minutes already, waiting for his arrival. Headset on, Jonathan began the evening's quest.

The group were about 45 minutes in when a news alert appeared in the bottom corner of his screen. Only half-reading the small text box, he registered that Scotland Yard were investigating an attempted assault on an MP - the attack thought to be racially motivated. Jonathan returned his full attention to the game, and before long it was almost two in the morning. A couple of his team mates were logging off for bed. His growing yawns were an indication that it was best to follow suit.

Showered and teeth brushed, he lay in bed trying to nod off, but for some reason he was not tired. He thought about how to optimise some of the tasks he had going on in the office, yet his mind kept drifting to the news alert from earlier in the evening. This was unusual for Jonathan; he was someone who had never developed a passion for equality. He tried to doze off, tossing and turning in bed but, before he knew it, his alarm was going off and the sunlight was piercing through his bedroom window.

***

Deborah Tate quickly ran up the entrance steps to the Inertia offices; frappuccino in one hand, bright Chanel bag in the other. Inertia, the advertising and communications agency, was based in the heart of London's West End, the offices occupying three floors of a stately old building. It had the type of grandeur that had been essential during the hedonistic heyday of advertising in the eighties and early nineties, but now had become a cumbersome expense for the once titan of industry. The company had been acquired a few years earlier by a large

US-based conglomerate, with Deborah getting promoted to Managing Director of UK operations. Her meeting with the Executive Committee would begin shortly, and she could not afford to be late. She sensed her opportunity for promotion to the Committee was nearing; maybe today would be the day for the good news.

The lift slowly scaled the building as she glanced at her watch for the third time in the last two minutes, happy she would have time for one last make-up check before the online call began. She had taken the large conference room for the meeting. She was pleased with the early start as it meant fewer people would be milling around the office, less chance of people seeing the board members on the big screen, which normally triggered questions from the nosier employees. She was the first to join, just the way she liked it. Not long passed before the rest of the committee arrived. There was some informal chit chat, and then it was time to get down to business.

"Debbie, thanks for making time. We know it's early for you guys," Arnold Johansson, the CEO, said with his trademark southern drawl. Deborah accepted this was the level of commitment needed to succeed and make it to the top.

"No problem at all. Early bird gets the worm, after all," she replied in her formal yet saccharine voice. For some reason that she never quite understood, her voice would become higher and more regal when speaking to her US bosses; nerves, she suspected.

"Deborah, we wanted to thank you for all of your dedication to the company over the years. You really are a shining light for the entire business," he said effusively, as he sipped a take-out coffee.

A smile beamed across her face: *maybe this really is the day.*

16

"Deb, I gotta be straight with you, if that's ok?" he asked rhetorically.

"Of course, sir," she replied.

"Our global numbers are soft... and, while you guys in the UK have been roughly on target, we need to do more across the business."

She nodded along, not sure how concerned she should be.

"If we don't hit our targets for the year, we're going to have to make some lay-offs and, of course, we don't want that."

Deborah was really beginning to worry now. Perhaps her job was at risk. Take her off the payroll, an efficient cut-back.

"Deb, our Global Insights team has looked into our public perception figures and we're not performing well. As you would expect, it's the same lefty PC bull-crap, but apparently our executive board is accused of being 'Pale, Male, and Stale'". This comment triggered a spree of giggling from the other board members. "We don't have enough people of colour in senior positions," he finished, rolling his eyes and waving his hands in the air to indicate that the assertion was ridiculous. "So, Deb, we're going to have push on 'inclusivity'" he said, making air quotes. A fellow board member leaned towards Arnold and whispered something in his ear. "Yep, sorry, *diversity* too... *Diversity and Inclusion*. The great thing is it's now a constant hot topic. There's always some kid getting shot or something. Even over there, you guys have your issues. I keep hearing about the MP those far-right nutjobs are trying to kill, so there's always something to play off. Ultimately, we need to be seen to be playing ball and upping our numbers. I need you to take the lead from the UK end and make sure we are seen to be being more... *Diverse*."

Deborah struggled to take it all in. She hadn't engaged with any of the coverage around that MP. She felt the media must have been dramatising events. "Right, Sir, well of course that's important, and we do already have a couple of—"

"No, it's not enough. We need more and it needs to be clear to everyone, internally and externally, that we are *Diverse and Inclusive.*" Air quotes were employed again for emphasis. "I'm going to get Genene from HR to set up a one-to-one to brief you on the details of the strategy, ok?"

She nodded deferentially in response.

"Perfect, you're a superstar! We'll check in again soon," he finished and the various committee members dropped off the call. When the call ended, Deborah sat in silence, mildly stunned, and slightly irritated the call didn't deliver the news she had hoped for. *They must trust me… that's something,* she thought, trying to make the best of the situation.

***

Jonathan arrived early to work, as he typically did, keen to settle in before the hustle and bustle of the 9:00 throng. By the time the majority of the company arrived, he would be deep into his work for the day. As Jonathan made his way to the desk, he was surprised to see Deborah in the conference room, seemingly deep in thought, pen on lips and eyes staring into the distance. The sound of steps brought her back to reality. She cast a broad smile his way, coupled with a healthy wave. *Strange.* Deborah had never acknowledged him in the past, not unless there was an urgent request for a last-minute design, and he certainly had never received such a keen greeting. Jonathan shot an uneasy, swift wave back, quickly hurrying to his desk.

***

Deborah tilted back in her chair and continued to think. She was struggling to remember the name of the design grunt she'd just enthusiastically waved to. The penny was slowly starting to drop: she realised she would have to get to know him much better.

Chapter 2

Keep Up

Dale and Andy were sitting in the corner of the St George pub, slowly nursing their pints. Robbo was due to arrive any minute now and they still hadn't come up with a valid reason for why the plan had failed so badly. Dale stared out of the window, distracted by an interesting puppy that was chasing after a Twix wrapper. Meanwhile, Andy stared at Dale with his usual mix of frustration and annoyance. "Dale... Dale!" he said loudly, but Dale was in another world.

Andy hit him hard on the shoulder. "Ow!" Dale shouted, more surprised than hurt.

"Get your head out your ass. What are we gonna tell Robbo?"

"I don't know, we can say the security was on to us or summin," Dale replied, shrugging his shoulders.

"On to us or summin?" Andy said with growing annoyance, hitting him again. He took a long swig of his larger to try to calm his nerves. But his mind continued to race. They couldn't afford another fuck up or they would be kicked out of the group entirely and then where would they be? Totally alone, totally worthless.

Bawdy George, one of the pub's oldest patrons, was asking a young barmaid to turn the television up as the afternoon's football matches were finishing and he was keen to check his accy. The additional noise did nothing to ease Andy's tension. At that moment the side entrance of the pub flew open. The boys couldn't see who was coming in but the energy change in the air confirmed it was Robbo. He walked past the two at an easy pace that carried both authority and determination with it: as if he always needed to be somewhere important. He cast his eyes at the pair and then straight ahead, enough of a gesture to get the guys to follow him hurriedly. They knew the drill: keep pace, but also maintain a respectful distance, and always, always, wait to be invited into his office. They made their way to the back of the pub, down the corridor with the bathrooms, and predictably had the office door slammed in their faces. Dale motioned to open the door, only to be met with a firm slap across the arm from Andy. "Wait, remember?"

After a few angst-filled minutes, they received the signal to enter. The office was packed with boxes, filled with different random items. A shimmer of light squeezed in through a small window above Robbo's desk. His office was never a place you wanted to find yourself. Robbo had his head down scribbling something in one of his dozens of famed note books. Despite his intimidating size, he was no fool; except perhaps when it came to trusting Andy and Dale.

"Come on then, what the fuck appened?" he asked firmly, slapping the A4 note pad with one hand, triggering a tsunami of dust to shoot into the air. The pair looked at one another, neither wanting to speak, but Andy knew, as always, he'd have to take the lead; knowing it would be safer for the both of them if he did.

"Thing is, Gaffer… well…" Andy began.

"Well, what? Get on with it," Robbo replied tersely.

Andy looked down at his shoes. Dale's head was

already cast down, not to be moving any time soon.

"We had a problem—"

Robbo interrupted again, "I know you had fuckin problem, the whole country knows you had a fuckin problem. I want to know what appened? When you told me it was sorted."

Andy's palms were sweaty. No matter what he said, he knew survival would be solely dependent on Robbo's mercy, nothing else.

"Gaffer, we fucked up, it was my fault, I gave Dale the wrong instructions and…" Andy said quickly, silently praying for a way out.

Robbo put his head in his hands. He knew Andy was lying, covering for his pal. The dishonesty irked him, but he respected Andy's seemingly inexhaustible loyalty to what could only be described as a complete liability in the poor excuse for a man that was Dale Cummings. "I should ave you both, you know that right?"

The room fell silent, for a moment. Dale had been in deep, silent prayer since the start of the meeting. He knew this was the moment of judgment. Which way would Caesar's thumb go?

"Gaffer, if you just give us another chance, I promise…" Andy pleaded.

"Don't fuckin Gaffer me. You're making us look like a right bunch of pricks! We're supposed to be showing this country that we're better than the fuckin darkies and queers, and you fuck wits can't carry out a simple plan!"

Andy looked at the floor again and waited.

"Go on, fuck off! I'm sick of the pair of you. On my life, you two cunts have one more chance – fuck up again, and I swear I'll dig your holes myself," he exclaimed.

"Thanks Gaff—" Dale piped up.

"FUCK!! OFF!!!" Robbo bellowed.

22

The pair took the hint and their stay of execution, and scuttled out of the office as quickly as they could. Dale's hand slipped on the door knob from all the nervous sweat. Andy clipped him around his ear, barged him out the way and forced the door open. They hurried away down the corridor, too terrified to remember to shut the office door.

"Fuckin alf-wits!" Robbo said in exasperation at the open door, as he turned his head to the heavens for strength.

***

Jenna sat quietly on the edge of a cafeteria bench, and carefully read her fourth article on the attempted egging at the party leadership announcement. Her heart rate began to rise, and beads of sweat slowly formed on her brow upon reading the victim's name. Trying her best to remain composed, not wanting to drawn any attention, she refocused on the article. The spate of racial hate crimes driven by the National Britain's First, or NBF, organisation did little to surprise Jenna, but she was still disappointed. She'd never believed the rhetoric that society was in a 'post-racial' era, irrespective of the number of MPs of colour elected; or the self-proclaimed assertion the UK was the most racially progressive country in Europe. She was determined not to care about the MP who was attacked. It being easier to believe he was more concerned with his own individual life progression than the improvement of Black people. However, she realised the attacks were indicative of the state of play, that there were still many out there who did not feel the need to hide their hatred; more so, were prepared to act on it.

Jonathan grabbed a cheese sandwich and headed to

the till, he caught sight of Jenna out of the corner of his eye. He thought about sitting with her, before pulling out at the last minute, opting for a simple 'Hello' instead. The prospect of trying to strike up an engaging conversation while simultaneously eating his lunch was too big for today.

Jenna gave him a passive wave in return for his hello, as she slowly grazed on her salad. *At least these guys were honest*, she thought. They lived their truth, out in the open; far better than those who lived behind fake smiles and contrived compliments. Jenna had lost count of the times she'd had to pretend to be thrilled with a 'your hair is so nice, is it all yours?' or, worse still, 'can I touch it?' But she understood the rules of the game; to not rock the boat, to get along, lest she be tarnished with the brush of the dreaded *angry Black woman*.

"There you are!" a voice from behind called. It was Charlotte. "I was looking everywhere for you. Didn't you see my messages? I'll grab some food. I've had a day!" Charlotte unloaded like a machine gun on fully automatic. She had appeared, splurged, and disappeared to the sandwich fridge, all before Jenna could utter a word. Jenna would occasionally question her friendship with Charlotte. They were different in many ways, but she was authentic, she didn't sugar coat anything, and Jenna respected that. She was also one of the few people to make an effort to make friends with Jenna when she first joined. Jenna felt like Charlotte saw her for her: no colour, or moniker of identification, just Jenna. It also helped that the only requirement of friendship with Charlotte was to listen. This was attractive to the more introverted Jenna – if talking had been an Olympic sport, Charlotte would be a gold medallist.

Charlotte returned as quickly as she left. "They never have anything good here. I tell you we need to start going out for lunch, get a cheeky Nando's or something!" she offered with her trademark cackle. Jenna smiled and nodded in agreement. "So, you know Mark from finance?" Charlotte continued at her usual rapid pace. "I've asked the guy for a simple breakdown of the Morris account and, I swear to you, all through the conversation he would not stop staring at my tits!" Charlie's candour made Jenna spit some couscous out of her mouth. She thought she should be used to her by now, but there were still moments when her directness surprised her. Charlie continued as if there weren't sprinklings of couscous salad everywhere. "I told him: Mark, I don't care how senior you are, keep your eyes up here, or I'll poke em out," she finished with in a fit of laughter.

***

Deborah was squeezed into a seventies-style egg-shaped chair in one of the small hub rooms, preparing for her meeting with Genene. As she wriggled for comfort, she struggled to remember why she'd signed off on the purchase of the 'cool' yet impractical seats. The hubs held no more than two, and, health measures considered, were better for just one. Deborah was an intelligent woman. She had to be to get to where she was in life. At a push, she considered herself more 'traditional' with a small 't' rather than 'Old School'. She came from a time when people brought themselves up via their own *boot straps*. There wasn't all this complaining that the younger generations seemed to be obsessed with. But she was still in-touch with the youth. As a young girl, she remembered hearing stories of the war and the countless lives lost at the hands of the Nazis, those who had given everything to save the world. But Deborah was also astute. She acknowledged that, in this world, it was not all about hard work, it was about towing the line, and while it annoyed her, if the party line was Diversity and Inclusion, then so be it.

She pulled out her pocket mirror from her make-up bag and checked her light lipstick. Deborah had long been programmed that a woman's appearance was as important, even more important, than what she had to say, even if she was speaking with another woman. She caught the crow's feet that seemed to be deepening and spreading from the corner of her eyes and quickly closed the mirror in response to her aging reflection. *Time to dial in*, she thought, hitting the join button on her laptop.

Genene's face filled the screen, on the call ahead of schedule. This was an unsettling start for Deborah who was used to being the first on a call; the power dynamic was already out of her favour. Genene had short cropped, dyed bleach blonde hair; she was filled with trademark bright, bubbly, Californian enthusiasm.

"Hi Debbie!" she announced vigorously.

Deborah naturally wanted to match her energy but wasn't sure if she had it in her, "Hello, Genene. How are you?"

"Amazing of course, and yourself?"

"Superb!" Deborah fired back, more loudly than intended.

"Right, so Deb, let's get down to it. We're going to be embarking on an exciting journey of Diversity and Inclusion. I'm so happy to be on this journey with you! How familiar are you with D&I?"

Deborah froze, trying to process the question. "Sorry, what is D&I?" she asked sheepishly.

Genene was shocked by the question. "Diversity and Inclusion."

"Of course, of course. I was joking. Had you going, didn't I?" Deborah said, attempting to laugh off the awkward moment.

"D&I is so important to our company. It's pivotal to the strategic direction of the organisation, and we want to ensure that all of our people know that. As you have been honoured with the task of rolling out this direction in the UK, we wanted to make sure you're prepared to complete this important task."

Deborah nodded along.

"I have a few simple questions for you to help pressure test where you are in this key area. Nothing to worry about," Genene said with a twee smile. Deborah felt there was plenty to worry about.

"Question 1: You need to select a candidate for a recruitment campaign, it is important that the candidate is representative of our company culture, do you choose:

A – A straight White male
B – A straight White female
C – A Black man
D – A Gay woman
E – A differently abled person."

Deborah considered the question carefully, she wasn't sure what E actually meant. She tried to remember the wording. *Representative,* she thought. Her mind flicked through the members of staff. "Well, if it's representative, I guess A," she answered, figuring that made the most sense.

There was a pause while Genene thought about her response. "You see, Deb, the image we want to portray to the world is one of openness and welcoming. I'm sure you can understand how a straight White man doesn't suggest that?"

Deborah knew she was supposed to agree with this statement but did not fully understand why. She had spent her whole career catering to straight White men… that was the bulk of her job. How could things have changed so much?

"Mmhmm," was the best she could muster.

"Let's try another," Genene said with renewed optimism. "Question 2. An employee comes to you with a complaint about a racial remark made by another employee. What do you do?"

Deborah's years of man-management experience kicked in, "Well, I get them both into my office and we get to the bottom of what has taken place." The look on Genene's face made her feel less hopeful about her answer.

"That's… good… but not quite what we're looking for. In our organisation, we want to make it clear that there is no place for racism, so what we would expect is swift and clear action against that perpetrator."

"But—" Deborah attempted to chime in.

"No buts, Debby, that's the environment we would like to create. Final question: you have two qualified candidates going for a position. One is from a minority background and the other is Caucasian. What things would you consider when making a decision?"

Deborah's confidence was low at this point. She didn't trust her gut, but was starting to pick up on the message. "The minority?" she said slowly, with a distinct mix of unease and uncertainty.

"Yes… but it's not completely straight forward. It also depends on the level of role that is being applied for. If it is a senior role, we need to take more consideration into the choice of candidate."

"Ah ha," Deborah replied, quite confused, but attempting to signify that she had fully comprehended the message. Deborah could tell she hadn't impressed; she decided to try and connect, woman to woman. "This

28

stuff is all a bit silly, isn't it? Especially for people like us, right? We're trying to break the glass ceiling. We know how hard it is, right?"

Genene stared blankly. "So, Debbie, this has been very illuminating for me. I think I have all I need to prepare my report for Mr. Johansson. We'll be in touch shortly," she said as she waved happily and closed the call. Deborah couldn't help but feel that Genene was trying to escape the disaster zone as quickly as possible. She really had work to do.

***

Jonathan was tapping away at his keyboard, thinking about what his team could achieve on tonight's quest, while also trying to recall when the next episode of *Narisha* (one of his favourite Anime shows) was coming out. His thought pattern was broken by Jenna walking past the Design corner on her way to the kitchen area; he swore he could smell her floral tones, even though she was several metres away. She gave him a little smile, as she sometimes would; he returned the gesture with much more enthusiasm, raising her a wave. She appeared to look away quickly, perhaps in embarrassment. Jonathan chastised himself for making her feel uneasy.

Freddy, one of Jonathan's fellow design geeks watched the entire incident unfurl. He was a heavy-set man who enjoyed a tight-fitting t-shirt, usually with a retro eighties logo stamped across it. Freddy had little regard for the smart-casual dress code. He was chewing on a Bic pen, preparing to share his unsolicited advice. "Mate, you gotta relax. Girls want to feel like they're lucky to have your attention, not that they are entitled to it," he finished, saliva now trickling down the side of his mouth. Freddy had an opinion on everything, but loved to talk about women, particularly all his success with women, usually from his travel to warmer, more developing countries.

Jonathan didn't disagree with his advice on this occasion, but still found it hard to take guidance on how to engage with women from someone he suspected hadn't had much real-life experience with the fairer sex that didn't stem from a financial transaction. He replied begrudgingly, "I guess so, Freddy."

Jonathan was still working on a design when Deborah walked up to his desk. "Hi everyone. Hi Jonathan, how are you doing?" she asked.

Jonathan was sure she wasn't talking to him, even though she'd used his name. He instinctively looked around, but everyone in the Design farm was looking at him. Freddy was giving him a piercing stare, imploring him to reply. "Hi... Hello... boss, Deborah, Mrs Tate," he uttered in mumbled, nervous fashion. "I'm well, thanks, and you?"

"Good, good," she replied with a broad smile, practically showing each one of her well-polished, shiny white teeth, "Well, just wanted to check in. Keep up the good work." She continued towards the kitchen.

"What the fuck was that?" Freddy asked, wanting to know why she had come over and also why Jonathan had lost his faculty for language.

Jonathan was still in a state of shock. "I don't know... you know, the weirdest thing happened the other day. I was in early, and she was in a meeting room. She gave me a huge wave. Eight years I've worked here, and she's never uttered a word. Now in the space of a week she's made two big efforts to engage with me."

"Maybe it's that new aftershave you've got on, mate! You just need to find one that Jenna likes!" Freddy said with a deep laugh that seemed to reverberate through his desk.

Jonathan wanted to be happy about the new found acknowledgement, but he couldn't shake the feeling that something was off.

Jonathan's Journal -15th

I know it's hard for people to acknowledge unless they're staring right at me, but I am Black. Sometimes I catch her looking at me, the proverbial head cocked to side look, assessing whether or not I actually am. I want to tell her it's not my fault, I was raised the way I was raised; that if I could change I would. Maybe it's in my head, she's not said this to me, it's just a feeling. I've walked in on her in the kitchen with Charlotte. You know when you know they've been having girl talk? My entrance changes the energy from flirty to sympathetic, and that's how I know.

Chapter 3

DFS

Dale and Andy sank into Dale's mum's ancient DFS sofa; a sofa that was once a second runner-up prize from a magazine contest. Despite its decrepit state, the sofa kept pride of place in Angie's, Dale's mum's, heart. *Countdown* played quietly on the telly, as the pair silently licked their wounds, while also counting their blessings that they made it out of the meeting at all. Andy expected a message would come in soon about the next mission, a mission he knew they couldn't afford to mess up.

"Do you boys want some tea?" Angie called in from the kitchen. There was a part of Angie that loved having her son around. Dale would always be her little boy, irrespective of the fact he was practically forty. But there was another part of her that wanted him to get out on his own, gain some independence. *I won't be around forever*, she thought, *but at least he's got Andy*. In typical fashion, Dale looked at Andy for guidance. Andy returned the enquiring look with a half-nudge/half-shrug that seemed to indicate acceptance of the offer. "Yes, Mum."

"Ok, Squishy, I'll bring it through in a bit," she said. Dale hated his nickname, which derived from his puppy fat as a baby, but his mum had kept hold of it his entire life.

Dale and Andy, like many of the men in the area, had found much more time to catch up with day time telly since the Ford factory closed about eight years earlier. Senior management had promised new roles would be found, that a new site would be built, but instead a location in Asia was chosen as the destination for reinvestment. 1,000s were left jobless, many of whom had only ever known factory life and lacked discernible transferable skills for other forms of employment.

Many of the men felt they shouldn't *have* to learn new skills. They were proud of what they had to offer. They actually built tangible things that people needed.

It was the country, and the stupid government that were wrong; driving the economy away from manufacturing and towards services and finances. The fallout for many of these now dilapidated labour towns was life on the dole and other benefits. Wandering from the pub to the bookie's and back again, a large collective of vulnerable men, ripe to listen to a narrative of victimhood and scapegoating. This, unfortunately, is how Andy, Dale, and many of the other former factory workers, fell in to the grateful arms of the NBF.

Before long Angie had appeared with the food; fish fingers, over-cooked oven chips, baked beans, and some lemonade. "Here you are boys, enjoy," she said warmly.

"Ta, Mum," Dale said.

"Cheers, Miss A," Andy followed.

A day of worrying and stress had made the guys hungry. Dale powered through his mum's cooking like it was his last meal. Andy was a bit more measured as he attempted to answer some of the questions on the quiz show while he ate. They were munching away contently when Andy's phone buzzed; it was a message from Robbo. They were summoned to attend the working men's club later that evening. While Dale happily continued to power through his tea, Andy had a sudden loss of appetite.

***

Deborah read the e-mail for a third time, trying her best to put a positive spin on the situation. She was an optimistic person, but even with her levels of optimism, she couldn't sugar-coat this pill. The e-mail was from Genene in HR, copying in the CEO, Mr Johansson, informing her that there would be a Diversity and Inclusion 'Sprint-Refresher' session for her and her Senior team to help ensure they reached the required standards to implement the D&I strategy across the organisation. This was the *pleasant* corporate way of saying that she was not yet up to scratch and required external help. Deborah would have to break the news to her team, rally the troops; *all part of the day in the life of a people leader*, she thought.

***

Jonathan returned from the kitchen with a round of teas. Jessie liked his very milky, while Elaine was like Freddy, preferring plenty of sugar. Jonathan didn't like his too strong, because he was caffeine sensitive and had enough trouble sleeping as it was.

The gang was gathered around someone's phone, captivated by a video. Jonathan announced the arrival of the tea, but was only met with outstretched arms as they remained focused on the screen. "What are you guys watching?" he asked.

"Shhh," Elaine said. "This is the funny bit."

Jonathan peered over Elaine's shoulder to catch a glimpse of the screen. It was a video of a group of men wearing NBF t-shirts burning an effigy; the dummy, mostly made of straw, was pretty much engulfed in flames, but Jonathan could make out the brown colouring on the dummy and he joined the dots.

"Watch, watch. The twats covered it in brown varnish!" Elaine exclaimed as the dummy fell on top of one of the NBF members, lighting his shirt on fire. The other men panicked and ran for water, and the video failed to give the threatening visage of masculinity that was intended. "These guys are such idiots!" she said, as the entire group burst into laughter.

"Racist bigots often are," Jessie said.

Charlie, another member of the senior team, walked past the farm and gave a disapproving look to the huddled group; it was enough to drive everyone back to their workstations. The NBF logo triggered Jonathan's memory of the MP story he'd seen the other night. He was aware the far-right group had been growing in influence in recent years, but in honesty hadn't taken much notice. They were clearly deluded people, and despite their racist rhetoric, he never felt threatened. It wasn't that Jonathan failed to identify with his race, it was more that, as a self-professed geek, he was used to being ignored by everyone, White, Black, and all in-between. It was only other fellow Geeks, irrespective of race, gamers, and Anime fans who had ever given him the time of day... those were his people.

***

The match had started by the time they arrived. The pair knew Robbo wouldn't want to talk until half-time, so this gave them a decent amount of time to collect themselves. A group of lads were gathered around the big screen, sat on fold-out metal chairs, watching Millburn take on

Chechester FC. Millburn were already 1-0 down after only ten minutes, to the displeasure of the keenly watching lads.

"These fuckin defenders haven't got a clue, fuckin fairies the lot of em," Alan offered.

"Just put a challenge in. It's a 50/50 and he's bottled it," another reflected on the mistake a defender made that led to the goal.

"It's not that, it's fuckin concentration levels! That's the thing with those lot. All muscle, no brains, fuckin gorillas the lot of em!" One of the tribe said, the rest of the boys grumbled in agreement.

Andy ordered two bottles of the cheapest larger that was already heavily discounted for the former factory workers. Dale was focused on the football when Andy handed him his beer. "Forget the fuckin game, mate. We gotta be switched on for this meeting. This is our last fuckin chance."

"Yeah, alright, I know. I'm focused," Dale responded.

Andy found it hard to believe that Dale had ever focused on much in his life. As Dale was pleading his case, a roar came from across the room. Millburn had equalised on the stroke of half-time. Dale turned away from Andy towards the noise and the replay of the goal.

"Get in!" screamed Alan, standing in celebration. "I tell you, that boy is rapid. They can't deal with him. Fuckin love it!" he gushed in renewed adoration for the young Black striker.

"Dale!" Andy called, trying to get his compatriot back to the matter at hand.

"Huh?" Dale replied, keeping half an eye on the screen.

"Dale!" Andy said again firmly, this time slapping his hand down on the bar, getting his full attention.

36

"Yeah, Andy," he replied innocently. At that moment, the bar phone rang. Jeff the bartender waddled over to answer. He nodded a couple of times before replacing the receiver.

"Go on, he's ready for you," he said.

The time had come, the pair trudged down the corridor towards Robbo's office. Andy knocked twice on the door and waited; Dale stood closely behind. Sweat began to form on the brows of the men as the seconds moved slowly.

"Come in," a deep voice instructed. They entered slowly.

"Alright, Robbo?" Andy began brightly.

"Shut it!" Robbo fired back.

Andy dipped his head in response. Dale followed suit.

"It's time for you pair of drips to make up for that mess the other day."

The pair listened closely.

"Now, I know you guys are footy fans so you're going to enjoy this one…"

***

Deborah was still reeling from her poor performance with HR. She knew, if she wanted to be promoted, she needed to do better to impress the executive committee. She sat in her study and pondered her situation. Deborah was used to succeeding. She was highly driven, motivated and, by all standards, had achieved a lot, particularly climbing the ranks at a time when women had few opportunities in the workplace. Her eyes tracked across her desk to a collection of family photos: her daughter, parents, former Prime Minister Margaret Thatcher, and even one of her ex-husband. Her mind went back to their final argument; him picking up and leaving half-way through dinner because 'he couldn't do it anymore'. She had sacrificed so much to make it to the top, and now she was being told there was another hurdle to overcome. *Where was D&I in my day?* she wondered.

Deborah opened her browser in search of topics to help her become more informed on a world that seemed to have become Diverse and Inclusive without her knowing. Trying to figure out what to look for, Deborah realised she had no clue where to start. For the first time in her life, she wished she was more social media savvy, then she'd have a constant beat on what was going on. More traditional media was the best she could go with. She typed in 'BBC' and clicked the website. The top story was about the upcoming Budget. She browsed the page and clicked on the UK section. There was more on the budget. Then a Black face caught her attention. The man was Calvin James, MP, who had recently survived a egg vandalism attack, supposedly carried out by the NBF. Considering the context of a politician being attacked, she knew this was big news she should be well aware of, but the story wasn't covered in much detail. She decided to head to her daughter's room for some tutoring. Despite all Deborah's attempts to dissuade her from becoming too caught up in social media and app life, she would now need modern expertise like never before.

The physical resemblance between Meghan and Deborah was striking, but in terms of values and beliefs they were worlds apart. Meghan was in many ways the archetypal Gen Z-er: informed, committed, and passionate about all forms of social justice, from environment to issues of identity. Ashamedly, Deborah had learned to tune out whenever Meghan began one of her rants about plastic in the ocean or the lack of diverse representation in the media.

She knocked gently on her daughter's bedroom door, knowing the ultimate sin was to enter without permission. There was no response. She knocked again more firmly: nothing. Deborah slowly opened the door and peered her head inside. "Sweetie?"

Meghan spun around on her wheely chair, hurriedly closing her laptop all in one motion. "Mum!" she shouted. "What did I tell you about coming into my room unannounced!"

"I knocked, but you've always got those headphones on," Deborah pleaded. Meghan rolled her eyes in frustration. "I've got a favour to ask, if you've got a few minutes for your mum," she said in an attempt at emotional blackmail.

"I'm kinda busy right now, what is it?"

"I wanted to know if you could direct me to some sources for different… people… different cultures…"

Meghan returned a confused look, as if her mother was speaking a different language. The lack of conviction in the request made her even harder to understand. "We're doing this Diversity project at work and I need to…"

Her daughter cut her off with a laugh. "Diversity project? You mean Diversity, Equity, and Inclusion, D E & I?" she said in a slightly condescending tone.

"Yep, that stuff. I need to brush up… things have a changed a bit since I was young," Deborah conceded.

"It's got nothing to do with age. It's about making the world a better, fairer place and correcting past mistakes." But Meghan could see her mum was struggling, and a pang of sympathy hit her. She had to admit it was nice to hear her mum finally take an interest in this sort of thing. "Ok, I'll send you some links. Can I get back to my work now?"

"Thanks, Button… oh and anything you can tell me

about this Calvin James chap, all the stuff that's been happening with him, that would be great," she squeezed in, realising her daughter's patience was wearing thin.

"You mean the harassment and assault of our potential first Black Prime Minister?" Meghan said in patronising fashion.

In truth, Deborah was unsure, but guessed that was what she was after; she nodded in agreement.

"Ok, now get out!"

"I'm going, I'm going, don't get your knickers in a twist," Deborah said with a laugh.

The digital efficiency of her daughter and her generation never ceased to amaze Deborah. Meghan had sent her multiple links before she made it back down the hall to her study.

She sat back in her plush leather office chair and opened the first link. She was taken to a site called SPICE, a page dedicated to key news topics and issues of the day. The author had written a feature length exposé on the growing under-belly of far-right nationalism in the UK, making reference to the same trend happening across Europe and beyond. The article centred around NBF's ongoing campaign of harassment focused on Minister Calvin James, or CJ as he was affectionally known. According to the group's messaging, Calvin James was a clear representation of what was wrong with the country and how the native Englishmen of Anglo-Saxon descent were losing control of their once Great nation. Deborah was slightly surprised people like this were still around and that they were so open. She knew she wasn't the most progressive person in the world, but presumed everyone had accepted that racism was wrong. The story detailed Calvin's humble beginnings on a South London estate, and how he had climbed the political ladder at an unprecedented rate to now be considered as a genuine potential candidate for Labour party leadership. There was also mention of how his taxing career had put strain on his marriage. After tying the knot with his childhood sweetheart, Calvin was positioned as the poster boy for progression in the UK by many on both sides of the political aisle. His charismatic personality and intelligence enabled him to charm members of the media and public alike. His bright smile and amiable nature seemingly put people at ease. However, there were some reservations from members of the Black community who felt he had not been vocal enough on issues of race, particularly the harassment endured by many young Black boys up and down the country. *An interesting man*, Deborah admitted.

She clicked another link, this time to a social media platform she couldn't pronounce. The video explained the importance of giving people the freedom to identify how they chose and the appropriate use of pronouns. There was an example of some of the most commonly used pronouns in current circulation, noting the list was not exhaustive. Deborah struggled to fathom how 'They/Them' could possibly work in reference to an individual person. Her head began to hurt.

She decided on one last link. The video opened; it was an animation. A cartoon squirrel explained how lack of representation could lead to negative perceptions of minorities and uninformed decision making. Deborah suspected this was created for people not long out of primary school and was likely a slight dig from her daughter at her current level of knowledge on the subject. Despite the subtext, she enjoyed the characters' antics and storytelling. "The next time you think negatively about someone from a different background, think about why that might be. Maybe you've developed an unconscious bias," the squirrel said with a wink.

41

She considered the story about Calvin James and reflected on how it made her feel.

***

Dale trotted slowly down the high street as he headed home. It was late and the road was quiet. Sadly, Dale knew that even during the day things wouldn't be very different. He stopped at what used to be his favourite sweet shop as a kid. Mr Saj would always give the kids a hard time for spending too long looking at the magazines but would also be kind enough to let them off if they were a few pennies shy on a chocolate bar or some crisps. It was all boarded up now, like so many of the shops on the street. The thought saddened him, a sadness that transformed into frustration when he thought about the speeches Robbo would give about all the immigrants to blame for the problems with the economy, the lack of good schools, NHS waiting lists and the rest. Dale had never heard anyone speak like Robbo; he was so convincing, so passionate. He thought about the social club, filled to the brim with his pals from the factory, everyone connected, sharing the same pain, and Robbo and the NBF offering a solution. But some of the things they said, the things they were doing, they had hurt people like Mr Saj. And he knew Mr Saj wouldn't hurt him: *how could it be right?*

***

Deborah hadn't slept well following her crash course in Diversity and Inclusion, but she knew it was time to be a leader and put on a show for her team.

"Well, that's what I told her: if she wanted a shot, she needed to stop whining and get on board," Deborah said with pomp to Trish, her secretary. She turned to face the door as her leadership team began to enter the room. Deborah checked her watch. To her annoyance, they were already a few minutes late. "Come on, come on, better late than never, I suppose."

Charlie, Rachel, and Edward feigned laughter in response to their boss's joke, as was customary in Deb's leadership team. "Alright, troops, we have an important item to discuss. It has come to the attention of myself and Trish," she nodded knowingly towards Trish, and Trish beamed brightly with the public acknowledgement. "It has become clear that we have not done enough to create a diverse environment in our company..." She paused for dramatic effect and to give her audience an opportunity to praise her virtuous revelation. There was little response, Charlie barely following along, Edward missing the message and Rachel unconvinced by what she deemed to be virtue signalling. Deb continued, "Not only is it the right thing to do for society, it is the right thing for our company. By nurturing diverse talent and new ways of thinking, we can foster a real innovation engine," she finished with aplomb, as if she'd rediscovered the wheel. Her declaration was met with immediate silence. Trish looked around awkwardly, beginning a desperate round of applause that was slowly picked up by the other team members.

Deborah proceeded to temper the timid applause with calming hand gestures, as if the rapturous ovation had already gone on for several minutes. The group happily obliged, with Trish once again left clapping alone. "To ensure *you* are all up to speed with this important topic," Deborah stressed the 'you', as if she were a long-term expert in the area, "and to ensure that we can effectively push the company into the future, we'll be holding a senior team workshop to help us develop a strategy," she finished with a big smile.

Charlie rolled his eyes. He was not impressed. To him, this was no more than Leftist pandering; a growing PC ideology that sought to target him and men like him.

Trish chimed in, "I'll check the calendars and put something in shortly. This is a top priority for us... now," she finished somewhat awkwardly.

Deborah was keen to end the meeting before any difficult questions came her way. *I can spend the time running up to the next meeting doing further research.*

But Rachel wanted some more clarification: "Deb, I just had a quick thought, if I may..."

"No, Rachel, there'll be plenty of time for that when we have our workshop. Go and brush up on your Tik-Toking and Insta-booking to make sure you're as Woke as possible," Deb replied, looking anxiously at Trish to help close the meeting. Deborah stood and headed for the door in an attempt to trigger the others to also move.

Trish gathered some papers. "Come on, everyone, we've all got work to do."

***

By the time Jenna arrived home from work, her younger sister, Yami, was already playing music in the kitchen. As was usually the case when she cooked, Yami's genre of choice was Afrobeats – loudly. She sang along as she prepared the food; way too much noise for Jenna's arrival to be noticed. Their dad had only allowed Yami to move out on condition she lived with Jenna and that Jenna was fully responsible for Yami; a responsibility she didn't always relish, but always honoured.

Jenna dropped her bag and coat on her bed, before sitting down to kick-off her shoes. She knew she'd have to head downstairs soon to make sure Yami did not get distracted and burn the rice, as she often would. However, she felt she needed to take a moment to collect herself before beginning the evening. She lay back across her mattress, legs swinging off the edge of the bed, like she used to when she was little. Jenna thought about her life. She could be accused of overthinking at times but, more than anything, she wanted to make the best decisions she could for herself and her loved ones. Was she in the right job? At the right company? Would she meet someone soon? When would she start a family? Did she really want one? These questions, and more, washed over her as she rested her eyes for a moment.

Yami thought she heard a sound. She checked the watch on her phone, determined not to get distracted by all the notifications luring her in. It was after six: Jenna would be home soon. Or maybe she was here already. It wasn't unlike Jenna to surprise her in the kitchen. She decided to shout up just in case. "Jay!" she called, before realising she'd have to be much louder or turn down the music; she went for louder.

Upstairs, Jenna heard a muffled cry. That was her cue to head down for dinner.

Yami could sense her sister was quieter than normal. She hoped everything was ok, but she had some key updates to share, which couldn't wait. "Sis, I know it's not really your thing and you're all work, business and saving the world or whatever, but I've bought us tickets to this Afro day brunch! It's gonna be all food, tunes and fine *fine* Yoruba men... maybe even a couple Yardies – just pure vibes!" Jenna opened her mouth to respond– "And before you say you're too busy or try and find some excuse, I won't take no for an answer. I see how hard you're working, and you need a little fun in your life. God knows when the last time was that there was a man in your room!" She gave a cheeky laugh, as she could see her sister was less than impressed with the observation. "That's how we work, remember? You do all the serious stuff and I provide the fun balance," she finished with her sweetest most guilt-trippy smile.

Jenna knew her sister was right, she did need a break, and, if it was a day thing, it would mean she could get to bed at a decent time and not lose the next day. She smiled back at her sis in agreement. There was one other reason; one she could barely admit to herself, let alone vocalise, and that was: she always welcomed a distraction from him.

"Yes! You're going to love it," Yami squealed enthusiastically. "I'm going to start picking outfits, or maybe I need something new! I've got a baby-t that would look great on you!"

Jenna was already beginning to regret her decision.

***

Jonathan was power walking home, repeatedly checking the time on his smart watch as he paced. If he was quick, he could get in two episodes of *Narisha* before logging on for the evening's adventure. The microwave pinged as the first episode was about half way through. He rushed to collect his meal: a soup tagliatelle that didn't much resemble the picture on the box. Jonathan eased the gloopy pasta out of the plastic basin and onto his plate; he quietly slurped and chewed as he watched the episode for what was at least the fifth time. One of the benefits of re-watching old shows, aside from the comfort and nostalgia, was the opportunity it gave Jonathan's mind to wonder and consider other things. Typically, this would be thoughts of new designs, Jenna, or battle strategies for Medi-Evil Quest. But this evening was different: he couldn't shake thoughts of his boss. Not only was she

46

being uncharacteristically friendly, but she also now wanted to meet with him – what about? He had no clue.

***

The day had arrived for the senior team's Diversity and Inclusion workshop, which was received with mixed reactions among the group. In typical fashion Trisha was enthusiastic and energetic, Charlie maintained his surly cynicism, Rachel was sceptical but hopeful and Edward was more interested in getting back on the Tennis court. Deborah took a moment to steel herself as she introduced Alicia, a diminutive West African woman with long braids, each capped with colourful beads. Deborah gave a Trish a nod to indicate the start of the meeting. Trish responded as expected. "Quiet down now, everyone, we're ready to begin," she said, placing an exaggerated finger to her lips as if she were a primary school teacher.

Deborah took over. "It's my great pleasure to introduce, Miss… Mrs…?" Deborah glanced uncertainly at Alicia.

"Miss is fine," Alicia replied.

"Miss Alicia Acoot… Acooty," Deborah tripped over the vowels.

"Acoate," Alicia corrected, as she stood to greet the room. She glanced towards Deborah with a look that suggested she should take a seat.

Deborah ignored the hint and powered through. "She is here to help us with our Diversity and Inclusion strategy, although many of us of course are already well-versed in this area," giving herself a metaphorical pat on the back for her limited pre-work.

"Hello everyone, and thank you so much, Deborah, for inviting me here today to help with your Diversity

Equity and Inclusion strategy," Alicia declared warmly.

Charlie responded with a distinctly audible yawn for effect, clearly demonstrating what he thought of this entire initiative.

But Alicia was seasoned. The disruptive and potentially entitled white male employee would not throw her off so easily. "So, I've been *invited* here today to help you guys with some important work that will be *critical* to the future direction of your business. I've worked with many companies, large and small, across a variety of sectors, and, I can assure you, you are all in safe hands."

Rachel gave a warm smile in support for their guest.

Deborah was on edge, keen to share her two cents, uncomfortable with not being in control of a meeting for longer than five minutes. "That's right, spot-on, this is critical, so everyone better pay attention," she stated emphatically. Alicia glanced her way in slight surprise at the interruption.

"So, to kick things off we're going to start with a quick icebreaker. I have cards with everyone's names on. You will be given a card with someone else's name on and you will guess that person's favourite colour. You will have to explain why you have chosen that colour – everyone got it?" Alicia was met with low energy nods.

Deborah couldn't resist the urge to contribute: "I've done stuff like this in the past and it's great because we will get to know–"

She was interrupted by a critical look from Alicia. The group commenced the task. After a few minutes, it was time to share feedback.

"Ok, Charlie, let's start with you," Alicia said, determined to show she was ready for any obstructive behaviour he may have in stock. Charlie looked unimpressed that he'd been called upon and that he even had to partake in the game. "I got Trish." Trish responded with an excited smile. "And yeah, I went for pink." He threw the name card on the table in front of him dismissively.

"And why did you go for pink?" Alicia asked, ensuring he wouldn't get off lightly.

"Because… because… she's girly… or is that not the *woke* term? Maybe 'feminine' is better," he responded in air quotes.

Deborah shot him a harsh look that told him he needed to play ball. "I think what Charlie means–" she began.

"I suspect Charlie knows what he means," Alicia responded, cutting her short.

As Trish was named, she was next up. "I had Edward. I went for white… because it just seemed to fit with him." She seemed less sure of her answer than when she began to give it.

"I hadn't thought too much about it, but that kind of makes sense," Edward conceded with a smile.

Alicia was slightly concerned with the response but didn't want to derail the exercise with a tangential discussion. "Ok, Edward, your turn."

"Right, so I've got Rachel," he began with the slightly smarmy smile that posh guys seem to have without trying. "I've gone with purple, because she's strong and stormy," he said in an attempted compliment. Rachel rolled her eyes, knowing the underlying intention behind the compliment was not genuine.

"No, mine is actually green. Geniuses pick green!" Rachel said, quoting the line from the film *Meet the Parents*.

Alicia checked her watch, realising the game had run on longer than planned. She was keen to get to the real work. "I think you guys are all warmed up, so let's get down to business."

The next session began with a short presentation where Alicia explained the value provided by creating a more Diverse and Inclusive organisation. The presentation was peppered with comments from Deborah, usually repeating what Alicia had stated, using slightly different words. Trish, as always, was on hand to support and affirm all of Deborah's remarks. Charlie continued to yawn and stare off into the distance, while Rachel was becoming more enthused by the prospect of actually effecting some positive change.

The next task was to develop a Bold Ambition that their subsequent strategy would work towards achieving. They were split into pairs to craft a one sentence ambition they had to present back to the group. Deborah and Trisha teamed up as always. Rachel was stuck with the tough choice of Charlie or Edward. She decided to go with Edward. That left Alicia to pair up with Charlie; a situation neither was particularly happy with.

Rachel's passion for the subject was nicely balanced with Edward's ambivalence and Charlie's distain, meaning she could easily take control of the task. "I think we need to articulate the importance of creating an open and inclusive working environment where everyone can truly be themselves and feel valued."

Edward nodded in response, finding it hard to imagine how anyone could not feel included or valued.

Charlie and Alicia were finding the task more difficult, or at least Charlie was making the task more difficult. "I don't see why it's needed. Isn't society doing enough to accommodate all these made-up groups of people?" he asked in frustration.

"That may be your opinion, Charlie, but we're here today to try and create something that will improve your company."

"I'm sorry, I just don't see how any of this will

improve anything. You say it's inclusive, but I bet guys like me are left out," Charlie said in defiance at the apparent exclusion of the White male from all things progressive.

Alicia sighed. "Yes, everyone will benefit from this, hopefully, but some people's attention is being focused on certain groups now because they have been neglected for too long."

"So why don't you ask them? What do I know about being a *minority*?"

"It's about creating something that everyone feels a part of, that everyone can get behind," she said in exasperation.

Deborah and Trisha were faring better, with Deborah asserting her new found knowledge in an attempt to educate Trisha. "You see, the thing is we need to ensure that we create a *culture* and environment that is accommodating of everyone, *despite* their differences," she stated grandly, as she tried her best to remember the Wikipedia page on inclusion she'd read earlier.

Trisha nodded along enthusiastically, even though she had never heard Deborah speak this way about people from different backgrounds; Deborah knew best and that's what mattered most.

Before long it was time to move on to the strategic section. There was a quick bathroom break and time for coffees. Charlie felt like he would need a flask of Espresso if he was going to make it through the rest of the day. Rachel made a beeline for Alicia, who was busy queuing up the slides for the next session. "Hi there, I wanted to say it's so great to have you here. I've been pushing Deborah and the team for work like this for years, but never managed to get any traction." She rolled her eyes.

"I'm happy to have your support, it really helps with

the transition process. There are usually some people on the team who find the... *adjustment*... difficult," Alicia responded, casting her eyes quickly towards Charlie, while still somewhat distracted by an issue with her slides.

Rachel got the message. "Exactly."

"Ok, time to get back to it, everyone," Alicia called, summoning them back to their seats.

"In this session, we're going to identify the strategic priorities needed to achieve our Bold Ambition. Which groups do we need to focus on and what do we want to achieve with them?"

In typical fashion, Deborah felt compelled to add her two cents. "That's right, Alicia," she began as she rose from her seat, splitting the attention of the room. "This is all about honing in on who we need to support, so we can really bring our vision to life." She finished with a warm smile in Alicia's direction, suggesting her comment added real value to the discussion.

Alicia returned a confused look at what was at best a redundant statement. "Ok, let's start the discussion. I'll capture thoughts on the white board."

The group looked around at one another, unsure what to say first.

Deborah felt as leader it would be best if she began. "Well, of course, it's important to focus on colo–" She caught herself: this wasn't the correct term. "People of colo–" She stopped again, almost choking on the word. She guessed again, "Minorities."

Trisha agreed, "Yep, definitely minorities."

Charlie looked decidedly unimpressed; Edward maintained a visage of neutrality.

Rachel wanted to chime in, but she was slightly uneasy. "I think... I think we also need to think about women, and also the LGBTQIA+ community."

"The what?" Edward splurged out in response to the

lengthy acronym.

"Yes, most definitely, the L-G-P-B-Q-I-M-+ community are important too," Deborah stated, determined to show her broad awareness and sensitivity.

"Can't forget the +," Trisha added in agreement with Deborah, as the two nodded together.

"And Women! Let's not forget ourselves," Deborah said with a sarcastic laugh that Trisha echoed heartily.

Alicia scribbled away, noting down the groups mentioned.

"I guess there's no place for White men in this New World Order?" Charlie asked sarcastically. The room fell silent at his frosty tone.

"There's room for all, that's the point," Alicia offered.

Charlie snorted in derision. "Yeah, I bet there is."

Alicia refused to take the bait. "So which groups would you want to prioritise and what do we want to achieve with each?"

The team spent some time attempting to agree on focus areas, but it was difficult; how can you say one group is more important than another? By the end of the session, they had a very rough plan. Alicia suggested they form a dedicated D&I team, including employees from the groups they sought to represent to be in charge of activities and further iron out their plans. She also promised to send through some additional resources to help them along the way. They ended with warm goodbyes. Even Charlie managed to force a smile, although it wasn't clear if that was driven more by the day's work coming to a close than anything else.

***

Across the city, Calvin sat in a dimly lit meeting room

with his communications manager and a couple of Senior party members. Calvin was disgruntled, still upset that a major moment in his career had been tarnished.

"Mr James, our report shows the vast majority of the public feels you handled the incident with grace; it may actually have been a good thing," the comms specialist said.

Calvin wasn't convinced. "I looked like a fool. At my own leadership announcement they made me look ridiculous!"

"CJ, it's really not so bad. The more these guys come after you, the more it shows the country needs *someone like you* to make a change," one of the senior officials said coolly from the corner of the room.

"Someone *like* me, or *me*, Bill?" Calvin returned in frustration.

"Not this again, CJ, you know there's nobody like you; you're the only man who can bring this election home for us."

"Tell my wife that, she still won't return any of my calls or texts."

"Flo will get over it, they always do. My wife was the same. Remember, you have an opportunity to make history. Think about all those young Black boys and girls up and down the country who could be looking up to you as Britain's first Black prime minister," he asserted.

Calvin hated the way people would use his race as a means of manipulation. He also disliked being called CJ by anybody who wasn't either a close friend or family member, but he had to respect the chain of command. Bill had been a guiding hand throughout his career. He knew he wouldn't have made it this far without him. But he felt uncomfortable with the current direction of travel. "Bill, I want to win because of my policies and credentials as a leader, not because I fit some British twenty-first century progressive narrative."

"I hear you, son, but when have I steered you wrong? We're making the best out of the hurdles that are coming our way. Listen, go home, make up with Flo, get some rest. We'll touch base in the morning," Bill said as he headed for the door, nodding at the comms lead to follow him.

Calvin took a sip of whisky. He grabbed his phone, opened the chat with Flo and began to type: *I'm coming home tonight.* His finger hovered over the send button.

Chapter 4

An Unexpected Knighthood

Nestled in her office, Deborah and Trish were deep in the midst of one of their daily pow-wows.

"I've got a meeting with her in a minute, so we'll see how she takes it. You just can't please some people," Deborah vented in mild frustration.

"Exactly, boss, and there's only so much you can do to motivate people," Trish replied as a knock came on the door.

"Come in," Deborah called. Trish sat comfortably in her chair awaiting the show before Deborah was forced to motion her to leave.

"Hi," Trish said bashfully as she slipped past Jenna and out of the office. Jenna was entirely focused on the task at hand. She knew the work delivered on the Armanzo account was top quality; she had all the ammunition she needed.

"Jenna, welcome, have a seat," Deborah said in her most inviting and accommodating voice. The unfamiliar tone and heightened deference caught Jenna slightly off guard.

"Thank you for your time," Deborah continued. "I wanted to personally congratulate you on all the good work you've put in on the Armanzo account; Mr. Joyce

56

called me personally to sing your praises – it has been noticed."

"That's great to hear. I actually wanted to speak with you too. I know you wanted to see more of my team leadership and customer relation management before considering my progression."

"Uh huh," Deborah replied, knowing the conversation would likely go this way.

"So, I was hoping to be placed on the shortlist of promotion candidates for the next round?" Jenna delicately queried.

Deborah cleared her throat. "The thing is, Jenna, while of course you've been doing great work and this Armanzo effort is a brilliant example of this, time and experience in role is critically important." She read the look of disappointment on Jenna's face. "The idea is to make you the most rounded professional we can, and to ensure that you're 100 percent, no, 150 percent ready for that next role. Patience is important. It is coming; you have to trust me."

"That's good to hear, I guess," Jenna replied in an attempt not to show how deflated she was; trusting someone who had done nothing to earn it was not an easy task.

"The take home message is you've done a great piece of work and it's been recognised… some reward points are coming your way," Deborah said with a wink, in reference to the internal reward scheme where points could be gifted for good work and then exchanged for vouchers, appliances, electronics and so on. "You should be very pleased with yourself."

"Yep. Is that everything?" Jenna asked, keen to leave.

"It is. Thank you again for all your dedication and commitment," Deborah said, but Jenna was already heading for the door.

Jonathan was early as usual for family time. This was the one activity that really got him out of the house, aside from going to and from work. It was time he kept sacred, moments that he cherished, afternoons with his gran. He was wrapped up as a kid, his gran seeing him as infinitely more delicate than the other children, an over-protective by product of traumatic times early in his life.

Jonathan entered the visitors room; the space was filled with a range of arm chairs and sofas, all occupied by older residents and visitors of various ages. The smell of tea and biscuits was strong in the air as carers patrolled the room, partaking in conversations with guests and offering refills. He scanned the interior in search of his gran, spotting her after a moment. She was not in her usual corner chair. For some reason she had taken up a new location. This was unlike her. He greeted her with a warm hug and a big kiss on the cheek. "How are you doing, Gran? New spot?"

"Mi good, my boy, you know me. Old Doris haffi nick mi seat," she said sharply. It always amused him that she considered everyone else to be much older than her, even if she was actually only a few years younger than most of the residents. In addition, her on again, off again friendship with Doris showed him that maturity didn't always come with age. At times they were as close as sisters, but on other occasions they were the worst of enemies.

"Why would she do that? She loves you, and you love her," he said light heartedly.

"That woman wouldn't know love if it hit her over the head. She bitter cos her grandson doesn't visit as much as you do – she *bitter*!"

"Come on, Gran, be nice. If she gets fewer visits, she'll need your friendship even more."

58

"How are things with you? Still working 'ard I hope and not spending every waking moment with your sketch pad?" she asked.

"You know I work in design?" he asked jokingly.

She responded with a sarcastic grin. "You work with design, but what you really need to be working on is getting me a great grandchild. How is *that* project coming along?"

Jonathan knew this conversation was coming, as it did every week, and each week his answer was the same. "I'm on the lookout for the right girl, but it's hard when you've set such high standards." In truth, he wasn't on the lookout. He never really had been. Nobody had ever taught him how.

Jonathan's Gran didn't appreciate being used as a cop-out for her grandson not being more romantically active. While she knew that he hadn't always flourished in that arena, she wished more than anything that he would meet someone.

"Have you been journaling and taking the medication?" she asked with sensitivity.

Jonathan looked away, hating the other, now predictable, part of the conversation more than the questions about his romantic life.

"Son?" she persisted.

"I have. You know I don't like how the meds make me feel."

"And the journaling?"

"It's not drawing," he said with a laugh that April couldn't help but join in with.

Jonathan steered the conversation in a different direction. They discussed the latest comings and goings in *Eastenders*, her favourite soap. He sank deeper in his chair and sipped the tea that had been dropped off by Karen, one of his favourite carers. He truly enjoyed their time together. Enjoying each other's company always brought him peace.

***

The values of hard work, commitment, and dedication were instilled in Jenna from a young age. Not just through her responsibilities as a big sister and often proxy mother, but in her school work, chores, and practically every other element of her life. Through her conscientious approach to life, she also learned the importance of independence and, to a certain degree, autonomy. It was through this lens Jenna sought to fix the problems of her community. She believed it was critically important to develop economic stability before any true societal shifts or changes could be made. This is what led her to start her own craft business, 'Cultural Crafts': crafts with an authentic African twist. Pads to purses, cups to calendars, all stylized with African prints. It was her dream to grow the business into something she could fully rely on, but, in the meantime, she would make do with it as a side hustle.

Every evening, after catching up with her sister over dinner, Jenna would head to her room for a few hours of work on the business. Whether it was designing new products, creating items, or marketing and sales, there was plenty to keep her occupied; often to the detriment of her social life. Her sister and friends would complain she was never available, that she was not living life to the fullest, that she was never in the moment. *How can you be in the moment if you're planning for the future?* she thought. Tonight was no different. After dinner and an episode of *Next Top Model*, she headed off to her bedroom for the night shift. Her sister shook her head in disapproval, before switching over to the next show.

***

"Come in, Jonathan, take a seat. Would you like a glass of water?" Deborah offered in her best welcoming voice.

Jonathan could feel a tension in the air. Water would have been great but for some reason he declined. He took a seat in a chair that felt like it was far away from Deborah's desk; he felt small. He tried to convince himself it was all in his head.

Deborah leaned forward slightly across her desk, almost attempting to bridge the gap. "I'll jump to it, Jonathan. You know that you are an incredibly important part of this organisation." Jonathan was unaware he was an incredibly important part at all. "And, of course, that you are extremely valuable," she declared grandly. He had never felt particularly valued. In fact he'd had to fight for some overdue time off in the last couple of years. "As a critical part of our organisation, we want to recognise you with a great opportunity." As confused as Jonathan was by all of this, it all sounded positive. "To help us deliver against our core commitments of Inclusion, Diversity and progress..." she glanced down at her notes, "...yes, commitments of Inclusion, Equity and Diversity. We will be creating a special role. A role that will be vital in helping shape the direction of this company," she finished.

Jonathan was trying his best to follow, but he was unsure if he was keeping up.

"This role... Chief... Chief Diversity and Inclusion... Ambassador... Officer," Deborah fumbled badly. She gave him a broad smile, imploring him to be enthusiastic about the offer.

Jonathan could tell it was his time to speak, but was unsure of what to say. "Thank you," he began, somewhat gingerly. Deborah gave him a nod to encourage him to continue. "It sounds like a great opportunity." His gut told him this was the right response. "But what would I be doing… exactly?" he asked, slightly embarrassed as if he should perhaps know already.

Deborah was perplexed. She wanted to say, *You know, Inclusion and Diversity stuff*, presuming he'd get it naturally. How could he be confused? Isn't this what all Black people were complaining about? "It's an opportunity for you to help… help make things better… fairer," she explained, uncertain herself.

"Ok, sounds great." What else could he say? *No, I don't want to help make things fairer or better?* Who would say that?

"Fantastic, we will announce it at a company meeting and get you up to speed with some of our plans. Welcome to the team!" she said enthusiastically.

It was as if he had just joined the company, he thought. *Perhaps for her, he had.*

***

Robbo sat in his crowded office, tilted back in an aging leather chair with a burner phone to his ear. "Alright, I got the full payment for the media job. Guess you're not fulla shit after all," Robbo said before taking another puff of his cigarette. "Another one? How much you got this time?" The sum offered caused him to drop the cigarette from the corner of his mouth. "Are you for real? You could buy a lot of sway with the lads for that alone… Yeah, yeah, I remember, that's not how it works… and we'll have to do what exactly?" He jotted down notes on the numerous pads on his desk. "Alright, I've got just the guys for the job."

***

The entire office was called into the large meeting room for the announcement. Jonathan was trying hard not to fidget in his seat, the imminent attention causing his palms to sweat, his anxiety causing his heart to race. Jenna and Charlotte were some of the last to arrive. Jenna caught his eye briefly before he looked away nervously.

"Alright everyone, settle down, we have an important announcement." The room gradually quietened. Charlie, whispering to a colleague, was the last person to finish speaking; Rachel shot a judgmental look his way.

Deborah slowly scanned the meeting room, making her usual mental note of attendance, before clearing her throat and starting proceedings. "So, as you all know, we have *always* been an organisation that prides ourselves on values of Diversity, Innovation and leadership. With those values in mind, I'm happy to announce we have appointed Jonathan Archer as our first ever Chief Diversity and Inclusion Champion," she paused waiting for a round of applause that wouldn't begin; instead each pair of eyes in the room was trained on Jonathan. He did not know where to look. Expressions ranged from confusion about the role to confusion about who Jonathan was. Trisha attempted to salvage the situation by instigating an enthusiastic clap of her own. This slowly picked up momentum from those in the meeting room as they tentatively joined in. Jonathan gave a nervous wave in response.

"We'll be tapping into Jonathan's *expertise* to help guide our D&I activities and initiatives as we look to better serve our customers and create a better working environment," Deborah tried to discreetly glance down at her notes to ensure she captured the message properly. "So, be on the lookout for some exciting changes coming your way soon. Any questions?" she asked, as she scanned the room for raised hands. She was met mainly with blank faces, mixed with looks of consternation, but only one hand. It was Charlie. She knew the question would not be productive so pretended to miss him. "Great, well let's all get back to it then. Plenty of work to be getting on with!"

Everyone slowly made their way back to their desks. Jenna shot Jonathan a supportive smile.

Charlotte caught up with Jenna. "Can you believe that? What was she going on about? And why bloody pick Jonathan? He's only a design guy."

"What's wrong with picking Jonathan?" Jenna asked earnestly.

"Well, he's not exactly a part of the team, is he?"

Jenna knew what she meant, but didn't share her view. "He *does* work here."

"They could have gone for you, if it had to be a... you know," Charlotte's no-filter approach had almost gotten her into trouble again.

Despite Jenna's dark brown complexion, some of the things Charlotte would say led her to believe she did not recognise her has a Black woman. Jenna always appreciated her candour. "Yeah, I doubt I was high on Deborah's list, even if it had to be a..." she finished with a laugh that Charlotte joined.

Jenna thought back to the first time she met Deborah. Deborah had been away during her interview process, so they made first contact on the job. Jenna had managed to hold the lift door open for Deborah while simultaneously balancing a stack of folders. Deborah slid in, barely acknowledging Jenna, let alone the effort made to hold the lift for her; she was too fixated on her phone. They attempted to exit at the same time, Deborah again paying little regard to the girl with the folders, as she forced her way out first. Despite Jenna spending a few years at the company, she had very little engagement with her boss. However, the small instances they did share, Jenna could tell that something was off; there was always a cool, if not cold, aura around Deborah anytime she was close. Jenna had seen her laughing with colleagues in the coffee area and suddenly switch as soon as she entered the space. She could not decide whether Deborah had a problem with Black women in general or just her. Either way, she was not surprised she was overlooked for this role.

Jonathan's Journal – 3RD

So, today was a weird one. I've finally won at something, something that wasn't a game anyway. Although I didn't actually have to do anything to win, nonetheless, I'm a 'Champion', a 'Champion' for Diversity and Inclusion. When I say I didn't have to do anything, I mean it was given to me, kind of pushed upon me… maybe its fate? Is that a real thing?

Deborah says I should be happy, that it's a real achievement, and that I should take the opportunity, but it's hard to have that feeling when you've done nothing to achieve the achievement. I feel a bit like Glisendor when he was appointed head of the Elder Trolls just because he was the last remaining Winter Elf. I don't really know what the opportunity is. Perhaps that will become clearer with time. The level of attention at the announcement didn't feel great. If it's going to be more of that, I don't think I want the opportunity. However, Jenna gave me a big smile, so there is some upside to the spotlight, I guess. I think when she says opportunity she means helping others, that's what the whole thing is supposed to be about; based on my quick Google at least. Helping is always good; I've never really been able to help anyone before.

***

St. Joseph's Primary School, 1994

April Archer burst into the quaint primary school reception with the frenzied energy of a Tasmanian Devil. A mild-mannered office worker tried to placate the situation, before showing her into a nearby room.

"It's ok, it's ok baby, Grandma is here," were the words he could barely hear over the melée of his shallow breathing, heart pounding in his chest and tears streaming from his eyes.

"Miss Archer, is it?" the frumpy woman with greying hair asked in an annoyed tone.

April looked her up and down quizzically, knowing this person could not be trusted to provide adequate care for her grandson.

"And are you the boy's mum?" the woman asked in an accusatory tone.

"I'm his grandma and main carer," April replied defensively.

"Right, well, Jonathan started freaking out and went into a bit of melt down when it was his turn to read in class. We didn't know what to do with him, so called you."

"Did you ask him if he was ok? What was wrong? Has this happened before?"

Miss Rudibaker paused while she tried to deliver her best answer, not prepared for an interrogation from the guardian. "As you probably know, we have a class of thirty-three students. It's hard for one teacher to focus on only one pupil for any length of time."

The room slowly stopped spinning and Jonathan realised his gran had arrived, the comforting reality immediately making him feel much better.

Months later a GP confirmed Jonathan suffered from anxiety attacks, typically triggered by stressful scenarios.

"What do you mean *anxiety*?" April asked.

"It's a form of emotional distress," the doctor replied simply, as if it was common knowledge.

"But what has he got to be stress bout? He's a child."

"It can be caused by many things: being in uncomfortable, pressured situations, perhaps a traumatic experience?" he said with more emphasis on trauma than he initially intended, almost suggesting that a childlike Jonathan was naturally bound to have experienced some trauma, even at an early age.

Following an attempt to simplify the complex condition, April began to get the picture. She considered his nature, something she had thought an organic expression of an introvert; she tilted her head in his direction, thinking about how much the absence of his mum may have already impacted her sweet boy.

Jonathan would never forget the look on his gran's face when the diagnosis was given, a look of resignation that seemed to acknowledge his life had just become substantially more difficult.

Despite his retiring nature, Jonathan sometimes enjoyed being around other kids in the neighbourhood. He preferred Spring and Autumn for socialising, not too hot or too cold. The doctors had encouraged interaction with his peers as a means to pre-emptively ward off anxiety attacks in social situations; the rationale being the more comfortable he was around other children day-to-day, the less shocking things would be in more stressful social situations. April would try to pitch the fun of playing '40/40' and 'It' out in the street, or football against the garage doors, but Jonathan was happiest indoors, pen in hand, sketching away; sometimes in front of the TV with cartoons on, occasionally in the kitchen while his gran cooked, or in his room just before bed when his gran would shout to turn the lights off. His doodles had been his creative outlet for as long as he could remember. For him, there was no greater peace to be found.

Chapter 5

Nation's Best

Andy checked the gate information for the third time, determined to get this right. The pair had been told to enter through gate M11, where a guard named Mark would let them in once they'd given the correct passphrase, 'He's no Terry Butcher.'

"M11, M11, no Terry Butcher, no Terry Butcher," Andy repeated to himself. Dale was caught up by all the furore outside the ground ahead of the big European Championship qualifying match between England and Hungary. Thousands of people were mixing and milling, chanting and drinking; there was a nice vibe in the air.

Andy could see that, as usual, Dale was not focused on the task at hand. "Dale, snap out of it, we're not here on a jolly, alright?"

"Yeh, but Andy, look at the little fella dressed up as a knight. He's got a sword and everything!"

Andy responded by clipping Dale around the back of his head. "Look, the gate we need to be at is over there," he said, pointing off to his right. Dale lumbered after him, weighed down by the large back pack.

They joined the queue and slowly made their way to the turnstile. As they approached the entrance, a security guard stepped forward to Dale. "Gonna have to see what's in that bag, mate," the tall Asian man said in a Cockney accent.

"Get the fuck off me! Raj!" Dale responded instantly. Andy shot him a stern look to make it clear this was not the time to mouth off and cause a scene.

"Sorry pal, he didn't mean anything by it," he interjected in an attempt to diffuse the situation.

"I don't care what he meant, I'm gonna need to take a look in that bag," the security guard replied sternly.

At that moment, a brown-haired security guard stepped in, "It's alright, Dev, these two are with me. Got em in on the old friends and family," he said with a wink at the security guard.

The guard stood down, disgruntled.

"Come with me," the other man said as he walked them through a side entrance. "Are you guys tryna fuck this thing up? I tell you what, I'm not answering to Robbo if this all goes tits up."

They followed quickly behind him into the stadium. "Sorry, this one ere is a few eggs short of a dozen."

"Oh yeah, the infamous Dale," the man said, rolling his eyes. "Alright, take this entrance down to the third block and your seats will be on your left. We've got you in with some of the other boys so you'll have a nice buffer."

They took their seats as the stadium began to fill up. Kick-off was fast approaching. Nerves were beginning to set in again. Before long, the teams were out and everyone, in the surrounding vicinity at least, was belting out the national anthem. Andy, Dale, and their compatriots bellowed out the song with right palms across their hearts. Just as the teams were due to kick-off, the England players took the knee in silent protest against racism in the sport and beyond. This act was met with loud boos from Andy and Dale's sector, only matched by those in the Hungarian end of the stadium.

The plan was to disrupt the game as much as possible with various acts that would commence with Dale's banner. First, it was hissing, whistles, and taunts every time a Black player was on the ball; then it was a barrage of bottles and flares, and finally, when there was enough attention from fans, players, and officials, it was the grand unveiling of the banner by Andy and Dale. The large banner read, "White Lions only, No Monkey's as Ministers, BFP!"

The disruption and banner were met with boos from the majority of the crowd, but the damage had been done. In protest, the England captain, in discussion with a few players and the manager, opted to remove the team from the field. This led to even greater unrest in the crowd. Police attempted to get to the banner but were met with a wall of patriots defending it. More officers were sent up; fans began to flee their seats for safety. Their job was done. Dale and Andy dropped the banner and made their way to an exit, trying their best to avoid the scuffles that most of their mates seemed to relish.

***

"Sorry folks, we're stuck on a red signal. Hope to be on the move again soon," the Tube driver shared over the speaker system to the dissatisfaction and groans of the passengers aboard. This was the third stoppage already, and Jonathan had only been on the train for two stops. He looked at his smart watch in frustration, acknowledging he was going to be late. This was disturbing because he was never late. *It's only been a day, and already this new role is not working out*, he thought.

By the time he reached the elevator, he was forty-five minutes late. His naturally over-considerate and polite aura did not come to his aid in the battle to get out of the station with all the other, also late, commuters; to top it off, the lift seemed to be rising particularly slowly. He clicked his knuckles anxiously, braced to burst out. Finally, he arrived at his floor and the doors slowly opened. He quickly made his way through the office and towards the graphics corner. The gang were already pre-occupied by their work; all except Freddy, who remarked sarcastically, "One rule for us and another for our new Champion, is it?"

Jonathan tried to dismiss the remark but, when he arrived at his desk, he was confronted by a very rough, childlike picture of what he could only assume to be him as some sort of superhero, with the D&I crest on his chest, like a low-budget Superman. "Very funny, guys," he said as he spun to face the crew who had all burst out in hysterics.

"We're only playing. I'm sure you're going to be great, Captain Diversity," Freddy said.

"No, no, it's Commander Inclusion," Jess piled on, to more rapturous laughter.

Jonathan decided it was time for a tea. He opened his drawer and selected a Rooibos, conceding that he would need something robust after the morning he'd had.

He tried his best to settle into his regular routine, but he couldn't help picking up on the change in atmosphere around the office. It was as if eyes were constantly on him. He tried to dismiss the feeling as paranoia but, for someone used to relative obscurity, it was easy to see when he suddenly became the centre of attention. Especially with Jenna.

Jonathan decided to grab his lunch late that day; his best attempt to avoid more newly interested eyes in the cafeteria. He successfully missed the midday rush. He opened his cheese sandwich and grazed slowly while scrolling through his phone absent mindedly. His Instagram page was a mix of gamer posts, character model designs, graphics, and the odd aspiring onyx model, all very colourful and creative, none particularly *cool* or *trendy*. A news alert popped up at the top of his screen, 'Cross party alignment of MPs stand together to reject acts of Racism following the incident at...' he clicked through to the summary, which outlined the collective parliamentary statement against all forms of discrimination. The message lacked depth or commitment but was much more positive than the tirade an anonymous source had uploaded from a popular radio show:

"Wait, hear me out," George Hopkins said with authority to the call-in guest. "We have good, honest, hard-working Englishmen who are merely exercising their democratic right to free speech with a banner and they're being lambasted by the PC Left, again!"

"I don't think it's that at all. It's inciting racial hatred and harm for no reason," the caller replied.

"Poppycock, how can a simple sign do that? And I'll never understand why the game had to be stopped. The irony is the liberal elites claim they want everyone to have a voice, for everyone to be included, but go into self-destruct mode when people actually do, like we saw at the match. Thanks for calling in, Gary. This is Sports Chat with George Hopkins, and it is a quarter to the hour."

Jonathan pondered the exchange while he ate. Indeed, things weren't so bad, he thought. He reflected on acts of racism he'd experienced, a couple of occasions passing drivers had shouted the N-word, drivers he'd graciously presumed were drunk.

***

Jenna sat at her laptop and played with different pattern designs. She was determined not to get lost in a media blackhole generated by the latest NBF attack; she had other things to worry about. The creative side of life usually brought her peace, but this evening was different. She was unable to shake her flustered feeling. She hated when she got like this; trapped in her thoughts, a negative feeling spiral. *Give it a chance, I should be happy they're finally doing something,* she thought, as she tried to unpick her consternation. *Be patient, I'm sure good things will come out of it, and Jonathan… Jonathan is a good guy.* She thought about the way he would always become awkward around her, endearing in his own way. Jenna's life had taught her that good intentions were rarely enough. To get things done in life, you needed more. Her mum would always tell her to have faith. *God has the master plan. We just have to play our role.*

She continued to switch between different colour pallets for a design she was working on. She was unable to decide whether it was the company's sudden interest in issues of Diversity and Inclusion, or the selection of Jonathan as the champion that made her most unsettled. Was she frustrated about being knocked back for the promotion? Or did she harbour some resentment at being overlooked for the role herself? *No,* she told herself, *that wasn't it.* She pictured Deborah's face in the announcement meeting, her fumbling over her words. How could a woman who could barely stand to be in the same room as her have an interest in all things race and equality? It didn't make sense. Jenna turned away from her laptop and went to get her vision book; this was where she would capture all her best ideas. She flicked through until she came to a page with ragged corners, a page she'd visited many times before. This special page was where she first captured the *market place*, her dream of cultural Black commerce, all thriving off one another, stalls for all needs, a community of sorts. *One day*, she thought. While that dream was still germinating, perhaps she could help Jonathan in the meantime. She thought about the look on his face in the meeting room, a deer stuck in the headlights, definitely someone in need of a helping hand. This could also be an opportunity to demonstrate some of her leadership qualities; at the very least help to ensure that Deborah's Diversity and Inclusion intentions were above board.

Chapter 6

Him, Her, and Him

As he made his way back to his desk, a familiar voice called his name. He turned to happy confirmation - it was Jenna.

"Hey, how are you doing?" she asked.

"I'm ok," he replied, in his most assured tone.

"I've been meaning to catch up with you to congratulate you on everything, on your new role. I think it's great... and I know you'll be great in it."

A broad smile beamed across his face with a warm glow. Recognition and validation from Jenna meant everything. For the first time ever he felt like she was truly seeing him. The feeling was amazing, something he wished would last forever.

An opportunistic brain wave suddenly hit Jenna, calculated without being Machiavellian; "I'm not sure if you know, but I do some mentoring with teenagers from the community, and I run my own African heritage business... I know how hard it is to get a different voice out there, so I'm behind diversity... and inclusion... if done in the right way," she caveated. "If there is anything I can do to help, just let me know."

Jonathan was delighted with the offer of not only a chance to spend time with Jenna but with someone who would actually be able to figure out what he was supposed to be doing.

"That would be great, it would help me out a lot. Let's just say, I'm new to all of this," he confessed. "Honestly, I'm not really sure where I'm supposed to start or what I'm supposed to be doing."

***

CJ returned to a dark house, something he was slowly getting used to, against his will. Flo seemed to have more reasons by the week to spend time at her parents; not just her, the kids too. Of course, the children were happy to spend time with their grandparents. He picked up the piece of A5 lined paper: 'At Mum and Dad's. There's some left overs in the fridge, F.' *At least she was willing to write a note.* There was a time when he would have to guess where his family had disappeared to, a situation he had to admit was self-inflicted, but did not fully regret as an image of her face flashed across his mind.

He pondered the evening of solitude ahead, in some ways welcomed following such a busy day, week, month. In truth he couldn't remember the last time things weren't hectic. He could finally take some time to peruse the media coverage of the NBF stunt at the England match. CJ felt better about positioning the personal attack as a *stunt:* it softened the notion of being the target of a hate group. As he scanned various articles, the balance of opinion once again highlighted the true feelings of large parts of the country. Commentary from everyday people attempting to perform ethical gymnastics to justify the approach from the NBF and political commentators who suggested we should be careful 'not to blow things out of proportion,' stated: 'If Minister James does indeed want to become the British Obama he will have to toughen up'. CJ questioned if the country were ready for an Obama, but did acknowledge that, either way, he would have to be tough.

I should eat, he thought, not sure when his last meal had been. Instead, he poured himself a glass of whisky and began to scan through the Dillon report on environmental sustainability. He found it hard to focus. The large five-bedroom town house in Angel felt haunted when he was alone. He checked his phone: perhaps she'd messaged. It sickened him in his heart that the only message was not one from his wife.

He sipped the thin brown liquid slowly, the alcohol's burn much milder than when he'd first started to drink back in the earlier days of his political career. The tonic was still soothing; a gentle kiss inside his chest, almost as gentle as when her lips would press against his body. His mind cast back to when they first met.

***

12 months earlier...

As usual, he was in a rush, running late. The morning's meetings had gone over and he would now be playing catch up the entire day. Colleen was briefing him in the back of an official party car, a long deep blue saloon. "CJ, you're going to be meeting some kids from Heybridge Academy. They're part of the *Better Start* initiative. This is one of ours from under Blair that has just about survived the Tory public sector cuts. But, I don't think it's got long left, so really important that we make the most of this opportunity while we can," she had said at speed.

CJ nodded along somewhat blankly, lost in thought about the latest argument he'd had that morning with Flo. He was struggling to understand how the person who used to be his biggest champion had changed so much now he was progressing in the career she'd encouraged him to pursue. He thought back to their late-night study sessions as law students at University, the evenings of debate and argument that translated into passion, and subsequently love. CJ had wanted to stay in the non-profit world, work on human rights issues. It was Flo who pushed him into the private sector and then public life with the promise that he could do more. Isn't that what this was all about? Trying to do more?

"Boss, are you getting this?" Colleen asked.

"Huh? Yeah, sorry, I'm just a bit in my head," CJ replied, glassy eyed, staring into middle distance, eyes fixed on nothing in particular.

"Everything ok?"

"Yes, nothing I can't handle," he replied with his default approach to life.

CJ and Colleen were rushed into a back entrance, through some corridors to a side door of the auditorium where the meet-and-greet event would take place. CJ couldn't help but be hit with nostalgia for his own school days at a school much like this.

"Everyone, come around. We're stopping a little earlier tonight because we have a special guest I'd like you to meet," Jenna said. The kids looked around at one another in confusion. "Trust me, you're gonna like it."

Colleen pushed the door open for CJ who was followed by a teacher who tried to scuttle in front of him and lead the way.

One of the kids shouted, "That man is from the telly!" pointing in CJs direction. This generated attention, although most of the kids were unsure of who he actually was.

CJ waved at the kids as he approached the group. Jenna was surprised by how tall he was in person. "Hi everyone," he'd opened warmly. "I hear you guys are working on some cool projects. Anyone want to show me theirs?"

Aiden came forward with his art piece, still unsure about who this person was, but knowing the teachers' change in behaviour meant he must be important.

"So, what do we have here?" CJ asked.

"It's where we play football."

"I see, these are the goals," CJ said, pointing to the metal nets on the caged pitch. *This kid has talent*, he thought.

Jenna watched closely, pleasantly surprised again, this time about how naturally at ease he was with the kids. She wondered if he was a father himself, realising she didn't know much about the political rising star.

CJ took his time speaking to all the kids, before making his way to converse with some of the teachers and mentors, including Jenna. His hand shake was firm but subtle, practiced but not insincere. The grip was warm, or maybe it was just her. He made her feel at ease. She guessed he was used to meeting 'normal' people.

"The work you're doing here is amazing," he gushed.

"Thank you, it's nothing really, just people who want to help, nothing like what you have to do every day."

"You're right, what you do is much more important," he joked back.

"No, no, I didn't mean that."

He laughed, "I know, I'm only joking," his warm disarming smile in action again. "You know, I'm keen to keep close to those who are helping out within the community. I run a private session with local community leaders once a month. You should come."

She could not believe what she was hearing. Mr. Shadow Chancellor himself was inviting her to a private meeting with community leaders. Clearly her prayers were paying off. He subtly gave her a card: *just drop me a line and we'll sort everything out.* Right on cue, Colleen pulled him away, informing him they had to leave for their next meeting. CJ had said his goodbyes and was back in the car before he knew it. Colleen was well into the next briefing, but his mind was still on Jenna. He really hoped she'd call.

***

There were days when it seemed like Jonathan's inbox would only grow, irrespective of how hard he was working, how determined or focused he thought he was being. In addition to his annoyingly stoic inbox, he was getting a higher than usual number of in person visitors to his pod. He didn't necessarily mind people coming over. In fact, a face-to-face chat often made requests easier to process. However, the downside was that the account teams, as ever, had little regard for the designer's time. Requests were often last minute and vague and, when the client was dissatisfied, the design team members were always the scapegoats.

The designers would work closely with different members of the accounts team but were particularly close to the Creative Directors. The Creative Directors, or CDs, were responsible for pulling the creative visual of different campaigns to life and would be the person who would relay the request to the designer. The need for scapegoating and what the design team would call an unfair distribution of recognition for good projects meant there was an ongoing rift between the two teams. The type of rift that pre-dated any of the current creatives or design team members; the type of feud that was automatically inherited by anyone who joined one of the teams. It would be unfair to suggest it was only the CDs who gave the design team a hard time; the creative team was practically bottom of the workplace Totem pole, only superseded by the administrators. Jonathan's introverted nature did little to combat the somewhat abusive office dynamic. He was a collaborative person who veered away from conflict and hostility. His gran would say that he inherited his calm nature from his mum but, not knowing her himself, he couldn't say for sure.

He caught Diane, out of the corner of his eye, heading his way in a rush; she was never easy to work with, worst of all when she was rushing. Before he knew it, he was being assaulted with details for a brief: "What we need is…" "You know, a bit like what we had for the Almondo account, but less frilly?"

He tried to interject: "Wait a second, the Almondo account, but that was about wearables…"

"I know what it was about. Pay attention. We don't have time for a back and forth, the client wants a mock up by end of tomorrow."

"Diane, I don't think I can do that. I have a dozen other things to do."

"Are they as important as this?" she demanded rhetorically

"I think they're all—"

"I can't deal with this, I'm going to Deborah," and as if by magic she was off again, as fast as she'd arrived, storming towards Deborah's office.

"You know, you can tell her to Fuck off?" Freddy offered, unhelpfully.

Jonathan returned a look that suggested he would like to do nothing more, but that it wasn't going to happen.

***

"And what about you, Rachel? Who's tickling your fancy

then?" Jess asked as she finished the remainder of her yogurt.

Rachel blushed, her pale skin and Celtic roots lighting up her face like the North Star on a clear country night. "I don't know what you mean," she protested.

"You need to tell your face that," Jess laughed.

"Hope you're not shy because you, because you like… what you like," Rachel said with all the care of a drunken bull in a window shop.

"What I like is my business, not lunch time gossip," Rachel stated as she picked up her sandwich and left.

***

The group descended back into confusion and talking over one another. Deborah knew her people leadership skills were needed to steer the group towards a resolution. "Calm down, we can't keep interrupting each other. We all can have a chance to speak. Perhaps if I try to summarise what I'm hearing in the room?"

"Great idea," Trish replied automatically, only to be met with daggers from the rest of the group.

"So, Rachel wants us to prioritise women because that's the largest demographic in the office, am I right?"

"Well, not only that, we're also half of society and to this day we still don't see enough women in senior leadership roles."

"Well, we have Deb as boss at least," Trish chimed in, missing Rachel's point entirely, while innocently undermining her position.

"What more do women want?" Charlie asked. "Trish is right: we have Deborah. Rachel, you're on this team, where is the imaginary glass ceiling you guys keep crying about?" he asked, mimicking a pretend surface above his head.

Rachel mouthed 'fuck you' in his direction.

"Women will be included, Rachel, but there are other groups we need to think about too, right, Jonathan?" Deborah said, attempting to give her champion an opportunity to speak up for the Black cause.

Jonathan was caught up in the to-ing and fro-ing but managed to agree. Charlie rolled his eyes.

Deborah said, "Right, so of course women and other groups like the Ls and Bs are important, but our focus should, initially at least, be around Black people – I mean people of colour. Superb." She co-signed her decision on behalf of the group. "Ok, so now that's sorted, can we agree on some of the activities we would like to take place in the short-term?" She was hoping to bring things to a swift close.

"If we're going to prioritise this way, we should at least do something of worth."

"Of course, that goes without saying. This is all about trying to help."

"Good," Rachel replied tersely. Jonathan apprehensively watched the back and forth between the two women – something akin to an aggressive Olympic table tennis match.

"Well, I think we need to ensure we have some support for the local community and ensure we get more diversity in the office," Jonathan said.

"I was thinking similar things," Deborah replied sharply.

"Great!" Rachel said with more than a hint of frustration.

"Yeah, Great!" Trish contributed blindly.

"Fantastic, we're all agreed," Deborah summarised, looking at Jonathan, who had his mouth slightly open, as if he was about to contribute.

"Let's get back to paying the bills then!" Deborah

closed the meeting in frustration.

Rachel and Charlie left particularly underwhelmed by the outcome, while Jonathan was grateful he didn't have to contribute too much to gain what he presumed was a win.

Chapter 7

Match Of The Day

While little additional impetus was needed, the incident at the England match had provided the perfect opportunity for Deborah and the Inertia team to roll out the new *No Space For It* campaign, with Jonathan at the centre.

Media hype had been bubbling since the failed attack on MP Calvin James, and the news of England fans derailing an important international match was a timely boost in a fading news cycle. Despite her early reservations, Deborah was really starting to get behind this whole D&I *thing*, and if it was going to be her ticket to the big time, more power to it. The campaign *No Space For It* was partly dreamed up by Genene from HR, with a little help from Deborah; who, while still learning, was experienced enough to spot a good opportunity.

***

An aesthetic design coordinator had been brought in for the photo-shoot, along with what Jonathan was sure were paid actors from different ethnic backgrounds to accompany him in the campaign photos. A large, converted warehouse housed the shoot; an array of lights, cameras, and clothing racks filled the cavernous space.

Jonathan imagined this must be what a Hollywood film set felt like. The amount of attention he received was overwhelming; although a part of him he was less familiar with was enjoying it.

"More blusher?" the willowy make-up artist asked with an inviting smile as Jonathan tried to get comfortable in the fold-out chair.

He was unsure how to respond: *did* he need more blusher? "Ok?" he said as he continued to wriggle.

Rachel looked on from the corner of the room, trying her best to take everything in. It was much, much bigger and, in honesty, better than she'd expected. *This is good*, she told herself. This is what she wanted, full support for Diversity and Inclusion. Yet something wasn't sitting right with her: this… this felt more like a circus.

Rachel couldn't help herself, her tenacious curiosity which, at times, could be construed as entitlement had got the better of her. She approached a flustered Deborah who was buzzing around set in a much more hands-on fashion than usual; a level of micro-management that was beginning to irk the shoot's Director. "Deborah, I just wondered…"

Deborah spun towards Rachel with semi-focus, clipboard in one hand, while murmuring into a headset. "Rachel, sorry, it's not a great time," she said, gesturing to the bustling set. "We need to get the guys out of make-up and ready before the players arrive. The players only have an hour to get everything done, and we won't be able to get them back for another three weeks. I'm sure I don't have to explain to you what it will mean if we miss our moment."

"I understand. I just wondered if this whole thing is a bit… reactionary?" she asked as she caught eyes with Jonathan, seemingly tied down to the make-up chair.

"Reactionary, whatever do you mean? Of course it's

reactionary. We're reacting to a moment. Carpe diem, my girl," she exclaimed triumphantly.

"But, but don't we need to be a bit more strategic in our approach...? And, of course, there are other groups too, which would also bene–"

"I hear you, don't worry. Of course we women are not going to be forgotten in all of this," Deborah said with a less than subtle wink. "Don't forget, I know how hard it can be. I had to make it before the 'leg-up' of Inclusion and Diversity, but it doesn't mean I don't want a fellow woman in arms to benefit now."

"Uh huh, that's great, but there are other groups, too," Rachel offered gently.

"Ah, the others. There will always be others but, as my mum used to tell me, *we can't all drink from the well at the same time*, can we?" Deborah with the wisdom of a rhetorically philosophical question as she rushed off towards Jonathan and the photographers, ready to issue more direction.

While Deborah was fully indulging in being back in the action, Rachel was left thoroughly unsatisfied.

***

"How are you doing, Champ?" Deborah said, hands clasped vice-like on Jonathan's shoulders as they both looked into the mirror.

"I'm ok, boss, Deborah," he said, unnerved by her grip.

"Do you work out?" she enquired.

Jonathan had a flashback to one January when he tried to adopt a New Year's daily workout regimen as a tonic of his anxiety; star jumps in his room that only led to complaints from the neighbours. He'd lasted six days. "Not really, no," he admitted.

"Right, right, might be something to consider." She turned away. "Jackie, do we have a tighter top please for Jonathan? We want to depict a shared strength and athleticism. I know we made wardrobe choices in advance, but I'm asking for a bit of flexibility here," she huffed.

***

Jonathan tried his best to stop himself from fidgeting as sweat proceeded to lubricate his palms. Stood side on with the rest of the 'models', he was unsure if the shoot itself or the famous footballers he was standing alongside were triggering his anxiety. Part of him wished it was the footballers but, despite how much the rest of the room fawned over them, he had no clue who they were. They were friendly, introducing themselves with handshakes and smiles, with the tone of people who expected to be recognised. Jonathan did his best to oblige with the expected level of enthusiasm. Three England players of colour – Marlon Bridge, Julian Hunter, and Jermaine Haywood – made it, alongside the White captain Dean Mason. The group joked among themselves while various assistants continually offered drinks and food. This catering was bolstered with subtle requests for signatures which the assistants hoped weren't picked up on by their respective managers.

The shoot was over much faster than Jonathan expected, especially considering all the hype and build up beforehand. Deborah closed the session by thanking the entire room, in particular the England stars who had given up their 'vital time to make a genuine change'. Jonathan caught Rachel's courteous applause and, more importantly, her dispassionate face which suggested she did not agree with her boss.

***

Jonathan arrived early to Reedmore, or as it became known as 'the home', even more anxious than usual to see his grandma. He needed to speak to someone about all of this, someone to help him make sense of what he'd signed up for. He tried to tell himself this was good news, but it had all happened so fast. He rushed into the waiting area, accidentally barging a man in a hat.

"Watch it! For fuck-sake!" Dale fired back at him as he spun off kilter.

"Sorry, sorry," Jonathan offered hastily. Dale had dropped his keys. When Jonathan crouched to pick them up for him, he noticed the MediEvil Quest key ring as he handed it back.

Dale gave him a suspicious look, the months programming kicking in. Jonathan didn't look like the hooded figures that Robbo and the others were always talking about, but he knew his type weren't to be trusted. He snatched the keys back and made his exit.

Jonathan felt his reaction was a bit dramatic, but didn't dwell on it too long: he could see his grandma waiting in the corner.

"My boy," she began as she hugged him tightly. She could feel his heart pounding when they hugged. She tilted her glasses to get a clearer look at him. He was sweating. "What's up with you? Someone chasing you?" she laughed.

Jonathan smiled in response, "No, was just looking forward to seeing you."

"Why so much? Am I going somewhere?" she asked in jest, looking towards the heavens.

"Don't joke about that, Grandma." He hated and admired how she was so at ease with her own mortality.

He dreaded the day he knew had to come.

"Ok, Ok, so what's new? Keeping out of trouble? Found me a granddaughter in-law yet?" she asked in her cheeky tone.

"No, not yet, Gran. I do have some news though," he said, unsure of how to broach the subject.

She looked at him lovingly. "Go on then, cat got your tongue?" she said, followed by a deep cough.

"I've been asked to be a... a Champ..." the word didn't feel right. "I've been asked to become an ambassador."

"That sounds very important, congratulations!" she applauded him. "Ambassador for what?"

He took a deep breath. "Well, this is the thing, it's not something I'm sure I should be even doing," he said self-deprecatingly.

She gave him a knowing look, the look she would give him as a child, the way she would always see him. "You were always too hard on yourself. Always."

"It's about Diversity and Inclusion. I'm the lead, I guess..."

"You know I'm old. You need to explain a bit more for your gran."

"It's about making things fairer, I guess, having more variety in the company, more people that look like *us*," he said.

She took a moment to ponder the proposition. Her mind flicked back to memories of Jonathan's parents; their life, their demise. She shook herself out of the moment of melancholy, and returned to the room. "Wait, so White people want more people like us around?" She burst out with laughter. "Times have really changed! Dem mad?!"

He wanted to laugh, too, but he knew it wasn't a joke to the company. He would actually have to do some stuff.

"The problem is, I don't know how to be a diversity and inclusion ambassador... I don't know much about history and race and stuff... You always said work hard and keep your head down... that I can do."

She could see the strain on his face. It was clear this wasn't a laughing matter to him. "Jonathan, I teach you the best I could. There was nobody fi teach me, we were fresh ere, new arrivals, it was different for us. We had to survive. Your generation now, you have new challenges, a different game." She took her hand and cupped the side of his face. "You have a good heart. Just try and do the right thing and you won't go wrong."

He'd hoped for more direction, but knew she was broadly right. *I don't have to be Malcom X.*

***

Posters from the shoot had appeared all over the office and beyond. The campaign had been pushed out across all Football Association social media channels, with the mainstream media also picking up and running with the story. Jonathan was again at odds knowing this level of fame and notoriety was something the average person clamoured for, while for him it was yet another thing to agitate his anxiety; not to mention the added opportunity for jokes from the Design team. He tried his best to slip into his chair unnoticed to try to avoid the tirade of abuse that was inevitably coming his way.

He had barely taken his seat before Freddy spun his chair around. "So, what is your favourite football team again, mate, I forget?" Jonathan attempted to ignore the comment. "I mean, it's not a big deal, but if you're red and I'm a blue, I'm not sure how this friendship continues," he said, trying his best to stifle his laughter.

Jess chimed in. "But you know I'm a green, right? That means I can't talk to either of you," she confessed, pretending to slap her own forehead at the revelation, before the group burst into laughter.

"Ha ha, very funny," Jonathan conceded in an attempt to diffuse the situation.

Freddy wasn't done. "But seriously, how is Dan Cole in person? It is Dan Cole, right? I bet he's breath-taking, those big manly legs. It must have been a dream to meet him?"

"Are you done?" Jonathan rolled his eyes and turned back to his work station.

"We're proud of you, that's all."

"Exactly, just happy with our Captain Diversity!" They began to laugh again.

Jonathan reached for his headphones, hit shuffle and turned the volume up to drown out his peers.

As he worked away, old-school Hip-Hop pounded through his over ear speakers. He was periodically met with a colleague waving in front of him to get his attention before pointing to a poster and giving him a thumbs up. To top a challenging morning, he had a lunch time session with Jenna, something he would typically look forward to but, with all the hype around the campaign, he was worried it would make things awkward.

***

"Let me get this right. You're his teacher? His tutor? I don't get it," Charlotte said as she sipped her coffee.

"No, it's not like that. I'm helping him, sharing a bit of wisdom. He's kinda new to some of this stuff," Jenna replied as neutrally as she could manage.

"Hmm, seems a bit weird to me. Isn't he supposed to be the expert in all of this? Why's he coming to you?

Unless this is some sort of sex thing; naughty teacher or bad student, whichever way you want it, it all works, right?" she said, nudging Jenna with her elbow, almost spilling her coffee, while cackling away.

"Stop. Not everything is about sex. It's just a friend helping another friend, that's all," Jenna protested, more defensively than before.

"I'm teasing, Miss. You can have as many friends as you like. I'm only a bit concerned, especially after things went bad with you and the mystery guy."

Jenna accepted her friend's apparent caring intrusion. "I'm fine, who needs men anyway?" she retorted defiantly.

"Well, you may not need them, but you've got one coming your way regardless," Charlotte said, watching a happy Jonathan walking towards them. "Good luck with the study sesh," she closed with a wink. She approached Jonathan. "Hey, Jonny, I know you're all in study mode, but, if you really want to lay teacher's pet, you may want to think about some exercise time too, ok, Champ?" She hit him firmly on his back, almost causing him to drop his notes.

The pair got settled in the meeting room and got straight to business. Jonathan was surprised Jenna didn't mention the campaign, and part of him was slightly disappointed; he'd hoped his spot of limelight might have gone some way to impressing her.

"So, what did you think of *The New Jim Crow*?"

Jonathan found himself distracted again, this time by her hair. He attempted to quickly gather his thoughts but failed to deliver a compelling answer.

"Everything ok?" she asked.

"Yeah, just people being a bit weird since the campaign and stuff."

"Oh yeah, I meant to say, you look good on the

posters."

The compliment made Jonathan's heart skip a beat. He tried to regain his composure and play it off as a small thing. "Yeah, you know, they hit you with a lot of make-up and lights."

"Ah, make-up… right."

He cursed himself for mentioning the make-up. "Got to meet some of the England Ballers, too." *Ballers? Is that the lingo?* Even if it was, it didn't sound right coming out of his mouth.

"That must have been cool. I quite like Kyle Coleman."

Jonathan tried to decode what the 'like' meant. Was it a *like* like or just an appreciation of his football talent? Of course, it was a *like* like. What girl comments on a guy's footballing talents?! He berated himself. He knew that comment wasn't PC in itself; yes, some girls watched football now for football's sake, even though he couldn't understand why anyone would want to watch it at all.

"Ok, so if you pick up here, next time we can discuss *Medical Apartheid.*"

He nodded in response.

***

Deborah eased back into her leather chair, tea in one hand, and perception report in the other; the initial findings were in. She glazed over the executive summary, focusing on the key figures. It had only been a month, but the results were striking. The shift in public perception in such a short time frame, resembled the results of a year-long campaign. They had received half a dozen Request For Proposals (RFPs) in the last week alone, and the number of new applicants had also shot up. "I guess this D&I stuff really works," she said to herself quietly. Deborah couldn't wait to show the findings to the board, announce the immediate impact and great success of all *her* hard work.

Chapter 8

Afrobeats

"If ur here ur here! Best whine that waist before the party dun!" screamed the DJ as he dropped the WizKid track and the party exploded. Jenna gave her sister a less than impressed, judgemental look. Yami had also invited her friend, Blessing, who was already assessing the talent, tipping her glasses down at a potential dancefloor candidate.

The day party venue was the rooftop of a typical restaurant in south east London. The layout meant the designated dance floor was of a limited size. People were crammed around the many large flower pots or seizing upon any empty wall space as sturdy support for an intimate grind.

"You said this was going to be a chilled motive?" Jenna questioned.

"Relax sis, it's a vibe. Get a drink and let yourself go a bit," Yami responded, winding her hips to the rhythm. The DJ cut in with the next track and a loud collective "eyyyyy!!!" came from the crowd as Sheriff the Traveller began to play. "This is *my tune*!" Yami yelled, almost in her sister's face. "Ok, let's go and get a drink,"

Blessing said assuredly, "Uh huh, not me. I'm going to see about this tall glass of chocolate milk in the corner!

I'll catch you guys later," as she made her way to her target.

This was no surprise to Yami who had witnessed Blessing's forthright approach to romance many times before. It was part of the reason she wanted to make sure she had Jenna: someone to party with at least for a little while before the guys got involved.

"Wait, where is she going?" Jenna asked.

"Don't worry, she's enjoying herself and we're getting a drink," Yami replied, hauling her sister towards the bar.

Yami unceremoniously squeezed herself between a guy and a girl. The girl shot some shade her way. Yami responded with her best unbothered face, her left arm still tightly gripped to her sister, who now had her face planted in the small of a large man's back. Sandwiched against another group of people, moving wasn't much of an option at this point. Jenna didn't want to move lest she touch him somewhere in appropriately or call attention to her awkward position. Meanwhile, Yami had managed to use her angelic voice to flag down the barman, someone who definitely met the cute requirement, even if he was perhaps a little short for her usual taste. She flirted with him as she ordered two passion fruit margaritas.

The tall, broad-shouldered man jostled with irritation at the jabbing pain in his back, but there was no way he was going to give up his spot now his drinks where on their way. He wriggled and turned, carrying the three drinks in his two hands, locking eyes on the short attractive girl. Jenna was star struck at the Adonis looking quizzically down at her. The best she could manage was a stammered, "Sorry."

"No problem," he replied, shooting a wide smile back her way. She hadn't moved. "Can I just…?" He used his shoulders to gesture that he wanted to move past her.

"Oh, I'm sorry," Jenna said, realising she was trapping him in. She did her best to create some space to let him pass. Her eyes followed him as he squirmed through the remainder of the crowd and onto the dance floor to meet his friends.

"Here you go," Yami called from behind her. "Come on, take it. Took me long enough to get these. What's got you distracted?"

"What do you mean?" Jenna replied, trying to hide the smile on her face.

"I know you, sis. Someone move to you?"

"Chill, it's not always about a man, you know."

"Mmhmm." They each took a sip of their drinks and made their way to the floor.

Jenna had to admit she was having a good time. It had been a while since she took some time to actually enjoy herself. The tunes flowed and the vibe was good. Everyone seemed to be enjoying themselves; no drama, no stress, and she had not thought about him. Only one thing could make it better: seeing her stranger from the bar.

Blessing made her way back to the pair with a friend in tow. "Hey ladies, this is Charles," she said happily, as if she were introducing her fiancé.

"Hey Charles," they both replied.

"You guys good?"

"Yeah, we're just jamming. Charles, you got any friends?"

"Yeah, actually. A couple of my boys were checking you guys out."

Blessing tried to subtly interrupt with the finger across the throat gesture.

"They're just over there," he said, pointing towards two short guys, who looked *different* to their friend. He beckoned them over.

The girls stared at one another with wide eyes, unsure of what to do next. Yami linked arms with her sister, spinning her away from the two approaching men. Blessing dragged Charles to the bar, not wanting to witness the fall out.

"Sweetness?" a voice called from behind them, which they pretended to ignore.

"Babes... lemme talk to u, init. I see u watching us," the other guy said. They walked around the girls to face them. The ladies were all out of moves.

"So, what you guys saying, tryna come to ours for the afters, yeah?"

The wannabe roadmen were the exact opposite of what Jenna was looking for. While Yami could handle a bit of road, these two were nowhere near cute enough to tolerate.

"No, we're good thanks," Yami said, sipping on the remainder of her drink.

Jenna was dying inside, unsure where to look, when a new, booming voice joined the conversation. "Hey, can I grab you for a second?" said the attractive stranger from the bar over the two guys, who didn't appreciate the interruption.

"Who, me?" Jenna asked.

"Yep, you," he said with a smile, before whisking her away.

"Sis...Sis!" Yami called out as she watched her sister leave her alone with the two sidemen. Jenna twisted back raising a finger to indicate she'd only be a minute, but the breadth of her smile suggested that she hoped it would be much longer.

Jenna struggled to reach the neck of her dance partner Se was happy with the stretch, not only because of the height difference, but in a strange way it actually felt good, as if the stretch in her spine was therapeutic.

Maybe she'd spent too long hunched over a desk. The DJ had hit the slow jams as the party drew to a close. Jenna felt a safety and comfort in his grip around her waist. She leant into his chest and found herself soothed by his slow, steady heartbeat. In a different scenario she could have easily fallen asleep.

***

The three girls squeezed into a cab, tipsy and in good spirits.

"We didn't think we would see you again without Charles," Yami jabbed.

"He got enough of my attention for one night."

"And you sis, off with the mystery man. Almost sad to see you at all."

"You know you need to give them something to work towards, right?"

They all burst into laughter as the car sped off.

***

"Yes, it was Mr. Fullop's secretary...uh huh... yes, Calvin, I double-checked," Flo said, rolling her eyes.

"You know, I know when you're doing that, even on the phone?"

"Doing what, sweetheart?" she replied innocently.

"Mmhmm. So let me get this straight one last time, *the* William Fullop wants to meet me at the Monarch Rooms this afternoon."

"That's right. You're not all looks, after all," Flo joked.

"This is huge. Do you know who Bill—"

She interrupted him. "Yes, I know who Bill Fullop is. I studied in the same library as you, remember?"

"The Bill Fullop Library," Calvin said, more for himself than his wife.

"Yes, the very same. He apologised for the short notice. I'm sure it's some sort of power play."

"Who cares. It's Bill Bloody Fullop," Calvin chimed in.

"Ok, ok, calm down. I know this is big but, if you're going to meet with him, you're going to need to relax a bit. Let me know how it goes. I need to pick up the kids. Love you."

"Love you, too," he said absentmindedly, still trying to get his head around the news.

CJ decided to take a Black Taxi to the famed Monarch Rooms. Better than the VW saloon which had seen better days and was in desperate need of a wash, or showing up sweaty on foot after an obligatory rush-hour tussle on the Piccadilly line.

For those in the know, the Monarch Rooms were about as legendary as Mogul and blue-blooded descendant Bill Fullop. The hushed corridors and drawing rooms of the Gentleman's Club were the venue of the inception and destruction of empires; where regimes and wars were plotted, where the country's largest power brokers met to wet their beaks. CJ had hoped one day his political star would shine bright enough to enable him access to hallowed places like this, but he never in his wildest dreams thought it would happen so soon.

He buzzed the door and informed a well-spoken voice of his appointment, more importantly who he was here to see. The large wooden door opened slowly. CJ was met with a grand marble entrance that had a small desk occupied by an attractive blonde girl. He tried his best to drink in the environment; the details were plentiful but subtle.

Kyle Powell

"Mr James," she said, as if expecting his arrival. "If you would like to follow me." Her tone was assured way beyond her years; her face looked as if it would be more at home on a yacht in Dubai, but her demeanour was far more serious. He followed her into a small lift, which descended slowly. CJ was unsure where to look, while she stared straight ahead blankly. He was about to make an attempt at conversation when a ping sounded their arrival. He was led past several large rooms, all bustling with hushed conversation, like a gentrified beehive. "Through here," she said, directing him into a smaller and much quieter room.

"Calvin, how are you doing?" Bill said warmly with an outstretched hand. "I can call you Calvin, can't I?" Calvin's honest thought was he could call him whatever he liked: this was Bill Fullop, Mogul and Icon. Calvin was simply happy to be in the same room as him, let alone be having a private conversation.

"Sure, Calvin is fine, or some people call me CJ," Calvin was surprised by the overshare. He only liked when people close to him used the nickname, ideally just Flo – his subconscious was clearly overwhelmed, too.

"Yes, CJ, I've seen the press run with that moniker. CJ, the local boy done good," Fullop said with a subtle laugh.

"Some outlets feel that fits with my... *branding*." The word felt uneasy and apt all at the same time.

"Ah yes, branding. What do you think of your branding?"

CJ was keen not to misinterpret anything or make a fool of himself. "I'm not sure how you mean, sir."

Bill studied him carefully, trying to read if the young upstart was more coy than he was letting on. "Well, perception is important, am I right?"

"Yes, of course, Sir."

"To ensure you have the best chance of success in your political career, we need to be certain you convey the right image. You have the potential to do great things, make history, untie people, but it has to be done carefully," Bill espoused.

CJ was completely won over. Not only was he sharing a whisky with a living legend in the Monarch rooms, but he was also now being complimented; Bill Fullop was talking about his potential, potential to do great things. *This can't be real*, he thought.

PART 2

Chapter 9

Professor J

And so it continued, the crash course on racial injustice; curated and instructed by Professor Jenna Kefore. At first glance of the reading list, Jonathan genuinely thought it was a joke. *She wants me to get through at least a third of the list by when?* He was pretty sure he hadn't read that many books in his entire life; definitely not, if comics and graphic novels were excluded. But he was determined to make it work. And ultimately it meant more time with Jenna; he would read a thousand books. They would usually meet after work. Sometimes they used the meeting rooms, but they would usually go to the library; Jenna stressed the importance of making use of the great local resource. Jonathan preferred their time in the library. There was no prying from Charlotte or childish teasing from Freddy.

Jenna started Jonathan off with what she described as a *light* mixture of antebellum African American history, supplemented with more contemporary summaries of challenges facing the African Diaspora, both in the US and the UK. Like an undergraduate attending a University tutorial session, Jonathan showed up to the evening library session with notes in hand, ready to discuss.

"So how did you find Malcom's autobiography?" she asked excitedly, enjoying the experience of reliving the books she'd read before.

"I mean, it was good."

"Just good, anything else?" she replied almost impatiently.

"I think it was interesting to see the journey made by Malcom."

"And what about what he stood for? What he fought for?"

"Yeah, I mean, I get it. Back then, things were tough, they... we didn't have anything."

"And that's where we would still be if it wasn't for people like him. That's partly why this work is important. We're trying to improve things for future generations."

He nodded in response. Jonathan wasn't short of words only because of the topic at hand: he was also enamoured by her glow, particularly when she was in her impassioned mood.

Jenna caught him staring. "Are you ok?"

"Huh? Sorry, yeah."

"Are you enjoying this? We don't have to if you're not, if it's not helpful?"

"No, no, I am. I'm learning so much, I don't know where I'd be without you. Though my Fellowship isn't happy with my 'lack' of commitment."

"Fellowship?"

"Oh, it's just a quest... a game... I play with some friends." He began to squirm. "It's nothing really."

Jenna could sense his embarrassment. There was a degree of endearment to his geek-dom, she decided to bring things back to work. "So here are the things I would like you to read before our next catch up." He sighed at the list. "Do what you can. Remember: you are our Champion," she finished with a laugh.

***

Despite her flaws, Deborah had ascended to her role through talent, hard work and commitment. Her position as Managing Director was something she valued, not only because of the dedication required to achieve her station, but because it allowed her to do what she enjoyed most of all, which was leading and developing people.

However, what she had failed to predict with the shift in focus towards all things D&I, was that the ascendence of a champion would be an opportunity to guide and shape Jonathan. He was not one of her direct reports. They had no formal check-ins, but in time spontaneous catch-ups became more frequent.

Jonathan was deep in sketch mode with one of his logo designs when Deborah appeared out of nowhere. "Champ, how are we doing?" she asked, leaning over the side of the pod.

Her powerful perfume and assured tone caught Jonathan off guard. "Hi, boss, I'm good thanks, and you?"

The rest of the pod kept their heads down and continued the show of focused work.

"I've told you about the boss thing. It's Deborah or Miss Tate," she said with a laugh. "Wondered if you fancied a quick coffee?"

Jonathan considered whether there was a world where he could genuinely reject the offer. "Sure, the kitchen? The nook?"

"Let's go to the nook, I think it's free."

The pair headed over and Jonathan fired up a couple of espresso using the cartridge fed machine, while furiously trying to figure out what mistake he'd made that warranted a coffee catch up. They sipped quietly, before his anxiety forced him to break the silence. "So, everything ok?" he asked nervously.

"Of course, wanted a bit of one-on-one time with my Champ. That's ok, isn't it?" she asked rhetorically.

Jonathan began to realise so many of her questions were rhetorical, it was hard to know when a response was actually required. He nodded in response nonetheless.

"You know I take a keen interest in all the guys here, but especially those who have a lot of potential." She practically winked in his direction, the compliment eliciting a feeling of awkwardness rather than anything positive. "I wanted to get your thoughts on your aspirations, your career trajectory? Where would you like to be in the next few years?"

"That's a tough question. I've never really thought about it that much, if I'm honest." He pondered for a few moments.

"I know you get along well with the design guys, but I presume you don't want to be one of the designers forever."

"I guess would like to have my own team one day, maybe run my own studio," he said openly, uneasy with the level of transparency he'd not shared with anyone before.

"I think that's a fantastic idea, and with a bit of work maybe we can start to make that a reality for you here. After all, you're doing so much for the company."

"I'd really appreciate that, bos–, Deborah."

"Fantastic. Well, I'll leave you to it, Champ. Don't want those logos to go undesigned do we?"

***

The kids left the hall in their usual cacophony of noise, despite every week being told to leave quietly by project leader, Kelvin. Kelvin had asked the mentors to stay behind for a quick chat after the session, something he'd rarely do. Jenna was helping to shepherd the last few remaining kids out of the hall as quietly as she could before re-joining the mentors. She felt a slight chill: the hall was almost instantly cold without the kids in.

Kelvin had already begun by the time she made it back to the group. "Thanks for staying on a bit longer tonight, guys. I'll keep it short. I know you all need to get on," he inhaled deeply. "Basically, the programme is struggling for funding and may not be able to continue." The news was met with disgruntled groans and murmurs. "I know, I know, not the type of news that any of us wants to hear. We are in discussion with the local council to see what we can do, but I wanted to keep you guys in the loop in case we end up in a worst-case scenario. Ok, thanks, and see you next time. Get home safely," he finished.

Jenna was shocked and upset by the news. She couldn't believe there was a chance the programme would shut down; the kids, and the mentors, enjoyed it so much. Her shock slowly morphed into frustration as she sat on the quiet Tube racing towards East London. *How could there not be funding for such an important initiative? They find money for things they don't need, millions for cleaning Big Ben.* Her mind wandered to the D&I activities at Inertia – fancy campaigning – but would any of it actually help anyone? A gut feeling told her it was unlikely. Her internal dialogue continued: *you don't actually know what is planned. Maybe there are some meaningful activities coming.*

***

Jonathan arrived with the tea, biscuits, and a smile on his face. His grandmother took a moment to appraise him carefully; there was something different about him, but she couldn't put her finger on it.

"How are you doing, Gran?" he asked brightly.

She continued to study him, not yet prepared to respond. "What's wrong, Gran?" he asked, starting to feel uncomfortable with her concentrated gaze.

"There's something different about you," she replied, finally.

The remark caught him off guard. " I don't know what you mean," he said, taking a sip of his tea.

She squinted into focus, "I know what it is… you have a new hair cut!" she said with aplomb, as if she'd cracked a murder mystery.

Jonathan burst out laughing. That was not the answer he was expecting after so much suspense. "Thanks, but I haven't."

She was visibly disappointed. "It must be summin. I know… you've finally found a girl! Congrats, mi boy!"

He had been spending more time with Jenna, but he knew they were a long way off a relationship. "No, not that."

"It's something, I can feel it."

"I don't know…" He thought about what had been happening in his life recently. There was nothing drastic: working, home, gaming, drawing. And then it hit him. Flashbacks from all his meetings: the attention, the focus, the smiling nodding heads. "Well, remember that new role I mentioned? It's been going… ok, I guess… Maybe it's rubbing off on me?" he finished, the acknowledgement causing him to revert to his more familiar, less confident self.

She knew her grandson well. She knew confidence was not something that came naturally to him. Glimpses of him starting to wear his novel, more assured shell so well were a pleasant surprise for her.

***

Deborah was particularly pleased with her *creation*; she was keen to show off her stallion to the board. There was a chance Mr. Johansson would be able to fit in a visit to the London office as part of a larger business trip.

Jonathan had been to a couple of D&I meetings with the leadership team to discuss action plans for various initiatives; however, he still felt like an imposter. He had done none of this work before, had no real frame of reference. And Deborah, Rachel, Charlie, Edward and the others were such dominating characters. They had an entitlement that enabled them to naturally command a room. He knew he needed to increase his expertise if he was ever going to be taken seriously.

"So... aside from the *teaching* stuff, what is actually expected of you and the team? Why was the role created?" Jenna asked, as she scribbled on her note pad.

"The company's 'Get To Know' sessions are only part of the strategy. There's a plan to help increase representation of different demographics, too."

"Hmm, so not just publicity for the company and our clients; showing the world how diverse we all are now?" she said sarcastically.

Jonathan found himself defending the initiative, not wanting Jenna to think he was associated with a superficial programme. "No, no, not at all. We are also planning on doing some real meaningful activities. That's what I'm most excited about," he proclaimed, somewhat honestly.

"Oh yeah, like what?"

"Like what? Umm like... like community activities, giving back. Also trying to get an internship and perhaps even a scholarship programme going," he finally remembered.

"That's actually really cool, I have to say. I'm pleasantly surprised. Wouldn't have thought meaningful work would make it through with Miss Tate leading the way."

"She's not so bad," he said, surprising himself. Jenna raised an eye brow in his direction. "She might surprise you." Jenna sustained the same look. "Ok, maybe not," he relented with a laugh.

"You know what, I have an idea. If there's a community element to this, my volunteering programme could use some support. It's perfect – we can see how committed Deborah and the team are to this whole thing," she said with a smile.

Jonathan began to regret his promotion of Deborah's apparently misunderstood altruism. "Sounds good. I'll ask about it," he said with as much enthusiasm as he could muster. "So what should we do for the first learning session?"

Jenna thought carefully. What would the office benefit from? What would Deborah benefit from? Her mind ticked over. "I've got it! Micro-aggressions!" she almost shouted.

"A micro-what?" Jonathan asked in confusion.

"A micro-aggression," Jenna replied, so close beside him, it made it hard for him to focus. "It's easy. They're a relatively small indirect or direct act or comment about someone's ethnicity that makes someone feel uncomfortable or ashamed."

"Ah ok," he pretended to follow, placing his hand to his chin in considered fashion.

"Don't worry, I'm going to give you all the definitions and source materials, so you only need to read up and practise. I'll also outline a suggested flow for the presentation, but of course it's up to you exactly how you would like to deliver on the day. Everyone has their own style, and you should feel comfortable. It's your presentation, after all."

"Thanks," he said, which he realised was insufficient gratitude for the level of support he was being gifted. "I really mean it, I couldn't do this without you. I almost feel bad taking all this help."

"Don't worry, I have some knowledge, read some books, lived the life. Actually a lot of the resources I'm giving you have come from work I've done with the kids down at the volunteering programme, not re-inventing the wheel."

"You'll let me know if I take up too much of your time?" he asked, hoping this would never become a reality.

"Of course. I still have my priorities. As cool as it is to finally get some representation around here, there are lots of ways we need to progress, and not just in the corporate sector." Jonathan nodded along, providing the visage of an equally well-informed and aligned peer. "Anything else before we finish?"

He thought. "Just one other thing. You mentioned being comfortable. I won't be comfortable. You might have noticed that I'm not exactly Steve Jobs when it comes to confidence and stage presence." She tried her best not to bite on the comment, instead providing a supportive nod and murmur. "So, if… *when* I get nervous up there, do you have any tips?"

"Well, you may have noticed I'm not a professional speaker either," she began.

But Jonathan was not in agreement. In his eyes, she was the embodiment of confidence and assuredness. She'd be great on stage.

"When I get nervous–"

"You get nervous?" he interjected.

114

"I do. When I get nervous, I try to take some deep breaths, slow down, and focus on the message I want to deliver. Remember, everyone in the audience is hearing the presentation for the first time. It doesn't have to be perfect. So take your time and you'll be great," she said with a warm smile and a rub of his shoulder. Jonathan blushed. His heart rate went up a couple of gears as his brain tried its best to hold onto to the sage advice he'd been given.

Chapter 10

Pitching In

Things were changing quickly for our D&I Champion; from lectures to the company, to now being added to a pitch team, his work life had truly transformed.

"What do you mean, they want you to go along?" Freddy scoffed with incredulity, while he casually chewed a 'healthy' protein bar.

"I don't know, it's like I said, they want me to go along. They want to showcase a more rounded team at the pitch stage," Jonathan shared, as he tried to maintain some focus on an e-mail he was drafting.

"But none of us have been invited along to any pitches," Freddy said.

"I don't know, I'm only telling you what Deborah told me. Apparently, it would be good experience for me as my role 'develops'," Jonathan said.

"What do you mean *develops*? You're a designer. What development is there?" Freddie finished the remainder of his snack.

"I don't know, I'm just telling you what she told me."

"This feels odd. Doesn't it feel odd?" Freddy asked.

"A bit, I guess, but it's not so crazy, is it? We support the account teams very closely. We are a big part of the teams. Why not include us more from the start?"

"Well, yeah, if they are really going to include us and…"

"And what?" Jonathan asked.

"And not just you," Freddy finished in a tone more bitter than he intended.

Jonathan was struggling with the awkward energy from his conversation with Freddy. After all, he hadn't asked for any of this, and he definitely wasn't looking forward to the idea of pitching; the mere thought of it had his heart racing. Deborah assured and reassured him that it would all be fine. He didn't even have to participate in all the rehearsals, he just had to show up and answer any design questions. *I can do that*, he thought.

***

University of Bristol, 1998

Crossed glances would always make a study session more interesting. Something CJ would always be on the lookout for on those initial rare occasions he was dragged to the library by course mates. While he appreciated the grandeur of the stately building that held the law books, the strict *no talking* rules enforced by Miss Whitmore and the statue of former slaver Sir Reginald Hargrave, were enough to put him off regular attendance; that was until he saw her.

Flo looked similar to most of the girls at Dunnanbry College: prim and proper middle-class types from various parts of the country. But there was something about her aura that set her apart. CJ loved how transparent her emotions were; the subtle rush of blood to her cheeks when they locked eyes, the way she would nervously chew the lid of her biro and attempt to make conversation with a friend to distract herself.

While he enjoyed the cat-and-mouse game across the study tables, he needed more. His natural assertiveness wouldn't be abated by what ifs. One day he saw her headed to the water cooler and decided to take his chance. He feigned a deep yawn before offering Collin, his housemate and study partner, a drink. He hurried over and tried to think of a funny introduction – cheeky jokes were normally his thing – but today he drew blank. *Could this be the effect she is having on me already?* he thought. She'd almost finishing pouring when he blurted, "Don't drink too much or you'll be in the toilet all afternoon."

"Sorry, what?" she said as she turned to see his face. He couldn't believe what he'd just said; it was his turn to blush.

"It's nothing... are you finished? Getting hot in here, right?" he said, sounding more like a bad rendition of the Nelly song than he'd hoped for. But she laughed, nonetheless. CJ was unsure if it was more out of pity than genuine humour.

"Flo!" a voice said from behind him. CJ turned to look. It was Collin.

"Hey Colin, how are you?"

"Good, as always. Are you going to the social later?"

"I'm not sure, depends how I get on with this coursework. I was just speaking with..."

CJ was totally confused. How did Collin know her? Maybe this was a middle-class White thing: they all knew each other.

"CJ," Colin interjected for his dumbstruck friend.

"Right, CJ, nice to meet you. Anyway, I better get back to it," she said before heading back to her table.

"You alright, mate? Not like you to be so awkward with the ladies."

"How did you... how do you know her?"

"Who? Flo? She's on the hockey team. We have

shared socials sometimes. Wait, mate, you don't like her, do you? I could have introduced you ages ago. But I wouldn't recommend her. She's a bit too fiery, if you ask me, all feminist this and human rights that. Who needs that, am I right? No, if you want some fitties, there are much tastier girls around." Collin could see CJ was still transfixed. "Mate if you like her that much she studies here every Sunday morning, or just come to one of the socials. I'm sure I can sneak a footy lad in."

"Sunday mornings," CJ replied.

Sunday was usually a pretty nothingy day, spent lounging around the apartment in PJs watching box sets and, if you were lucky, perhaps doing a little bit of work. It didn't go unnoticed by Colin that CJ was up and out early on Sundays now, textbooks in hand. Things were easier now they'd had an introduction and Sunday mornings were quieter than during the week, so the pair quickly transitioned from glances across a shared table to study partners. CJ loved her mind, her passion and robustness. Her entitlement was not expressed in the same self-indulgent way as most of her peers. Instead, it fuelled an altruism in her to demand more for those who had less. It was an intoxicating and inspiring energy to be around, and closely aligned with his own core values.

***

Waves of frosty air and harsh neon light washed over the two anxious novices.

"I really don't get why I'm here. Not like I'm pitching," Freddy said as they stood side by side looking into the large mirror of the free weights area of 'Your Time Gym'.

"Really, you have no idea why you might be here?"

Jonathan said, looking at his tall friend's pot belly squeezed into what looked like an old PE vest.

"What? This?"

"That," Jonathan said, staring at the tire shape around the midriff of his rotund friend.

"Some ladies like a more robust gentleman. Girth can be seen as a sign of opulence," Freddy said.

"Well, my spindly arms need some help." Jonathan shook his straw like arms in the mirror. "So, you can help me focus on that."

"Is this about Jenna again?" Freddy provoked.

"No," he protested.

Freddy returned the questioning look Jonathan had sent his way earlier, before tensing and flexing what muscles he had. "I guess it wouldn't hurt to get a bit more *stacked*."

The pair were happy the gym was beginning to empty out, following the after-work rush. They were grateful to have fewer prying eyes on their novice journey into the world of exercise and fitness.

"So, what weights do we use?"

"I don't know, keep trying until it gets too heavy?" Freddy advised.

They collected sets of dumbbells and began to bicep curl. Without any real frame of reference, Jonathan was disappointed that his maximum was 8kg. He saw a girl on the other side of the mats managing the same weights much more comfortably than he was. Freddy, on the other hand, could comfortably handle the 14kg, "I told you size counts for something," he said, tapping his belly as he worked. The pair went to the matted area and began to follow an exercise video focused on body weight. The guy in the video demonstrated a range of push ups, which the boys struggled to imitate. "They can't be this hard," Freddy complained as he went down to his knees.

"Yeah, maybe we're doing something wrong?" Jonathan agreed.

"Start that video again. Slow it down. Let's see his technique," Freddy said. The instructor demonstrated a diamond push-up. "What the fuck is a diamond push-up?" Freddy was getting frustrated.

Jonathan looked at his watch. "Maybe we've done enough today?"

"Maybe we have," Freddy agreed. "Let's have a stretch or something. Or, fuck it, we can just go."

They headed to the changing room. Freddy sat and watched Jonathan undress. Jonathan had his back to him. "Maybe next time we try some legs stuff, what do you think?" he asked, spinning around, expecting Freddy to also be in the process of changing.

"What?" Freddy asked. "Are you not changing, thinking about having a shower?"

"Are you checking me out?" Jonathan asked with unease.

"What? No, don't be stupid. Can't two guys be in a locker room together without it being weird?" he deflected, getting a quick look at Jonathan's manhood.

"No, I think I'm going to shower at home," Jonathan decided last minute.

"Me, too."

Pitch day rolled around. Jonathan looked different to the pristine professional façade of the rest of the team, with his mismatched loose-fitting Blazer and trouser combination. He could feel Diane's glare as they rode the lift towards the pitch room. She clearly wasn't prepared to politely ignore his attire, not even for the sake of team spirit.

She sighed heavily. "Guys, you know what we have to

do. We all have our roles. Let's get it done!" she exclaimed triumphantly, though not to the reception she was hoping for. They shuffled off the lift. Diane grabbed Jonathan by the arm. "Just wanted to check that you're super clear on your role?"

Jonathan began to sweat. "Support you guys… stay quiet and answer any questions on design."

"Right, the 'stay quiet' part will be support enough." She patted him on his shoulder as if she'd just delivered a motivational team talk; Jonathan only had further motivation to get through this performance as quickly as possible.

Jonathan followed the rest of the group in shaking hands with their prospective clients. He stood on the far-left hand side of the group as the presentation took place. He regularly glanced up at the clock, only to be met by stubborn hands, a face that happily reflected the slowly dissipating seconds.

"Any questions?" Diane said after her closing.

The questions came in, the 'core' team happily fielding the enquiries when a young-looking man with greying temples stepped up. "We haven't heard much from you, I believe you're the design lead, right?" he asked, glancing at the team organisational chart at the back of the pitch booklet. "What do you feel are the biggest design challenges we face, and how can we best address them?"

"Well, I think–" Diane attempted to step in.

"I think I've got it, Diane," Jonathan said quickly, surprising himself.

"Of course," she replied in mild shock.

The heat from the spotlight started to build. Jonathan took a deep breath, tried to clear his mind and began to speak. Before he realised it, he'd finished and was met with a warm smile from the greying questioner. Shortly after, they were shaking hands again and heading back to the lift.

"Good job," said Greg, an account manager on the team.

"He answered one question," Diane said.

"Alright, it's a team effort. Not like he was given much opportunity to do more," Greg countered.

Something told Jonathan he should chime in and account for himself, but he could tell they were fine to have the conversation without him; *why wouldn't they be?*

Jonathan's journal – 21st

It doesn't feel natural yet, but it feels good. I'm starting to see why people like to talk so much. Or, I guess, more when people have to listen to you... choose *to listen to you. Jenna says I'm coming out of my shell. Who knew life could be fun outside the shell! Obviously, I don't want to get too carried away and end up like Hogroth when he found the Emerald Gem of Enlightenment and thought he should become the superior samurai, but this is good. For the first time I'm feeling less anxious in group situations when I have to speak up or present.*

I don't know if I'm imagining it, but it feels like Jenna is starting to pay more attention to me. Maybe it's because she's helping me learn and we're spending more time together, but it feels like she's actually starting to see me, not just look at me from time to time.

Thinking about cutting back on the meds a bit, not sure. I know Gran would say speak with Dr Phillips first, but surely I should just do it if I'm feeling better? The whole point is to be ok without them.

It's not only Jenna, it's everyone. The whole office seems to know me now. There are some people I'm struggling to recognise. Deborah has also taken a greater interest in me, keen to see how

I'm doing, checking in on me, giving me tips and stuff. Let's see how things go, but this whole Champ… (I've always wanted to be a Champ to someone) Champion thing isn't so bad.

***

"So, Champ, how is everything going?" Deborah asked. You pitched for the Delanti account the other day, right? That's really great exposure, the type of thing that would benefit an aspiring design team leader."

Jonathan smiled. "Yep, I think it went fairly well, but I don't have any frame of reference. The team was happy… at the end, at least."

"How do you mean?" she asked, picking up on his tone.

"It's nothing. I think some of the guys were a bit stressed with it all."

"Were they not welcoming?" Deborah asked in her most concerned tone.

"I think maybe I rubbed Diane the wrong way or did something wrong."

"Leave it with me. That's unacceptable. I know you did a great job."

"It's nothing, really."

"Champ, leave it with me," she said firmly, but supportively. "I know you have the microaggression talk coming up, too. Are you all ready? Happy to run through the slides with you in advance, if you want," she offered apprehensively, hoping he wouldn't take her up on it.

"Thank you, I appreciate the support. I should be fine with the micro-aggression stuff. Jenna is helping me."

Deborah picked up on his affection by the way he said her name. "Ah Jenna, ok… If there's anything I can do, let me know. I'm sure it will be a great session."

***

April turned away from her bedroom doorway as she coughed deeply, wary Jonathan would reappear with their water while she was in the middle of one her fits which were becoming more regular. As ever, she was steadfast in maintaining her role as his protector, which meant ensuring he didn't have to worry about her health. The truth was she didn't know how much longer she had left. The doctors were vague, trying to protect her from any unnecessary concern; but despite their reassuring words and hushed whispers, April knew something was wrong. She spat some discoloured saliva into her napkin just as Jonathan shouldered the door open.

"I hope you ask the waiter to mek mine strong. You know how I like it, triple rum," she laughed, triggering another coughing fit which this time she was unable to hide from her grandson.

"Are you ok? Drink some of this," he said, passing her the plastic cup.

She sipped, waving her free hand to suggest there was no problem. "I'm fine, mi made of sturdy wood," she said, wracked by some smaller coughs.

Jonathan could tell something wasn't right. "Maybe I should get one of the nurses?"

"No, no, it's fine. Tell me, how are things at work? Your promotion?" she enquired with genuine interest, while also trying to change the subject.

"It's not a promotion, Gran, it's like an extra role. I'm still a designer."

"I know, but you're helping people with this role, right?"

"Yeah, I guess so… trying anyway."

"Mi proud of you, you know that."

"I do," he said reassuringly.

***

The bell icon flicked over on the third screen spoiling Andy's triple win.

"Fuck!" He banged the side of the fruity in frustration.

The three other men in the bookie's slowly turned his way before switching back to the horse race on the fuzzy Toshiba.

His phone buzzed: it was Kelly. 'Need dat money 2day, these r ur kids, remember!'

He returned the phone, shoved his hands back into his faded, stone wash jeans and was fishing around for some coins when the doorbell twinkled into life and Dale's head popped in.

"And, ready to hit the Jobby?" he asked.

Andy pulled some lint from his pockets and nodded in his direction.

The Job Centre was a depressing place. The grey seventies- style building, peeling wallpaper and lingering smell of cigarette smoke didn't help and neither did the lethargic and unmotivated Job Seekers team. Andy hated the fortnightly visit. It was a regular kick in the stomach reminder of the failure his life had become. Dale on the other hand was much more positive. He still couldn't believe they got money for nothing – practically nothing: they had to prove they had applied for at least three jobs in the past two weeks.

As Dale began his fortnightly consultation, Andy sat, arms folded, on the small, sticky plastic chair attached to the wall; he was crammed between a young mother who was trying to calm her crying baby and a gruff looking man who smelt of old beer and urine. He closed his eyes,

126

bent his head forward and placed his palms behind it in an attempt to mentally escape the room.

"Dale Cummings is it?" the consultant asked.

"It is," Dale replied warmly.

"Right, so how's the search been these past weeks, Mr. Cummings?"

Dale enjoyed being addressed as Mr. It was probably the only time he'd ever experienced that. "Ok. I applied for six jobs on the site, even a couple I found on the Job machine here," he said gesturing to one of the arcade looking console machines that were used to find roles.

"Good, good," the consultant said, stamping his payment collection form. Dale was delighted that he'd comfortably surpassed the minimum requirement, feeling like he'd sufficiently earned his pay. "Take this to the counter and we'll see you in two weeks."

"Just one thing. I have a strong interest in writing and wondered if you had any advice on how I could get something in that area?"

The consultant re-opened Dale's file in disgruntled fashion, keen to move on to the next seeker. He inhaled deeply as he perused the screen. "Mr Cummings, how do I say this? I think that would be difficult for someone of your... experience."

"But I write a lot at home, fun stuff, action and that - I can even show you some of my work."

"I'm not sure you're getting me. You only have one GCSE and it's a D grade in Religious Education... you don't have the qualifications to be a writer."

"Oh," Dale responded despondently.

The consultant could feel the drop in his energy. "Look, perhaps you can look at a local college course or GNVQ. You may have to demonstrate some of your work. Check the site, there are some links."

The guidance perked Dale up a bit. "Ok, thanks. See

you in a couple," he said as he headed to hand in his form at the counter.

Andy was relieved to hear his name called. He wrestled his way out of the tight confined space, only to be met with the kissed teeth of the mum who didn't appreciate his aggressive movement, triggering another crying fit from her young one.

"Mr Dewsberry, how are we today?" the elderly lady with bright pearls and tinted purple hair asked with slight judgement.

Andy wondered how someone who could afford pearls could also be working here. *Must be fakes.* "Yeah, ok, will be better when I'm out of here."

"Mmhmm. And exactly how many roles have you applied for?"

"Enough," he shot back, not enjoying the interrogation and getting flashbacks of telling-offs by his headmistress in her office; 'you'll amount to nothing,' she would say, apparently accurately.

"Enough isn't a measure I can add to the system. Care to try and give me a number?"

"Care to sign off on my fuckin cheque?" Andy suggested aggressively

"Mr Dewsberry, we do not tolerate that kind of language here. If you can't cooperate, we will have you ejected from the building," she said, looking at the portly, security guard stood at the entrance, chewing gum, "and you can forget your allowance."

Andy realised he had to rein it in. He needed this money badly, not just for him, but for Kelly and the kids too. "Alright," he offered in concession. "I've applied for four jobs, two on the box over there. Not heard anything back."

"That's better. Are you applying for appropriate roles?"

"What does that mean? You mean the shit ones fit for me? Yeah I think so," he said, temperature rising again.

"I mean roles that match your… qualifications."

"I think we both know my qualifications, two decades at the factory. What does that get me? Fuck all, especially when there's all this… competition." He tried his best to temper his language as he cast his eyes around the multicultural room.

She gave him a look before stamping his form. "You know the way. Next!" she called.

Dale was stood outside with a cigarette, waiting for Andy. He was watching a group of kids kicking around an empty beer bottle. "Go ok, And?" he asked sincerely, offering some of his cigarette, knowing his friend found these trips harder than he did.

"Nah, tryna cut back. Got the money, so guess so," Andy said in frustration. "Look, I gotta go to Kells and drop her some cash. Will catch you later." He left before Dale could reply.

***

Jonathan sprang up covered in a cold sweat and tears. It was the same nightmare he always seemed to have when a nerve-wracking event was coming his way: an exam, interview, presentation, sometimes just a social engagement. It had become a predictable precursor to times of impending stress.

The dream always followed the same format: Jonathan sat in the back of a car while his mum and dad rode up front, one of the only memories of his parents that he had. It began as many dreams do in pleasant enough fashion; low music playing, a feeling of warmth accented by indecipherable talking, or maybe singing from his parents. But things would change, the music would fade, his parents would be arguing about something, their indistinct yelling becoming louder and louder, before a shriek of terror followed by what felt like floating in an eternal limbo. A feeling that would be abruptly interrupted by a mix of flashing lights and cries in the darkness that brought him back to the world.

Chapter 11

Tiny Grievances

The majority of the office huddled into the large meeting room after collecting their choice of sweet treat provided by the D&I committee. Charlotte had saved a seat for Jenna, to the annoyance of some of her peers. "We're not in secondary school any more, Charlotte," Beth said in a deliberately childish voice.

"Well, maybe you should stop wearin your hair in pig-tails, babe," she fired back with peak sarcasm.

Jenna finally arrived as proceedings were about to begin. She spotted Charlotte who waved her over to the free seat, giving Beth a death stare in the process.

"Where were you, babe? Thought you were gonna miss your man doing his thing."

"I had to run through a few final things with him. He's a lot more confident now, but he still gets a bit shaky in places… *and* he's not my man."

"I'm sure you did have to run through some final things," Charlotte said with a cackle. "I'll admit he is more attractive now, since he's become all …" Charlotte struggled to think of a reference.

"All what?" Jenna prompted, realising she was leaving herself open for a cringe worthy moment.

"Mmm… all Obama," she finished, bursting into a

131

laugh.

Jenna was compelled to join her stupid friend in hysterics.

At that moment, Jonathan walked in and the room fell into a quietened hush. Leaning into his new found gravitas was becoming easier by the day.

Deborah stood in preparation for the introduction, as Jonathan waved to the audience in almost stately fashion. "We're looking forward to having our very own Jonathan Archer talk to us today about the micro-aggressions!" she declared in a happier tone than was appropriate for the subject matter. Jonathan began to open when he was interrupted by his trusted leader. "And I want everyone to pay close attention. This stuff is really important. For *all* of us," she said, wagging her index finger for emphasis.

"Right, yes, thanks Deborah…"

She'd already thrown him off his train of thought. Jenna could tell he was starting to struggle.

He felt the baying eyes of the audience locked on him; he panned the audience in search of his anchor. At first, he saw Charlotte's peroxide blonde hair, but quickly found a safe space in Jenna. She gave him a warm smile and an encouraging nod, and he continued. "Thanks to everyone for joining in today's lunch time talk as part of our 'Get To Know!' series, as mentioned, I will be talking to you about micro-aggressions."

As he spoke, he tried to make eye contact with members of the audience to help maintain engagement, just as Jenna had guided. Jonathan briefly locked eyes with Charlie, who was squashed in towards the back of the room. He responded by pulling out his phone and scrolling in boredom.

"So, what is a micro-aggression?" Jonathan flicked a slide up. "It is a statement, action, or incident regarded as an instance of indirect, subtle, or unintentional discrimination against members of a marginalised group such as a racial or ethnic minority." He gave the room some time to digest the definition, finding it intriguing how much facial expressions gave away about who was genuinely interested and who was trying to stay awake. To his surprise, the majority of the room seemed to be intently focused. Even Deborah was scribbling away on her notepad. Jonathan went on to provide some examples of what microaggressions could look like in real life. These examples led to murmurs among the group. Jonathan wondered if people were discussing their own potential past micro-transgressions. "It's important to know mistakes can be made and that's ok, it's part of the learning process. So, any questions?"

He was met with silence. He scanned the room again, anxiety rising. Why was it harder to stand in silence instead of actually giving the presentation? He would have happily closed the session, but he remembered another pearl of wisdom from Jenna: *if messages have landed, there is likely to be some engagement with questions and a discussion. Also, even if people are unclear, it's a sign that they're interested if they ask for clarifications.* He held on for a few moments longer before Barbara from accounting raised her hand.

"Great presentation, Jonathan, thanks for sharing this with us. I had a question around intent. A lot of the examples you described I feel could be innocent mistakes. What if you intend to pay someone a compliment, let's say by complimenting on their hair or skin colour? I love the look of Jenna's hair, for example."

"Right, so there's a lot to unpack there..." He glanced at Jenna, partly out of habit and partly because she'd been mentioned. "I think intent is really important, but even with the best intentions we can still be inappropriate and hurt people's feelings." He looked at Jenna for verification he'd given a good answer. She nodded subtly in response. "I'd also add there's a way to pay a person a compliment without racializing the person or over-stepping boundaries. Saying you like my hair is fine. Touching my hair without an invitation or permission is a violation of my personal space."

"Ok, Harriet Tubman over here," Charlotte whispered.

The initial question had the desired effect of opening the flood gates. The enquiries began to rain in.

"So, I dated this Asian girl once and she liked when I called her Brown Batina. Guess that was ok, right?" Brian from IT asked.

"Yeah, that's not okay, Brian. Next question?" Jonathan shut down the line of questioning quickly before it became an HR issue. He saw Rachel: *safer ground,* he thought.

"Thanks for this, Jonathan, you know I love all the work you're doing. I think you've touched on some important subjects there, but wondered if you could have included more examples from the LGBTQ+ perspective, or even from a female perspective, because we also experience micro-aggressions."

He paused. She wasn't wrong but he thought she would have understood why he would focus more on examples based on race. He didn't want to end the meeting on a sour note. "Yes, you're right, Rachel. I'll take that on board." She had a satisfied smile on her face, but Jenna was clearly not so impressed at her colleague's attempt to refocus attention onto herself.

The session ended with a large round of applause. Jonathan was relieved and proud of himself for delivering the session. He hoped the enthusiastic claps were confirmation of a job well-done, but recognised they could have been because the session was finally over and people were happy about the choice of cakes still available.

***

The Giphar account on the whole was more exciting than most of the accounts and teams Jonathan had contributed to; however, like all the others, the weekly team meetings were something he never enjoyed. He typically hated these environments because they would trigger his anxiety by forcing him into the uncomfortable position of having to contribute to discussions with often competitive colleagues. The effect was compounded by the fact the teams were built up of confident, charismatic account handlers and creative planners who all seemed to have particularly loud voices and who were primarily concerned with being heard. The slight upside being that, as the design guy, he wouldn't have to contribute for too long, but there was always a time where he would have to explain his mock-ups and drafts, to prepare the account handlers and managers for their conversations with clients.

With everything going on in the D&I space, Jonathan had fallen behind with some of his day-to-day tasks. He hadn't put the usual level of love and attention into the graphics for the Purdue campaign. This particular campaign was around the launch of Purdue's new fitness shoe range for women. Jonathan scanned through his mock-ups as Diane, the Account Director, began the meeting. Jonathan expected he would have some time to add final tweaks while the team went through their usual back-and-forths and client gossip, but this meeting was different. A difference he would have picked up on earlier if he hadn't been so worried about the quality of his work.

"Jonathan, we'd like to hear from you," Diane said begrudgingly. The request was heard by Jonathan but the unusual timing of it meant it went unregistered. She cleared her throat and tried again, a little louder, "Jonathan... we would like to hear from you?"

His sub-conscious processed the request at second time of asking. He peered up from his laptop screen to a sea of faces looking eagerly his way, all in anticipation of his response. "Sorry, did you say something?" was the best he could muster in response.

"Yes, I was asking for your input on the strategic approach for the campaign."

Jonathan quickly and carefully processed the question. He had never been asked for input this early in the meeting and never about anything beyond design concepts; he certainly had never seen Diane or any of the other team so excited to hear his input on things. It was more typical to see his team mates conspicuously yawning or on their phones by the time it was his turn to contribute.

Now the pressure was on, he had to make a useful contribution. "Well... I guess... I like the approach... perhaps we can have more emphasis on the girl from the Middle East," he said cautiously, unsure if this made any sense at all. To his surprise, his words were met with positive nodding heads and broad, somewhat saccharine, smiles.

But this was only the beginning. This pattern was repeated across all his teams. He was asked for contributions more frequently than ever before, and everything he said was gold: he couldn't miss. For the first time in his life, he felt like he was being seen and heard; it was exhilarating, intoxicating.

The attention didn't stop with the team meetings. It

extended to his entire work experience. People who had never spoken to him began to say hello, offer to make him tea. It even felt like the cafeteria staff, who were typically less than enthusiastic about their job, were now more cheerful with him. His world had totally changed. The impact of his meteoric increase in his colleagues' respect began to change Jonathan himself. His posture seemed to improve, he spoke in a more commanding way, with more conviction and authority, he held people's eye contact, even his handshake became more robust.

***

"And when are you going to find yourself a nice young man, eh? You know you work too much. Work, work. When I was your age I had you, your sister, and was expecting your little brother."

"Yes, Mum," Jenna replied, attempting to stop her mother telling the well-trodden story of how and why she was able to be a 'young' mum and raise a family.

"Eh eh, you see your daughter? She thinks she knows so much; these English schools and work, they think they know everything," she shouted to Jenna's father. "I am trying to give you wisdom, but you don't want to know?"

"No, no, go on, Mum."

"Oh, so now you give permission. If I was there, I would show you permission eh. I had a family because I had a good, god-fearing man willing to support me, you hear?"

"Yes, Mum, I hear," she said, rolling her eyes.

"I can see your eyes you know!" she said, kissing her teeth. "Where is your sister? I bet she is on her phone no doubt, the internet superstar. She is too beautiful, that's her problem. She has her mother's looks eh?"

Jenna was relieved her interrogation was over, for now at least. "Yami, Mum is on the phone."

Her sister came into the living room and took the phone, "Mama eh, how is everything?"

"Aw my baby girl, everyting is wonderful. How is God blessing you?"

Jenna headed to her bedroom, not wanting to hear her mother swoon over Yami; she knew if she had decided to become an influencer, her mum would not have shown her the same level of support. She sat and opened her laptop with a spreadsheet of businesses and contact details: it was nearly time to move to the next phase.

***

Jonathan's star continued to rise. He was getting more attention and gaining more traction. Jenna knew she was playing a key role and didn't mind she wasn't necessarily getting the public credit she deserved. Aside from the superficial showboating, some good work was getting done; however, she was keenly aware that the big-ticket items, 'core activities', were yet to be delivered. Jenna had mentioned this to Jonathan a couple of times before but was wary about coming across too maternal. Ultimately, she wanted to be supportive and not rain on his parade.

***

"I know it's not easy, Mrs Archer, I really hate having these conversations, but the recommendation from Dr. Roberts is we move you to a room with the necessary medical equipment."

"I fine," she said with a cough.

The nurse took a second to reposition her approach.

138

"Perhaps, if you have a conversation with your grandson, I'm sure he would be more than willing to help with what's needed."

"My grandson have enough to deal with in his life, he does not need to worry about this," April fired back.

"I could speak with him, if you prefer?"

"Mi say no! I will be fine."

***

Jonathan carefully cradled the teas to what was his favourite meeting of the week. They exchanged pleasantries and he gave Jenna the drink.

"Jonathan, there's something I've been meaning to talk to you about." She wanted to frame it correctly. "You've been doing amazing work."

He chimed in, "*We've* been doing amazing work."

Jenna smiled. "Yes, we, but I think we need to push for some of the more impactful projects and initiatives. You know we spoke about trying to make meaningful differences. All this educating the office stuff is good, but that can't be where it ends. Remember the volunteering programme? And that's only one example," she finished, not wanting to seem self-serving.

Chapter 12

An Apple Far from the Tree

A rumble of low voices and bass music was coming from the living room when Deborah arrived home. Meghan had friends over; this was not an unusual occurrence as the combination of being a lone parent and years of Meghan being away at boarding school had led to her growing up quickly, and finding an independence her mother not only respected, but also identified with. Despite their ideological differences, Deborah knew, if worst came to worst, Meghan would be ok; ultimately, as a parent, this was her greatest achievement.

She gently opened the door, peering her head inside; she wondered how long it would take before she was noticed. On this occasion not long.

"Fuck! Hey, Mrs T," Otto, Meghan's friend said in surprise as he saw Deborah's face and dropped tobacco all over the beige Persian rug.

"Hey, Mum," Meghan said without looking up from her *building* duties. Deborah tried her best to hide the look of judgment from her face, but she was too late. Otto was accompanied by Tilly. Both of whom decided they'd spent enough time at Meghan's and it was time to go.

"Catch you on Twitch later, M," Otto said hurriedly,

as he struggled to find his shoes.

"You guys don't have to go," Meghan said lazily, casting an equally judgmental look back at her mum. Tilly was still quite confused, but Otto was on hand to help guide her to the front door.

Deborah opened the door to a sparse fridge. "Meg, what happened to the Waitrose order I asked you to put through?" she shouted through to the living room.

"What?!" Meghan replied.

"Waitrose! The order! What happened to it?"

Meghan lumbered into the kitchen. "Oh, yeah, I forgot, sorry. You don't have to shout, you know." She opened a bottle of water and gulped deeply.

"Do you guys really have to do that stuff in the living room? Your bedroom is big enough for your friends."

"I know, Mum: you wish you'd had your own room growing up, let alone one as big as mine," she said tapping her mum on the shoulder.

Deborah returned a look that said 'touché'. "Should we order something?"

"Mmhmm," Meghan said, drinking, realising how hungry she was.

The pair had divvied up the Indian takeaway and were happily grazing in front of the television. Deborah loved these moments with her daughter, moments that were happening less often these days. She was keen to capitalise on the opportunity, "No, Meg, did she just say that? That's a definite *microaggression*," she said as the white model on TV complimented the black model on her hair. There was something unnatural about the word; it stuck to her tongue.

Meghan looked at her mother in surprise, mouth full of food. "A what?" she mumbled.

"An aggression, a micro aggression, right?" Deborah replied.

"Who taught you that? I'm pretty sure I didn't send you a link to *that*."

"I do my own research, too, you know."

"So what else has my woke mother learned?"

The pressure hit her suddenly; she may have over played her hand. She desperately scanned her memory for more information, but she was coming up short. *I need to start making notes*, she thought.

"Well, of course these are small things that could be misunderstood and taken the wrong way."

Meghan rolled her eyes. "Misunderstood?"

"Yes, misunderstood."

"Mum, it's not a misunderstanding." Deborah looked blankly, pretty sure she remembered the definition correctly. "It's a manifestation of privilege to not have to understand how our words and actions impact others."

"Privilege?" The word caused her skin to crawl.

"Yes, Mother, things we have without working for them, you know, like this house?" she said in provocation.

"I've worked very hard for everything, this house included!" she replied, taking the bait as she always did.

"Oh no, that dress is not the one!" Meghan shouted at the TV, spilling some korma on the rug.

***

CJ adjusted his tie for the umpteenth time while listening to the final briefing.

"And remember, always, full smiles please. Half smiles can look disingenuous or sneaky; not a look we're going for," Colleen said.

"Alright, I got it, smile and smile again," CJ replied with a mock smile.

"This is important, Calvin, you're going to be meeting

with some key campaigners and there will be press."

"Yes, press, press."

Colleen gave him a look a teacher would give a troublesome student. "I'm glad you're in a good mood, but we can't mess this up. Need I remind you the election is only around the corner?"

"Ok, I'm serious, I'm focused," he said with a laugh.

They arrived at the designated street in the heart of a shaky constituency seat, exactly the type of place that would need to be reclaimed if the party had any chance of winning the election. CJ approached the first door with Colleen, camera team, and security close behind. He wrapped his knuckles on the door and an elderly voice shouted back. "One minute, one minute." A short woman carefully opened the door and was taken aback by all the faces in her walkway.

"Hi there, I'm Calvin James, Shadow Minister and Leader of the Opposition for the upcoming election. I wanted to talk to you about the election, if you have a moment?" he said softly, acknowledging the shock in her face.

"Oh why yes, do you want to come in?" she offered as she tried to collect herself.

"That won't be necessary, mam, we can talk here. Wouldn't want to dirty your lovely carpets."

She smiled at the compliment.

"Do you know who you will be voting for, mam?" CJ continued.

"Oh, I'm not sure. There's the girl from up north, she seems nice, and then there's the other chap… and you, of course."

"Definitely lots of strong candidates. I wanted to personally let you know that a vote for Calvin James is a vote for your community. We're keen to ensure your needs are met."

"Oh that does sound good, I guess… what did you say your name was again?"

"Calvin, Calvin James, madam."

"Ok, great," she said with a smile.

"Can we count on you?"

The lady hesitated.

"What if I give you a badge and a mug?" he added jokingly.

"Oh, I could do with a mug," she replied. The pair had a photo taken with her holding the mug, wearing the badge and him warmly embracing her.

"That wasn't amazing, Let's hope the next one is better," he whispered to Colleen as they approached the next door. "Hello, I'm Calvin James, here to talk to you about a vote for PM." He delivered his practised introductory spiel before trying a different tact and asking the young woman what she wanted from the next Prime Minister.

Kelly was star-struck by the cameras and CJ's warm smile. "I don't know, Mr Prime Minister, there isn't much work round 'ere anymore, not like there used to be."

"Of course, I know there's been a big problem with employment, especially since the local factories have closed… Oh and I'm not the Prime Minister yet, but maybe with your help, I could be."

She blushed, lighting up like a beacon, as she heard shouts from her kids in the house. "Well it's good to know you care. My fella, well my ex," she corrected as she fixed her fringe, "he's been out of work for ages now and the government aren't helping at all. You know, it's all these new lot that get the jobs, not like me and you." She tried to whisper the last part, before shouting at her kids to be quiet.

CJ stilled himself internally, he'd been expecting this. "I understand. Rest assured a vote for James is a vote for more jobs and a better economy," he said, offering her a badge, before posing for a photo. Kelly got as close as possible to CJ, inhaling his aftershave deeply.

CJ made a subtle but quick exit for the next house.

"Better?" Colleen joked as he approached the next door. He fired back a look acknowledging the joke, without embracing the timing.

At the final house a small South Asian woman opened the door. Wrapped in traditional clothing and rocking a small child, she was happy to answer a couple of questions, but said she couldn't be long as her elderly father was about ready for lunch.

"Of course, so let me ask you, what concerns you most? What keeps you up at night?"

She thought carefully. "I think I worry about my family, my husband mainly, who is working two jobs at the moment. Sometimes this area doesn't feel safe. People say stuff... sometimes worse."

CJ appreciated her candour and recognised the sensitivity of the situation. "I hear you, we should all feel safe in our communities, no matter where we're from."

"I've seen you before, on the TV. You seem like a trustworthy person. I believe you will fight for people like us," she offered, somewhat hopefully.

'People like us' resonated with CJ. "Of course, I will do all I can. I don't want to keep your father waiting, I'm sure you have a lovely lunch prepared. Any going spare?" he joked. She smiled and touched his hand. They took the mandatory photo. The young child was angelic throughout.

The car sped CJ and Colleen back to HQ. "Now *that* was better," he said to nobody in particular as he stared out of the window.

Chapter 13

The Bentalago Job

Jonathan was unsure why the emergency meeting was called or what his role would be, but hoped he would be able to contribute.

"Thanks for joining, everyone," Deborah began. "We have a real emergency, and a genuine opportunity to really help."

The D&I squad listened intently, all except Charlie of course. "Here come the Diversity Brigade to the rescue," he jabbed.

"One of our most important clients has reached out for us to help with a little bit of… reputation management," she continued. "Bentalago are a leading design house, with over a century of heritage in providing luxury items for consumers around the world." There were nods from around the room in recognition of the famous brand and the work Inertia had supported with in the past. "There's been an unfortunate incident. A product range depicting an… old fashioned image… has caught some bad social media and subsequently some online outlets."

Jonathan was trying to deconstruct the message. He looked around the room, the majority in attendance seemed to understand the situation. People were beginning to look his way with reassuring eyes. Jonathan interpreted the growing attention as solicitation for his input. Bowing to the pressure, he asked, "What was the image? Why has it caused so much trouble?"

The question made Deborah feel uneasy. Unsure how to answer, she connected her laptop to the screen and loaded an image of one of the t-shirts from the product line. The bright white eyes and even brighter large red lips of the early twentieth century caricature filled the screen. The wincing in the room was almost audible.

"Oh… right," was the best Jonathan could muster.

"It was an honest mistake," Deborah quickly replied to the growing judgment in the room. "We know the best fashion is often *daring*… This perhaps is pushing the boundary a little too far."

Jonathan tried to buy into the accidental creativity narrative that Deborah was suggesting, but it didn't feel right. He wondered what they would be expected to do to help with this fiasco.

"So, we need to help. Any ideas?"

Murmurs began around the room.

"Maybe, if we leave it, people will forget?" Edward said.

"Exactly how are we helping if we 'leave it'?" Deborah asked. "No bad ideas."

"No bad ideas," Trish echoed.

"An apology?" Rachel suggested.

"Yeah, an apology is always good," Deborah said, happy that progress has been made from *maybe if we leave it*. "An apology, right, anything else?"

"A gesture?" Rachel continued.

"Wait, wait, wait, just an apology? Like a statement? Is that enough? Genuine?" Jonathan asked.

"That's why I said gesture, too," Rachel returned.

"What about if we get someone else to help with the

apology?" Trish added.

"How do you mean?" Deborah asked.

"Somehow make it more genuine, someone that validates and corroborates it," Edward said.

"Like a celebrity?" Trish asked.

"A rapper?" Deborah shot out.

"Or a Trapper?" Trish added.

"What's a Trapper?" Deborah asked.

"Hmm… I don't actually know, but I've heard it said," Trish pondered, finger on chin.

"Ah, I'm not sure a rapper was quite what I was thinking," Rachel continued.

"An actor?" Charlie offered ambivalently.

"People do like actors," Trish said.

"I think what Rachel is saying is that perhaps a celebrity isn't the best option," Jonathan contributed to Rachel's agreement.

"But if they're not famous, how will people know to care?" Trish asked.

"Yep, so a public apology, supported by someone with gravitas, and maybe a bit of a gesture. Good, good, right, let's get to it, get this into action. Time is important." Deborah dismissed the team while Jonathan and Rachel exchanged equal looks of unease. "Trish, so who can we get? What's Coolio up to?"

***

"What are you guys working on now?" Jenna asked with interest as they packed up from another study session.

"This Bentalago thing," Jonathan replied.

"Benta-what?"

"Bentalago, the designer?" he said confidently, as if he hadn't only recently learned the name.

"Oh, the label that Undoubted and Confounded

148

wear?"

"Yeah," he replied, pretending to know who Undoubted was.

"What is it? Will it actually help the community?"

He paused. "Not exactly, it's more about an apology, I guess," he said coyly, slight shame around the project seeping into his speech.

"An apology?"

"Yeah, this is about creating a credible apology to limit reputational damage… I think."

"Right, sounds very impactful!" she snorted in derision.

Jonathan looked at the floor. "I know, but Deborah, she comes up with these things and we have to jump."

"What about all the actual work that was planned, the stuff that will help people?"

Jonathan was silent again, no satisfactory answer to hand. His best recourse was an attempt to change the subject. "Should we head to the library?"

The rain poured heavily as Jonathan attempted to shelter Jenna under his mack as they approached the library steps. They pushed against the large library doors. But they were locked with a damp *Closed* sign struggling to stay attached to the handles. Jenna was starting to shiver.

"Maybe we should cancel this week?" Jonathan offered.

Determined as ever not to let circumstances get the better of her, Jenna said "We can go back to mine, it's not far."

Jonathan couldn't believe his ears: an opportunity to go to Jenna's. "Yes," he replied before Jenna had a chance to finish the suggestion.

The pair walked back into the rain in determined fashion. "Do you drive?" Jenna asked.

"No… I never got round to it," he said ashamedly.

"Oh, that's cool. You don't need to drive in London, anyway. I gave up my car. The insurance got too much, but on days like this I miss it."

"Yami, you here?" Jenna shouted as she took her shoes off in the small hallway to no response.

"Shall I take mine off?" he asked cautiously.

"If you don't mind," she replied, looking for signs of her sister's presence.

Jonathan eagerly absorbed his surroundings: this was where the love of his life resided.

"Let's go through to the living room. Looks like my sister isn't back yet."

He passively followed behind. The small but neat living space was well decorated with family photos and various artefacts and artistic pieces. They sat closely on the cosy two-person sofa and began to discuss the learnings for the week.

Something seemed off with Jenna, he wanted to find out what was ging on but didn't want to pry. It was hard for him to see her like this, to know something was up. "Is everything ok?"

"Of course, why?" she replied automatically.

"You just seem a bit off, a bit quieter than usual. Normally, you're all over me about my lack of enthusiasm for the work."

She paused and considered a viable response. "A bit tired, I guess," she said, trying not to think of the real source of her problems.

"You sure? I know we're not close like you and Charlotte, but you can tell me things if you want."

She dreaded the idea of sharing this information with Charlotte, knowing the type of blunt advice she'd be given; even her sister would no doubt have similar

150

feedback.

"It's ok, just personal."

"Are you healthy?" he shot out without thinking.

"No, not like that, it's... man... boy trouble."

The confession hit Jonathan like an anvil. *Of course of course, she had someone in her life, how could someone so beautiful not?* "Oh," was the best he could muster. Not wanting to seem insincere, he doubled down on his previous offer. "Still, if you want to talk, I'm here."

Jenna appreciated the gesture. She knew he cared. As she was about to reply, the front door opened.

"Sis, I am home!" Yami shouted as she wiped her shoes on the matt and slammed the door. "It's horrible out there, honestly, I don't know why I'm in this country sometimes," she continued as she entered the living room. "I didn't realise we had company!"

"This is Jonathan, we're working a bit together. We've probably done enough for today," Jenna said, glancing at the Africa-shaped clock on the wall.

Jonathan got the message and gathered his stuff as Yami carefully studied him.

"Don't leave on my account. I can give you guys some privacy. I need to do a couple of tutorial recordings tonight, but I can do them in my room. Are you on Insta, Jonny?" she asked salaciously enough to make Jonathan's heart beat rapidly.

"I am, but I don't really use it. Mostly to follow some anime–"

Jenna interrupted him. "You don't need to worry about that," she said.

"See you tomorrow?" he suggested as he was practically pushed towards the front door.

"Yep," Jenna replied, arms now folded across her chest.

"See you. Jonny!" Yami shouted as the door shut.

151

"Look at you, bringing boys home when I'm not around," Yami jested cheekily.

Jenna rolled her eyes. "Put the rice on from yesterday."

"Yes, Mum!" she fired back sarcastically as she headed to the kitchen.

***

The wind blustered and howled as Deborah forced her way up her road and onto her path. It was the type of weather to cap the type of day that you wished would end as quickly as possible. By the time she entered her quiet home, she was desperate for nothing more than a hot bath and a large glass of wine, not necessarily in that order, perhaps best together.

"Meghan?" she shouted. No response. Deborah presumed she was out at a friend's, as usual. She took off her damp coat and kicked off her shoes, allowing herself a sigh of relief for the very stylish, but pinching heels. She climbed her plush staircase with her glass of wine in hand, and heard faint music. *I guess she just didn't hear me*, Deborah thought as she headed towards the bathroom. *I'll pop in and say hello before I get in the bath*, she thought, and she headed back down the hall to Meghan's room. The music became louder as she approached. By the time she reached the door she could hear whispers and giggles emanating from the room. Deborah remembered the countless chastising lectures she'd received from her daughter about privacy, but her curiosity had taken over. Meghan shared very little about her love life, despite her mother's constant attempts of interrogation. If she caught her in the act, at least she would have a boy's face to work with... maybe even a name.

She made the call to proceed, pushing open the door.

"Evening, Princess, wanted to come up and say hi before getting in the bath. I've had a hell of a day… hope I'm not interrupt–"

"Mum!" Meghan shouted in surprise, as if she'd not only lost track of the time, but also completely forgotten she was in her mother's home.

"Meghan, who is that?" were the only words she could find as she dropped her wine glass.

"It's no one. What have I told you about knocking! Boundaries!" she exclaimed as she prodded around in an attempt to find a t-shirt to cover her exposed breasts.

"It's a *girl*," was the next best attempt of her shock-stricken vocabulary.

"Yes, Mum, it's a girl," Meghan replied as she picked up the wine glass and ushered her practically paralysed mother out of her room.

"Meghan, I think we need to talk about this," Deborah said as her daughter closed her in the bathroom. "At least let me get another glass of wine," she shouted again, realising the wine was even more essential than before.

"I'll bring you one, just get in the bath." Meghan rushed her guest out of the house before delivering the new glass of wine and accompanying bottle to her mother, realising one glass probably wouldn't cut it.

***

CJ's study was dark, the house deathly silent once again. He drained his third tumbler of whisky in nervous anticipation for the call.

"You saw the footage?" CJ queried anxiously.

"I did," he replied calmly.

"And?"

"Well, it was okay," Bill offered.

"Ok isn't great," CJ clarified.

"It isn't."

"Any more detail?" CJ asked impatiently. There was a pause, "Bill?"

"We may need a little push to sway the... doubters. We can't afford to be seen as too *soft* on certain issues... given your... background."

CJ pondered the assessment. "Right."

"Don't worry, we'll get it sorted. I have some ideas." Bill ended the call.

'Fuck!' CJ shouted internally. He reached for the bottle of whisky and poured another glass. He grasped his phone again and checked his messages. Nothing from Jenna, nothing from Flo; he gulped deeply.

***

Deborah watched on in silence as Jonathan went through the messages he'd helped craft with the respective guest speakers. She wondered if his growing gravitas was genuinely built on a maturing confidence or more blissful naivety at working with minor celebrities. His naturally unassuming aura was well balanced with those who craved the lime light. Deborah could see him doing more work like this in the future, as long as he was willing to be a true team player.

"Let me know if you're uncomfortable with any of this?" Jonathan said to the speakers, in slight hope someone would challenge the approach. He was met with understanding nods. "Ok... well, we can ..." He saw the young rapper, Undoubted, was about to say something. "Yes?" he invited.

"So, we need to say the messages exactly, kinda word for word?"

"Good question. I think you can say things your own

way, as long as the sentiment comes across. Does that make sense?" He was met with more silent nods. "Great, you'll get the call to go up soon."

"But who's perfect, really, anyway?" Undoubted said, as he leaned back against the brick wall of the designated estate style stage. "And you know, for me, that's where I come from when I look at times like this," the shot switched to a gang of boys in black baggy tracksuits murmuring along in agreement.

"So, from when we can all say, yeah I make mistakes too, we can forgive the people at Bentalago, and God tells us to forgive, so you know what it is already… oh, and the clothes are dank still," he finished as the video apology moved to the next star, this time to comedian Kofi Ati. Jonathan watched on in awe from the audience, awe that this was the decided upon tone and awe about how quickly they managed to pull together the stellar cast of Black celebrities.

Kofi picked up the baton. "You know me, I like a joke as much as the next guy, but sometimes jokes go too far." The shot switched to an image of the contentious hoody with a red x over it. "Like a good comedian, Bentalago have the awareness to know what is and isn't a joke and when to apologise for things that have gone too far."

The video switched to the final star, footballer Kyle Coleman, who began with kick-ups on an urban green before catching the ball and spinning to the camera. "When a team mate makes a mistake on the pitch, you don't tear them down. No, you help them up. Once they've apologised, you help them to do better. That's how we win together," he finished with a toothy smile.

Deborah started a round of applause that was echoed by the rest of the panel and the journalists in the audience. She took the mic at the podium. "Not only are Bentalago apologising, they are donating 50 pairs of their new Entrustiso shoe to teenagers from deprived areas." She led another round of applause. "So, you'll see we have a couple of stars from our movie here, along with representatives from Bentalago. We can take a couple of questions. Sure, you in the blue."

"This isn't the first time a major fashion house has been caught up in this type of... *incident*. It's not actually even the first from this company. When do you think lessons will actually be learned?"

Deborah looked awkwardly at the rep from Bentalago, who slowly began to speak into his collar mic, "I think, we in the fashion world are always trying to be cutting edge and daring..." Deborah stared intensely at the rep to suggest that was the wrong line of messaging. "...but we're always trying to learn and do better. This is a constantly evolving situation and we need to continue on our journey."

"Ok, how about one from one of our celebrities?" Deborah suggested.

"How did that piece by Bentalago make you feel?" the journalist asked in an empathetic tone which felt slightly strained.

The three celebrities looked awkwardly at one another, before Undoubted decided to take the reins. "I can't lie, I didn't even notice it first time. I just saw the news drip and was like, yeah, but then my people told me about the racist shit and I was like, nah, can't be that."

"Well said," Deborah affirmed. "And with that, we have to end our session for today. You can send any follow up questions to the e-mail address on the handout," she finished quickly, desperate to end the event before something damning was said.

***

"Champ," the voice said from behind as Jonathan headed for the lifts.

"Hey boss– Deborah," he corrected.

"How do you think it all went?"

Jonathan's mind whirred into life looking for the most diplomatic response. "I think we set out to achieve what the client wanted." He surprised himself with the political correctness of the answer.

"I thought we did, too. You did well helping organise all of this in such a rush. And a great job on the logo. I appreciate the commitment. It's not going unnoticed – definitely showing leadership credentials. You know, as we look to develop you further, there's some training I think you will benefit from."

"Training? I didn't think the design team received training."

"They don't," she said with a smirk.

Chapter 14

Politically Correct

Andy banged the front door with his fists. "Kell!" he
shouted. He waited a moment and looked up and down
the street. He could see curtains flicker as people spied
from their living rooms. He began to bang again. "Kell!
Kell! Let me in or I'm gonna kick the door in!"

"Shut it!" a voice shouted from down the street.

"Fuck off and mind ya business!" Andy returned.

A silhouette approached the door. Andy heard the
series of latches adjust.

"Just get in," she said as Andy pushed into the house.
"You stink of booze, again!"

"Was in the St George with Dale, wasn't I," he said
rhetorically.

"Of course you were. How much money have you
come back with, then?"

"I gave you a bit, didn't I? Can't I have a drink? What
else have I got?" he slurred.

"Quiet, you'll wake the boys."

"Good, I wanna see em," he said, as he teetered,
looking starry-eyed up the stairs.

"Not like that, and you're on the sofa tonight.
Coming in at this hour, in that state and with no money,"
she said in disgust as she headed back upstairs.

"Kell! Kell!"

"Shhhh" she replied as she continued to climb, back facing him all the way.

Andy stumbled in the dark living room as he fished around for the light switch. He was instead met with the sharp edges of a pointy action figure that shot a sharp pain through his foot, causing him to shout in agony. He finally managed to settle on the sofa, having to use his jacket as a blanket as the cold night breeze blistered in through a panel in the front room window he had cracked the month before and only poorly patched up with masking tape. He looked at his phone, hoping for warmth from the glow of the screen; a news alert flicked up: 'PM candidate mingles with locals'. He clicked through to see an image of Kelly cosied up with CJ. His blood began to boil, the intrusive cool breeze no longer a problem.

***

Deborah's frustration grew as the call continued. "I think that's a good idea, of course, but it would be a different area of focus for us," she offered with muted optimism.

"Deb, Debby, Deb! That's what we do at this level: think about the bigger picture, identify the bigger opportunities. Leave that to us," Mr. Johansson said.

"Of course, sir."

"Ultimately, we want to be helping, right, doing the right things?"

"Definitely."

"There you go. It's all good, then. I know you'll execute expertly as always," Mr Johansson finished happily.

Deborah closed the call with a deep sigh, something that was becoming a more regular occurrence.

***

Jonathan slumped into his gaming chair, tired enough to fall asleep. He glanced at the stack of reading he needed to do, and then across to his computer. He reminisced about when his evenings were simply hours of online questing. He decided to quickly log-on to check if anyone was online. *I'll only be a couple of minutes.* His desire was met when he clicked on to find three of his former team online. The chat function buzzed into life, the group pleasantly surprised to see him active again. Some were worried something had happened to him. He allayed their concerns by letting them know he'd taken on an extra role at work, which meant he had less time. There was a pang of nostalgia as they chatted. They updated him on recent quests. He congratulated them on the levels that had been attained. Invitations followed for an evening adventure. He looked at his watch, then to the stack of books, and begrudgingly declined. *The things we do.*

***

The following morning, Deborah called the squad together. "Alright team, when it rains, it pours, am I right?"

The group were unsure what she was referring to. "We have a new project in, and it is an important one, could represent a new *avenue* for the organisation," she stressed in her best French accent; Trish was the only one to chuckle along. "We are going to be helping PM hopeful Calvin 'CJ' James on an ad and potentially in the run up to the election."

A hush fell over the room. "But this is not a D&I project," Rachel stated.

"No… but we do need a level of *expertise*. Jenna, I understand you've actually worked with the candidate on this, so I will be putting it on you to run point."

Jenna was struggling to process all the information. Jonathan picked up on the consternation on her face.

"Any problems, Jenna? I'm sure Rachel can help as needed."

"No, no problems," Jenna replied quickly.

***

"He seems to be a bit, I don't know, fake?" Jonathan said in his most ambivalent tone.

"Ha, why fake? What's fake about him?" Jenna queried, intrigued to get another person's perspective on the man she knew so well.

"Pshh, just look at him. He's a bit too polished, and the little jokes he's always making."

"I don't know, people seem to think he's quite funny… charismatic… charming." She'd let her natural enthusiasm for CJ take over.

"Charming? More like cheesy."

Jonathan's natural defensiveness made her laugh. The delicateness of male pride had always fascinated her. "Well, we'll have to agree to disagree on this. Ultimately, we're getting a chance to help. That's the main thing, right? I mean as long as they stick with the bigger objectives of the plan."

"I guess so," Jonathan replied begrudgingly.

"By the way, I don't think I'll be able to make our session on Thursday."

"Really? Why not? I was hoping we could go over the Unconscious Bias work," Jonathan whined.

"I've got a life. I do have other things going on aside from helping you be Deborah's champion," she snapped.

Jonathan was taken aback. "I'm sorry. Sometimes I forget how much you have on. You seem to have time for everyone. I still don't know how you do it. How are plans for the Black Business Fair going?" he asked sincerely, but also in the hope of tempering her feelings.

Jenna inhaled deeply. She knew he didn't mean to be demanding. It was her nature to want to help, to want to do all she could, all the time. To be a super-woman felt innate, but she often wondered how truly natural it was. Had she simply bought into societal programming? "It's going ok, still a lot to do, but I'll get there."

"I know you will." He had complete faith. Faith that only grew with more time they spent together. "I'm hoping to have my own studio one day, too," he added automatically, his subconscious seeking connection.

Jenna was surprised by his dream, having clearly underestimated his level of ambition. "That's really cool. Who knows, maybe one day we'll be moguls together," she said playfully.

***

Yami came into the living room, kitted out in brand new fitness wear. 'How's my favourite sis? You like?" she said, posing for her endorsement.

"I'm your only sis," Jenna replied dryly. "What's all this? Since when are you a gym girl?" she asked with a laugh, knowing her sister was usually against most things that could ruin her make-up.

"New year, new me. And this is important for my brand. If I'm going to be a proper influencer, I need to have the full package: make-up, body, and the hot topics. Going to start a podcast with Blessing."

"Yeah, but it's not the new year and I'm sure it's the same you! I want to believe all that, but I'm still sceptical about the influencer stuff. Are you actually going to stick at this project?"

"What does Mama say, have faith?"

"As long as it's not misplaced," Jenna returned.

"I saw a Tik-Tok about meeting guys at the gym. You know my girl, Kendra? She put me on, too. Said there are loads of fine eligible men ready to help you with your form and all sorts down at the gym. *And* you have instructors, too. So I thought why not pop along and see what's what, right? Also, I need these curves to be tight if I'm posting more content, so it's not *just* about the boys."

Deep down, Jenna enjoyed her sister's vivacious approach to life. Part of her enjoyed the opportunity to live vicariously care-free through her adventures; part of her wished she had more of that for herself. "Right. I guess. And the face full of make-up, like you're hitting the club, isn't a problem?"

"Did you not hear me? I'm going to meet men. No man is going to want some plain-faced bait ting, come on."

"They're probably not going to want a sweaty mess, either."

"Don't hate, you know I'm cute," Yami said, rolling her eyes. "Anyway, what happened with you and that guy from the shoobs?"

Jenna considered her response. "I don't think he's right for me."

"What do you mean, what could be wrong for you? He's six-foot-three, broad shoulders, hands like plates and skin like a black hole. Are you crazy?"

Jenna couldn't argue with the description her sister had painted. "I don't know, the spark wasn't there, and he was *very* traditional. Like some is good, but he was barefoot-and-pregnant type."

"BS. You're always going on about god-fearing men.

I know what it is, it's that *neek* from work you keep hanging with, isn't it?" She walked around to face her sister, so she could look her directly in her eyes.

"No, Jonathan and I are just friends."

"Psshh, I invented 'just friends'. Friends don't make you blush – Yeah, I can tell when you blush. Is he even from GH? Naija? No, he's not a Yardie, is he? Sis!"

"*Go to your class*!" Jenna demanded, throwing a cushion at her sister.

Yami left, singing a Burna Boy track as she closed the door. Jenna tilted her head back on the sofa. Maybe her sister had a point. *Was* she developing feelings for him? Maybe they were spending too much time together. He wasn't her type, it didn't make sense, and he still hadn't delivered on what had been promised.

***

Jenna toyed with her phone, while trying to stem the growing feeling of frustration. 'Did you arrange this?' was the message she finally sent to CJ.

'I know I might be the next PM, but I'm not a magician. Believe it or not, I didn't want to do the ad, let alone work with your company. What do you think Flo would say if she knew?'

Jenna knew he was right but found it easier to believe he was leveraging his influence rather than the universe was bringing them together once again.

'I'm sure you don't have to work on it, anyway. You probably won't even see me.'

'Funny thing… I'm running point,' she finished with an emoji covering its face with its hands, aptly describing her feeling.

A huge smile materialised across her screen. 'I promise to not be too demanding on set.'

164

'You, a diva? Never,' she texted back, remembering the time he gave a waiter a dressing down for bringing the wrong bottle of wine.

***

Shoot day rolled around quickly. Time was of the essence with the election looming. Jonathan was on set as consult, demonstrating the company's commitment to CJ's inclusive platform. He could see Jenna was off. He tried his best to reassure her. "It won't be that bad, I promise."

"I know, but, if we're going to be doing this D&I work, we need to be doing it properly. No more of this superficial show stuff, pampering politicians. We need to be making impactful change, the real things that will actually make a difference."

Jonathan was captivated once again by her passionate delivery and floral scent. He didn't recognise this perfume but enjoyed it nonetheless.

"Wait, J, so we're really going to do all of these scenes?" CJ asked Jenna with genuine confusion.

"Not J," she fired back in a hushed voice, not wanting anyone to hear him address her with a nickname.

"What?" he replied in confusion.

"Not J, not at work," she said, looking at her surroundings in an exaggerated fashion, until he got the message. She got the conversation back on course: "Our guidance was very clear. We need to show you're comfortable in different worlds."

"I mean, yeah, but, really?" CJ re-checked.

"It'll flow. Do you trust me?"

"Of course."

"Trust me, then."

"Mr. James? CJ? Can you sip the pint?" Deborah

suggested as deferentially as she could manage.

CJ glanced towards Jenna for support. She looked backed at him and gestured with her hand to her mouth, mimicking a drinking action. CJ braced himself to drink the stout, not his drink of choice.

"Got it!" shouted the director. "Let's go to the next shot."

CJ spat the mouthful into a nearby glass. "Oh, man up!" Jenna said sternly, as she ushered him to the office set.

Deborah and Jonathan caught the abrasive comment and seemingly familiar interaction. "Jenna, a moment?"

"Uh huh," she replied.

"I know your style can be a bit more... direct... but let's remember this is a client, and not only a client, it's potentially the future Prime Minister, so a little respect please," she instructed, before chasing after CJ to reassure him.

Jenna held back her desired response.

The team regrouped at the office set, a scenario CJ was more comfortable with. "So, what we're thinking is, you're typing on the computer, and then the phone rings and you deliver the line," Deborah said.

"And the line is 'As a business owner, I understand the importance of a solid economy, so that's why you can count on me to keep the pounds in check.'"

Deborah nodded and smiled. "That was actually one of mine," she said proudly.

CJ looked for Jenna; Jonathan monitored their interaction. Jenna gave a helpless but somehow reassuring shrug.

"Ok, take two," the director said.

Jonathan watched Jenna and CJ talk and walk; there was an ease with one another that he hadn't seen before, and was something he longed for.

The rain and wind swept across the field as the cameraman struggled to keep the lens on CJ, who was fully decked out in what he thought resembled an out-of-date PE kit. "But I don't even like football," he pleaded to Jenna.

"That doesn't matter, people expect you to like it; you're the young, fit, active candidate," she countered.

"And what am I going to do with this?" he asked, looking at the football.

Jonathan felt his pain.

"I don't know, kick-ups or something," she offered, the suggestion getting a thumbs up from Deborah who was wrapped tightly in her Burberry mack, rapidly losing interest in the previously critical filming project.

CJ awkwardly kicked at the football as the majority of onlookers clapped and cheered encouragingly, all except Jenna who looked more concerned than anything else.

"Is that enough?" CJ asked in frustration.

"I think we can do something with that," the director replied.

CJ was hoping he would now be able to get some alone time with Jenna, when Colleen ran over with a phone. "Sir, we need to go. Urgent call from Headquarters."

"Can't it wait?"

Colleen gave him her serious face. CJ gave Jenna the same helpless shrug she'd given him earlier in the day, something she was used to seeing. Jonathan couldn't shake the feeling something was up. Perhaps that was the type of guy she liked: someone more established, more inspirational. He began to think about his upcoming training.

***

Jonathan sat quietly with his pen hovering over his journal, unsure how to begin this entry. His mind continued to race back to the ad filming, the interaction between Jenna and CJ, subtle looks, and even perhaps, *tension in the air? No that's too much*, he told himself, hoping it was just a sense of paranoia. He struggled to put his finger on what was bugging him so much about the whole situation; he began to jot down questions instead of a proper entry. *Maybe it is CJ? The way he's so 'charismatic'*, as Jenna described, or apparently *committed to the issues* that Jonathan was only now discovering. His mind continued to wander. He thought back to when he was young, a time in his life he rarely allowed himself to reflect on, a time that was practically locked away. Those moments when he stood beside the two large oak boxes, each one containing a parent. Parents he never knew, people he would never have a chance to get to know. April wouldn't speak much about her son or daughter-in-law, and it was a dynamic Jonathan grew to accept, not knowing any different. But, despite all the love provided by his Gran, it could never fill the void. *What have I missed out on? What would my parents have taught me? How different would I have been?*

PART 3

Chapter 15

Onsite

Dale sprinted, or at least his best attempt at sprinting the over-sized boots he'd borrowed from Andy would allow. Andy was smoking outside the café when Dale arrived. "You're lucky the driver was running late," Andy said, stubbing out his cigarette. "I wouldn't have waited for you."

"Come on, And, you try moving in these things," he said, looking down at the large steel capped boots.

"Trust me, you'll be happy you have them when you're walking around a construction site."

"Yeah, I'm grateful, of course. What are we gonna be doing, anyway? Building a school or summin?" Dale asked naively.

"What do you know about bricklaying? No, we're not gonna be building a school, we're just gonna be on clear-up. And we should be happy we have that; it's a hundred quid cash in hand, no questions – Robbo has done us a solid with this."

The van pulled up and the half a dozen workmen piled into the back. Dale and Andy were sat opposite each other on wheel shafts as the van bumped and jolted to their destination. Dale could tell Andy wasn't in a talkative mood, so tried his best to keep himself entertained and his boots on. They arrived on a busy construction site about forty-five minutes later. They were given hard hats and high vis jackets, and then broken into smaller groups. As expected, Dale and Andy were part of clean-up responsible for moving excess debris from the building site to the skips and bins at the other end of the site. Craig, who had been splitting the men up, informed the clean-up team Pavel would be in charge. The other men all seemed to be chatting with one another when Andy realised he and Dale were the only English people in the group. Andy suddenly heard one of Robbo's passionate speeches in the back of his head. He grabbed Craig: "Mate, any chance you have something else for us to help with, something maybe with the other lads?"

"What other lads?"

"You know… the English boys," he said at a low volume.

"Right, well we all work together on this site," he looked down at his clip board, "and I believe you guys have no prior experience so the best we can offer is clean-up. That is clean-up," he said, pointing to the Polish group.

"It's come to this, has it? Not looking out for each other anymore."

"I don't know what you mean. Do you want the job, or not? I've got plenty of lads looking for a day's work."

Andy relented. "Clean-up, it is."

Clean-up was not easy. Both Andy and Dale struggled with the back-and-forth heavy lifting. Many of the broken tinder blocks that required moving needed to be carried in pairs. So long out of work and not much physical activity to speak of, by mid-morning the pair were exhausted. The group rested against the wall and sat curb side with their teas while, to the amusement of the rest of the group, Andy and Dale were taking deep breaths and chugging on Red Bulls.

"This is so embarrassing," Andy managed to force out between deep inhales.

"Huh?" Dale replied struggling to hear over the sound of his own breathing.

Pavel looked on and tried his best not to laugh. "Guys, I have a suggestion. How about we keep you two near the bins and skips and the other boys can pass the stuff to you? We create some kind of a chain, yes?" he offered compassionately.

"Sounds great," Dale replied quickly.

"Makes much more sense," Andy responded between pants.

The rest of day was significantly easier, Andy convinced it was because the pair had an opportunity to warm up. "We were a bit stiff from being out of work," he proclaimed to the rest of the group as they collected their wages for the day and waited for their ride home. Andy hated to admit it, but the day with the Polish guys wasn't so bad.

Surprise visits were not his forte, Jonathan found. Following a planned schedule helped his anxiety much more than spontaneity. But today was an exception. He was unable to shake thoughts of Jenna and CJ, thoughts about his parents. He had to ask some questions.

"Hey, Gill, is my gran about?" he asked, spotting the carer close to the communal kitchen.

"Oh hey, darling. April should be about somewhere, maybe check the games room?" she suggested, pointing towards the activity space.

Jonathan poked his head in, but his gran was nowhere to be seen. He waved to some of the other residents and continued his search. He checked all the

172

communal areas but she was nowhere, so he headed for her room. The door was closed, but he could hear coughing and muffled voices from inside. He pushed his ear close to the door and listened more carefully, still unable to make out the chatter. He decided to knock.

"Come in," a voice called.

He opened the door only to see a doctor and nurse crouched near his gran, asking her to breathe into a device. "Did you bring the spirometer?" the doctor asked without turning around.

Jonathan was taken back by the scene. "What's going on?"

The doctor and nurse both turned to face him. "I'm sorry, you can't be in here now."

"I'm her grandson, her next of kin, of course I can."

The nurse gave the doctor a pleading look. "Ok, we'll just be a moment, but please take a seat over there."

Jonathan sat and waited for the examination to finish. His gran gave him a thumbs up from her bed. "Is everything ok?" he asked.

"Perhaps we should step outside for a moment." The group left room. "Your grandmother has been having issues with her breathing. We've run a few tests and we're concerned that it could be pneumonia. Has she spoken to you about this?"

Jonathan shook his head, trying his best to process all the information.

"We'll continue to monitor for now, but... this is hard to say: she requires some extra support, which will require additional fees to her current support plan. I suggest having a conversation with her at some point."

He nodded blankly, finding it hard to concentrate on what was being said. He re-entered the room.

"You didn't say you were visiting today?" she said with a cough. "Unless my memory is going with my breathing," attempting to make light of the situation. Jonathan tried his best to laugh along, but struggled to force it.

"What's on your mind, son?" she asked, picking up on the worry in his face.

For the first time in his life, Jonathan found it difficult to look at his gran, a totally unfamiliar feeling he had no control over. He wracked his brain for the right words, level of reassurance, but was coming up blank. "The doctor said we should talk," were the words that fell out of his mouth unceremoniously.

"Did he now? Well, I'm ok. You know mi strong. You nah affi worry!" she said.

Jonathan could tell she didn't want to be pushed. Unsure of her actual state of health, he did not want to push her too hard. He decided to change tact. "Can I ask you something?"

"If it not about mi health," she replied with another mini-series of coughs that caused Jonathan to wince.

"I wanted to ask something about my parents. We never talk about them, not even how they died. I wanted to know why?" The question triggered another coughing fit.

April stared out of her window. "I guess I shoulda av say somting sooner... but you know losing my son and your mum was so ard. An you was so young... I was trying to protect you and me from reliving everything." She looked his way as if to ask if the answer had made any sense.

"But what happened?"

"We don't know for sure. Ur parents, dem were inna some tings." She gazed off fondly. "Nottin bad, but bad in a way cah it make dem a target."

Jonathan struggled to follow what she was trying to say.

174

"Like what? Crime, drugs?"

She began to cough again, while laughing. "No, mi wish in a way, would be less attention. Them were inna dem freedom fighter tings you know, some organisation deh Panter dem, Black Power ting. They were trying to help, but in dem days you couldn't do dem tings, you couldn't say too much or you would become a target, you see?"

Jonathan nodded along, trying his best to follow.

"So many people dem days, dem people who were tryna help with the movement, help with the community, dem kill off." She shook her head in sadness, painfully reliving the memory once again. She looked back to Jonathan. "Dem take mi son, I couldn't let dem take you too." Tears began to fall from her eyes.

Jonathan embraced her. "I'm here, I'm here."

"I was stupid."

"You could never be."

"I was," she shouted. "Stupid and scared, too fraid. I kept everyting from you, tried to make sure you wouldn't get dem ideas and end up like em. I wanted to protect you."

Jonathan again struggled to comprehend the message. "You did protect me, you did," he said, hugging her tighter.

***

'J, I know we shouldn't be talking, but this is work related, right? We can discuss work', the message read.

'I guess so,' she replied faster than intended.

CJ smiled at the speed of the reply. 'Ok, tell me what you honestly think about the ad. It's too cheesy, right?'

Three dots appeared and disappeared as Jenna edited her response. 'I think it communicates the messages your

175

team wanted.'

'But in a good way? Authentic? Genuine?'

'I guess that's for the voters to decide,' she replied with a tongue-sticking-out emoji. She realised she may be being too playful. 'Honestly, you know what it is, they want to push the narrative if it serves them, but do they really care? Our company has been doing some D&I stuff, but when it comes to the big things, the real commitment, it's not there.' It hit her, after pressing send, she really had to speak to Jonathan about that.

Her thoughts of D&I were short-lived as the fact was she was slowly being drawn into the irresistibly insatiable black hole that was Calvin James. She clicked onto his profile picture from the message thread. The picture almost came to life as it enlarged: CJ, his wife, his two kids, and a wave of emotion.

She would never forget the first time she saw that picture. As was often the case with their time together, spells of secluded bliss were marred by an intrusion of reality. On this occasion, a lovely meal had turned sour when that very family photo had fallen out of CJ's wallet as he attempted to pay the bill. CJ's misfortune triggered an inevitable conversation about their future, the future he had promised.

***

"J, I'm working on it," CJ said, in response to a question that hadn't been asked, at least not verbally; the look of dejection across Jenna's face said more than words ever could. She sighed.

"It's not easy, she's the mother of my kids, and there's…"

"What, CJ? What else is there?"

"There's perception, image to consider." The

comment lit an incredibly short fuse in Jenna. "No, I mean, in the public eye, it's expected, to be a family man, you know."

Jenna maintained control, managing to refrain from the explosion that was bubbling inside; in any case, she refused to give the clientele at the posh restaurant the pleasure of watching her lose her shit.

She managed to cling on to their romantic dream for longer than she would care to acknowledge. Admittedly, something that was easier to do without the reminders of real life. CJ did his best to maintain the illusion, but at times it proved impossible; one evening, in particular. Jenna had stayed late to help Kelvin clean up after the session, something she would often do. Kelvin didn't want to keep her longer than necessary, as usual having to insist that she head home. Jenna checked her messages as she exited the large steel school gate, only to hear someone shout.

"Jenna! It *is* Jenna, isn't it?" came the question from the large chrome SUV, as she looked at the photo of CJ, Jenna and the other volunteers from the charity website, which CJ had reposted.

Jenna was unsure how to respond to the mysterious female voice emanating from the large car; curiosity fuelled her approach, "Sorry, who are you?"

As soon as the words left her lips a familiar face came into view.

"I'm Flo, Flo James." The emphasis placed heavily on the surname. Jenna wanted to run, but her legs wouldn't move. Flo could tell by her reaction that she'd been recognised. "I guess I don't need to waste any more time with further introductions. I know this isn't all on you, in fact you may have even been innocent to a degree, but, whatever he's said to you, it stops now. This is over." It sounded like an instruction.

Jenna was having trouble believing this was actually happening to her. "It's not what you think," was the best she could offer.

Flo raised her hand to physically halt any further lies. "He's married, he has a family, and he has much bigger things ahead of him than you." She put the car into gear and sped off.

Jenna was in a state of shock. She felt liked she'd been punched in the stomach, while having a glass of ice-cold water thrown in her face. She was shaking, unsure what to do next. Part of her wanted to call CJ and lay into him for allowing this to happen, while another part wanted to chase down the car so she could give a better account for herself; *maybe your man wouldn't stray if he felt heard at home.* No, this was wrong, she was so much better than this. How would she feel if that was her husband, the father to her kids.

She began to walk home slowly, and a particularly piercing wind seemed to pick up out of nowhere, as if this night wasn't bad enough.

***

"Dale!" shouted the muffled voice from downstairs. Well attuned to distant beckons from his mum, he leant over his hi-fi system, turned the volume down and paused *FIFA*.

A pang of guilt hit him as he walked past his underused notebook at top of the stairs. "What?"

"You want a cuppa?"

"Yeah."

"Come down then, it's brewing."

"Now?!"

"Yes, now!" she bellowed back.

Dale trudged downstairs and took a seat at the

kitchen table as the kettled boiled. His mum had laid out some digestives and custard creams; Dale grazed absentmindedly.

"How's the job search, son?"

"Huh?" Dale replied, now thinking about how long he had left to get back into the game he was playing.

"Job, son, how's the search?"

"Oh, yeah, fine. Applied for a few things… the job support officer seemed happy enough."

The kettle bubbled to life and she filled up their mugs. "Son, you know you can stay here as long as you like. You'll always have your room. But you've been out of work for a while now," she said gently.

"I am trying, Mum," Dale replied, crumbs falling from his mouth.

"I know you are, son," she relented, as Dale grabbed his tea and headed back to his game.

***

Jonathan felt even more confused now. His core screamed out to challenge Deborah on what the squad's activities and priorities were, but now he had to think even more about what that might mean for him and his future. His gran needed him more than ever now. Could he really risk getting on the wrong side of Deborah; potentially losing any future hope of having his own team one day?

Jonathan's anxiety meant that at times it was hard to determine if what he was observing was real or just inflated paranoia. The pressure to pin Deborah down on the need to commit to *real* D&I work was growing, and with it, apparently her elusive nature. He'd tried his best to catch her around the office for a quick chat, but their previously frequent informal catch-ups were drying up.

She had suddenly become elusive. No more popping over to say hello, or tight embraces. To him at least, it was almost as if she no longer worked at the company.

Knowing Deborah barely acknowledged Jenna's existence, so she wouldn't have much luck, he decided e-mail was the next best option. He carefully crafted the message, spelling out in detail why it was important to honour the commitments that had been made; ensuring the company maintained its integrity and delivered for those who needed it. After a thorough review his finger hovered above the 'Send' button, he wondered what the response would be, what the backlash would be; but he was committed now - he hit send.

Dale and Andy liked to sit towards the back of the room at the monthly NBF get-togethers, unless a game, or a fight was on and they wanted to be closer to the screen. Sitting further back of course meant there was less chance you would be called upon in the discussion, and wouldn't have to be as enthusiastic with the cheering; although on occasion Robbo would call Andy irrespective of his seating position. This meeting's focus continued the trend of shining a light on the growing threat of the new potential prime minister and the dangerous change in direction the country was moving towards. Pictures of CJ on the campaign trail flicked up on screen.

"This is actually happening. I warned you, didn't I?" Robbo bellowed. The crowd groaned in agreement. "He's on our patch, coming after our families with his Lefty messages. Do we want our community infected with that?" he shouted.

The images sent a shot of rage up Andy's spine. "No!" voices returned.

"He can fuck right off," Andy added, the suggestion

greeted with cheers.

"Yeah, he can," Robbo agreed. By now Dale would usually be swept up in the furore of the room, but he felt different.

He clicked again and the screen changed. CJ's face popped up and the campaign ad began to roll. Murmers and insults continued as the ad played. "Is this what we want our country to be? Is this what King George wanted for our people?" Robbo continued, as he was met with shaking heads and more belligerent swearing. Dale considered if he had any opinion about what King George would have wanted; he wondered if anyone in the room would have known what King George would have wanted.

"Right, so we need to make sure we do something about it, don't we?"

"Yeahh!!"

"Good, cos I don't want my kids growin up with a darkie as Prime Minister."

"Yeaahhh."

The plenary part of the gathering ended and the most appreciated part of the meeting began: discount beers, darts, cards and an extra treat this evening, some adult entertainment courtesy of Robbo.

Andy and Dale were happily swigging their beers when Andy received a tap on the shoulder. "Oi, the boss as a message for yous," the barman relayed.

"Me?"

"Yeh, you and the simple one," he clarified.

"What is it?"

"Come to the bar. It's for your ears only."

"Dale, we're wanted," he said to Dale, who was caught up in a joke.

"Huh?"

"Just follow me." They headed behind the bar out of

earshot of the rest of the room.

"He says, there's something big coming your way, and it'll be worth your while, be ready."

"Is that all?" Dale asked, only to be hit by Andy for his disrespect.

"If Robbo says be ready, we need to be ready, and I don't know about you, but I could do with a bit of extra change," Andy confessed to his compatriot who was in a similar situation.

Chapter 16

Training Day

The majority of the group, dressed in casual business attire, were congregating around the hot drinks. Jonathan felt uneasy as the only person already sat in the circle, so decided to join the rest of the group and make himself a tea. He steadied his hand with the flask of pre-made tea, wary about spilling it everywhere: that's not how he wanted what would already be a challenging day to start. He eavesdropped on the small talk amongst the group, the mix of girls and guys were introducing one another, sharing job titles and company names.

"How about you, pal? What's your story?" a guy asked in a friendly Northern accent that Jonathan was unable to place.

"Me? I'm a designer from Inertia."

"Woah, you hear that," he said to another member of the group. "We've got a designer from the famed Inertia. Didn't think designers came to these things. Times must really be challenging over there," he said with a laugh and a firm strike on Jonathan's back, causing him to gasp for air.

The group were summoned to the circle to begin the training session, following more formal introductions where everyone got to hear Jonathan's unique background. Jonathan told himself the intros would be the worst part of the day; if he could get through that, the rest would be more straight forward. He remembered his breathing exercises, focused his mind, but was still unable to shake the thought that most of the group were judging him for his differentiated role.

In the morning, the group was given a case study to work on, in which they all had to present a section to the wider contingent; Jonathan was wrong, the intro would not be the worst part. His sub team mimicked many of the account teams he'd worked with in the past, loud voices and large egos vying for attention and control. Jonathan was left with a small section to present towards the end, a short duration he was not mad at. While the others seemed to be happy to network during the break period, Jonathan was keen to practise his section, repeating the words verbatim to try to commit them to memory. The delivery wasn't terrible, but he was definitely more stilted than the rest of his team. Willow, the course organiser, suggested he try again without his notes, which he kept referring to, and instead focus on the message of the slide in his own words. Jonathan was at first reluctant to stand and present again – he'd thought the nightmare was over – but after some encouragement from the group, in particular his Geordie (he was backing on Geordie) friend, he tried again with the guidance and found it much better. He was met with a round of applause and a warm feeling of satisfaction, similar to the one he felt after the micro-aggressions session.

Following his conquering of the presentation summit, Jonathan found himself engaging with the group at lunch, chatting relatively freely about their companies. He found people were fascinated to hear about his life as a designer and that he was broadening his skillset. The afternoon was more his speed, smaller team work, mainly in pairs and threes, about the importance of motivating team members in discussion, empathy, and providing constructive feedback, things Jonathan could naturally lean into.

***

"Sorry I'm late," Jonathan said, running up to the library desk where Jenna was sitting.

"No problem, I was just doing some work," she replied, removing her headphones, able to predict what he would say without actually hearing him.

"Deborah had me on this training session today, something to help with future leaders."

"Oh cool... Deborah is investing a lot into you," she said with a mildly sarcastic undertone.

"It's nothing that huge, just some presentation skills and team motivation ideas. You know how I am about public speaking."

Jenna nodded. "I guess if you guys are getting closer it's good for the programme. You'll be able to nudge her towards some of those bigger projects."

"Yeah, I'm going to try," he offered in his most convincing voice

"Good," she said. "Should we get to it, then? I know the micro-aggression session went down well, but I think we can deliver an even better session on unconscious bias. What do you think?"

"Do we think this is the best next step? Is this the topic we need to focus on now?" Jonathan replied confidently.

Jenna was taken aback slightly by his challenge. "Uh, well, I think it follows quite well from micro-aggressions. The two can sometimes be connected, with an unconscious bias leading to a micro-aggression."

"That makes sense, I guess."

"Good, I have some resources which might help."

"I also know a couple of places that should have some good information," he responded quickly.

"How about we both bring our ideas to the next catch up, unless you would rather use your own?"

"I didn't mean it like that; the more ideas the better, right?"

"Yes. I hope you're bringing some of these ideas and energy to Deborah and the D&I squad, too," she said, making some notes and not looking directly at him.

"How do you mean?"

"You know we could be doing more with the programme, not just covering up for designer fashion labels."

"I know. It's not so easy to influence."

"I guess it'll be good practice, if you want to be a team leader, Champ," she said with emphasis.

Jonathan received the nickname loud and clear. He sensed a shift in mood following this back-and-forth. There seemed to be less discussion. Jenna appeared more distant, seemed to be spending more time on her phone; or maybe it was all in his head. He was supposed to be reviewing some flash cards in advance of a pop quiz, but his eyes kept wandering above the cards and towards his tutor; he caught a smile. "What are you looking at? Something entertaining?" he asked innocently.

"Oh nothing, just a clip of CJ, I mean Mr. James, on a chat show. Are you ready for the quiz?" she asked, quickly flipping her phone over.

All Jonathan heard was 'CJ'. "You guys seem to get along well. I guess up close he is quite impressive."

Jenna felt herself blush. "He's fine. I mean he's ok. He's planning to do some good things. I think he means what he says. I think he will deliver," she said pointedly. "I hope so, at least," she conceded.

"Yep, me too," he replied through gritted teeth. "Let's get to the quiz. I need to head back soon."

***

He was exhausted by the time he arrived home. As the kettle boiled, he wondered if all the extra work assigned to a 'champion' was actually worth it. He checked his watch to see if he had time to quickly join the gang on MediEvil Quest. The kettle bubbled into life, and he filled his noodles and headed to his room. He sat his noodles on the desk and sunk into his gaming chair. He felt the weight of the day on top of him. After several deep breaths, he brought himself up right towards the cooling pot of noodles; the pressures of recent weeks continued to spin in his mind. To the left of his noodles was his journal. He was overdue an entry. He switched his attention to his laptop and then back to the journal, alternating between the two, before picking up his pen.

Jonathan's journal – 7th

I think I'm growing, but things seem to be getting harder – is that the way it's supposed to be? I'm doing all I can to meet the expectations of this... role, but it's still not enough, not enough for her, at least. Somehow, I'm not yet hitting the mark, but Deborah seems happy so I may have an opportunity to move up, help Gran...

But why do I feel like I'm falling short. Is this one of those 'great power, great responsibility' things? Or am I just doing it for her? I guess I need to say something.

***

Things move quickly in the world of politics. CJ had come to know this but, with each passing year, each ever more senior role, time moved faster. In the throes of the campaign there were precious few moments for reflection, but there were those occasional moments, when he was alone, when he could reflect on a simpler time, before he made it, or before he was made.

There were two further meetings at the club before things were formalised. CJ would have happily had several more. He was growing accustomed to the scotch and the cigars; even the stares that lasted a bit too long were beginning to bother him less. This meeting didn't take place in the smoking room. Instead he was taken to a secluded room at the end of several corridors. Bill was sat behind a large desk. He had a glass of whisky ready for CJ.

"My boy, how are you?"

"I'm well, and you, sir?"

"Apologies for the venue change, thought we could use a bit more privacy for this chat."

"Something important?"

Bill sipped his whisky. "Important, yes. You know we believe you have a lot of potential, and I know you have done some… meaningful work, which I'm sure you want to continue, right?"

"Of course. I came into politics to make a difference, I guess we all do?" he asked rhetorically.

"Of course. But this is the big leagues now and to achieve what we want, to make history, we need to satisfy all sides of the aisle, across the spectrum. We will need to make sure people believe you are strong on the economy, ensure the markets believe you will make the right decisions, while convincing the public you are serious about immigration… all while, of course, also being the progressive candidate."

"Right, so all things to all men?"

"Ha, you are a smart and talented man, CJ, you know this. You have a uniqueness that will allow you to be… *most* things to *enough* men."

Chapter 17

Systemic Interference

Deborah embraced Jonathan as he entered the meeting room. To the untrained eye they could have been best of friends. The group took their seats for the standing review meeting. Deborah, as usual, could not wait to showcase the excellent results from their campaign efforts so far. "Settle down guys. I know you are all keen to get the latest performance update. I'm pleased to share this is our best month yet. Our Q scores are through the roof, and our share of voice continues to increase.'

Jonathan was psyching himself up for the big ask. He hadn't felt the need to give himself an internal pep talk for a while now; it was almost unfamiliar. Despite his new found platform and prominence in the company, he was yet to make any real demands; this would be a first request. He tried his best to wait patiently for the right moment, but his nerves encouraged him to get it out of the way.

Deborah was in the midst of a self-congratulatory spiel, highlighting how, if it wasn't for her vision and bravery, much of this important work would have never been released. Jonathan carefully raised his hand. He was ignored. Deborah continued. He tried again. "Excuse me?"

Rachel looked his way. "Deborah?" she asked.

"Not yet, Rach."

Trisha affirmed her response by putting her fingers over her lips.

Jonathan's frustration was beginning to build, his confidence kicking in. "Deborah, I've got something important to raise," he said loudly and firmly.

Everyone turned and looked his way.

Deborah was shocked. "Ok, please, our Diversity Champion wants the floor." She made an exaggerated gesture of invitation with her hands.

Jonathan felt the pressure to deliver. "I wanted to highlight that, while we're doing some great work and the results are fantastic, I feel like we've been neglecting some of our bigger promises… and commitments." His words brimmed with passion and frustration. He paused, allowing the message to land.

He was met with silence and confused faces. The room was taken aback by the force of his delivery.

"What do you mean?" Deborah asked. "We've done the campaign, we've been running the workshops… appointed a champion." She gestured towards him with grandeur.

"We have, but we also discussed some other things. We discussed helping out with community initiatives, offering scholarships and internships, increasing representation across all levels of the organisation, but we've enacted none of this."

She was caught off guard. In truth she couldn't remember half the things he mentioned. Her leadership qualities kicked in: delay, divert, and regroup when she was better prepared. "Time, my boy. Sometimes things take time," she replied with her most disarming smile. The awkward mist which had descended on the room still hung.

Without realising he'd risen in the heat of the moment, he sat back down slowly.

"So, where were we? Quarterly figures show…" Deborah picked up where she left off.

***

Deborah slowly climbed the stairs, heels in hand, the prospect of passing out on her bed the motivation driving her forward. As she prepared to flop across her pillows, she realised something lay in her path; instead of being met with a comfy mattress, she was met with rigid corners. She removed the obstacle: a hardback book with a post-it attached. The note read 'Read this! Will help with the broader view, Meg xx'. The book was titled *On Women, Race, and Class*. She flipped the book over and saw a second post-it: 'There's also a good summary on YouTube by Femi Artur #timesaver'. She smiled at how thoughtful her daughter was. Deborah perused the blurb; on second pass she believed she'd got the message on the importance of the connection between the three areas. She reached for her phone, ready to fire up YouTube, and then she thought about Jonathan's comments. She sighed, headed back downstairs, poured herself a large glass of red and returned to the bedroom to open her new gift.

***

"Can we take a break?" Jenna asked between breaths.

"Break? What break? We've only just started the warm up phase," Yami returned energetically, as they followed the instructor's moves on their table exercise video. "Listen, you're the one who said you weren't ready for the gym yet, so here we are. We need to get you up to a certain level of fitness. Can't have you out here embarrassin man, not in front of the man, you know," she said, kicking her leg high in the air, accurately reflecting the action of the instructor on screen. Jenna was not unfit, but she could barely lift her leg twenty-five degrees off the ground. She had no idea how her sister or the terribly enthusiastic lady on screen were kicking so high.

She tried her best to keep up, but was struggling.

"Come on, sis, you can do all that work and studying, but you can't kick your leg. You need to spend more time working out with me and less time playing sexy teacher."

"You don't know what you're talking about. Just focus on the exercise," Jenna said bitterly.

"Psshh, I know that boy loves you."

Jenna ignored her comment, instead focusing on maintaining consciousness as the instructor shouted, "Now we're nice and warm, we can kick it up a few gears."

***

Deborah had stayed late for this meeting, ensuring the office was practically empty. She knew this wouldn't be an easy conversation to have. In her experience, her superiors didn't respond well to demands; this would take some diplomacy.

The screen sprang to life, the faces of the Executive Committee filling her field of vision. "Debby! Baby! How are you doing? How is it on the other side of the pond?"

"All good, thank you, Mr. Johannsson. Still raining as much as ever," she said in an attempt to warm her audience up.

"Of course, that classic British weather. Between that and the food, I don't know why anyone would want to

193

live there, honestly!" He tapped a colleague and triggered some giggles. "But Deb, I know you're a busy woman," implying that he was busier, "so you must have brought us together for a reason, am I right?"

"Yes, Sir, you are. Some concerns... I've had a request," she began.

"Concerns and requests are never good. The King is alright, isn't he?" he joked, to more laughter from those on the line.

She laughed along as required. "As you know our D&I... our *DE&I* work has been going well."

"I'll say. Our figures are going through the roof. You Brits are definitely more ready to accept the Big Bad White Wolf than some of the guys on this side, I'll tell you that for free."

"Right, well, it seems there are certain members that aren't happy with the work we've been doing. They think we could be doing more."

"*More*!? Are they insane, didn't they like the campaign? What about the guy we gave the new role to, the Captain or whatever? You can't please these people! They get their freedom and now this, am I right?" he said to more laughter and shrugged shoulders from his team.

"We made certain promises as part of our strategy. Some of those have also been communicated publicly..."

"Let me stop you there, Deb. I'll give you a quick lesson in leadership. We are in charge. We run this company. Those employees, they work for us and do what we say, does that make sense?" he said with a sinister change in tone.

"Yes, Sir, but–."

"No buts, that's it. If we give in to this, what else will they want next? This whole idea was supposed to benefit the company, the company that pays their wages and puts food on the table. On top of it, they got an opportunity to feel good about themselves and wave the finger at bad Mr White Man, but a reality check is needed. If they don't want to play ball, we can get someone else. We can always hire more black people, am I right?"

"The unemployment figures suggest that's the case, sir." Oscar the CFO chimed in for more laughs.

Mr Johannsson sensed Deborah was slightly misaligned with the vibe of the call. "Deb, I know you're trying to do your best for your people, but you have to keep your eye on the big picture too; think about that promotion. When you're part of the EC you won't have to worry about Black History Month or whatever. Ok? Good job, good talk, go home to your kid." He ended the meeting without saying goodbye.

Deborah admitted defeat. She wasn't the deft negotiator she'd hoped she was. *Maybe he was right*, she thought, *keep focused on your goals. I've worked too long to risk it all now.*

***

Jonathan re-read the email. 'The Executive Committee carefully considered your important suggestion and feel that at this time it is best if we maintain our current activities, which are aligned with our broader company strategy. We may have the opportunity to reassess our current comprehensive programme of DE&I activities at a later date.' It was a long-winded way of saying no. He was unsure of his next move, how was he going to break this to Jenna. He'd have to figure it out quickly, as they were due to meet in five minutes.

Jonathan stammered around the point, his confidence wavering again. "Just say it," she said, watching him squirm.

"They said we can't do the core activities. Apparently,

they're not aligned with the 'broader company strategy', but they'll 'reassess… at a later date'."

Jenna was met with that familiar feeling of disappointing reconfirmation of the world they were living in.

"I'm sorry."

"That's it? You're sorry? We give up just like that?"

He looked sheepish. "What else can we do?"

"All the work we've put in. How much time you've spent educating yourself, training all. Just to give up at the first no? No, that's not good enough."

He didn't know what to say.

She checked her watch. "Meet me after work, I've got something to show you."

***

Bill sat comfortable in the deep cushion of his study's luxurious chair. The amply-sized room was his most cherished space, his inner sanctum; a perfect place for his machinations to flourish. Chopin's *Études* played quietly in the background as he scrolled through his mental to-do list. One of Bil's greatest acumens was his ability to jeep track of multiple tasks. Not just tasks, but entire worlds of information. He cerebrally flicked into CJ's, down the imaginary list of actions and stopped about a quarter way down – he reached for his phone and dialled.

"I trust you know who this is?"

"Yes, I was told you would be calling," Flo replied.

"Perfect. Flo, I can call you Flo, can't I?" he asked in a slightly intimidating way that can only be mastered with years of experience of a position of influence.

"I guess so," she said awkwardly.

"I wanted to touch base with you to ensure all those in our man's camp have his best interest at heart, make sure we're aligned. I trust someone of your education and background understands the magnitude of the opportunity he has in front of him. It would be a terrible shame if he were to waste it over childish ideals of righteousness or morality."

She remained quiet.

"As I've stressed to him on multiple occasions, he has the opportunity to make history, to change the country like never before, perhaps even the world, but he will need to *flex* on certain things; it's the way of the world, you understand?"

"Yes, I think I understand."

"Superb. Continue being the great wife and partner you have always been and, if he ever needs a nudge in the right direction, I know I can count on you to do it."

He ended the call without saying goodbye. Flo sat back in a mild state of shock. *Did that conversation really just happen?*

***

They approached the 'academy' from the rear entrance. Jenna punched in a code and pushed open the heavy steel door. Jonathan followed closely behind. He wasn't sure why they were at a school and felt slightly uneasy being an unannounced adult on school premises. "Are we allowed to be here?" he asked.

She ignored him and carried on down the hallway. A somewhat scruffy looking, and clearly over-worked teacher walked towards them. To Jonathan's surprise, they were met with a warm wave and hello, at least Jenna was.

"It's through here," she said, directing them to her left through a large set of double doors which led to a large hall filled with kids who looked to be in their early teens. They were broken into smaller groups, with adults in each. The adults wore different outfits. None really looked like teachers. Some were too well-dressed and some were under-dressed for school.

"This is it," she proclaimed.

"Ok," he responded, unsure of what he was looking at. "And what is it, exactly?"

"This is what we are working for... the next generation."

"But they're just kids?" Jonathan said redundantly.

"Yep, *now*. But we want them to grow up in a world that is better than the one we did, where they have more opportunities. As you know, one of the pledges was to fund this programme, help give these guys a better chance. That's been taken away. The programme will have to close in a couple of weeks because there is no more funding."

Jonathan studied the room in closer detail. The kids seemed to be having a great time in their groups. A lot of the kids resembled him in his younger days. He wondered how much he would have benefited from something like this.

"This is why we need to fight. This is why we can't take no for an answer. They don't get to benefit from our trauma, our stress, and not give anything back."

Jonathan nodded silently; he understood.

***

6 months earlier...

"I don't see the problem. This is high level politics. We've spoken about this?" Flo said, cradling the head of her husband from behind as he reviewed the policy amendments.

"Like this? They've slashed the public spending budget. This isn't why I got into politics."

"Baby, listen to me. You are a phenomenal man! You're my hero and you have an opportunity to be a hero to so many others," she said as she ushered him out of the dining room chair, carefully bringing him to his feet. "I know this isn't exactly how you wanted it, I know it's not perfect, but life rarely is. You have a chance to help people if you get in, but you *need* to get in first, and that may mean adjusting your approach in the short-term."

"Flo, that's not me," he retorted in frustration. He wondered what had happened to the woman he fell in love with, the privileged altruist who wanted to make the world a better place at all costs. He thought about Jenna; she wouldn't ask him to compromise, she would encourage him to stand on his principles, to push back.

Flo put her index finger on his lips. "You may need to make some short-term concessions for long-term impact. You've always been strategic. Now more than ever is the time for patience." She kissed him on his forehead and brought his head towards her chest.

This was his favourite place, a trusted oasis of tranquillity. He knew she had his back, he had to have faith.

Chapter 18

To The Rescue

Jonathan was in search of something soothing. Time with his gran usually provided this. He flicked on an episode of *Ninjita* on his phone while he waited for his gran to arrive.

"You are too big to be watching those dam cartoons. I don't know how many times I have to tell you that?" she said with a laugh, knowing full well it wouldn't be the last time she would be saying it.

"I thought life was about trying to be happy?"

"It is."

"Well, this makes me happy," he said, leaning to kiss her forehead.

Various elderly residents were sat around the room engaged in light conversations with their loved ones. Jokes and old stories being told and relived. Jonathan noticed there always seemed to be more women than men. He wondered if women naturally lived longer. As always, he noticed the few people who were alone, those who had nobody to comfort them. On occasion he would chat to a couple of the solitary figures, even at times have a game of checkers or ludo. Mr. Riley was his favourite of the solo crowd; he had the best stories about his days as a young heartbreaker in the marines.

Travelling the world, fighting the bad guys and getting the girl.

The person who knew him best could sense something wasn't quite right. "Tell me, son, I can see that brain working."

He wanted to subvert the request, but also wanted her guidance. "You ever feel like you're trying your best but it's not enough? Or you don't know if what you're doing is the right thing?"

"Mi nah understand, speak clear."

"Some things are not clear, or not easy."

"I think you need to trust yourself more. It's partly my fault, I should have done more to build this into you... your heart is good, follow that."

Jonathan, like most, never enjoyed clichés. Clichés were often wise, but rarely practical. He was still without a simple fix to his conundrum.

He temporarily zoned out while his gran was on a splurge about the time she went to see Bob Marley in Brighton in the sixties. One of the lone figures caught his attention. It was Doris; she seemed to be struggling to say something, her hand to her throat. It took him a couple of seconds to realise what was happening: she was choking. Instinctively, he leaped out of his chair and rushed over. Jonathan hadn't been trained in CPR, so instead began hitting Doris on her back. After a few firm strikes, a small egg-shaped object shot out onto the visiting room carpet. It was a yellow peanut M&M. Doris was gasping for air, and the nursing staff rushed over to help. The commotion had drawn the eyes of all in the room. Jonathan had saved the day.

As the drama subsided and Jonathan returned to his gran, she had a strange look on her face conveying multiple emotions. "What's wrong?" he asked

"Did you have to save her?"

"What do you mean?"

"She can be such a pain in mi ass sometimes!" she said, bursting into laughter

Jonathan should have seen his grandma's humour coming.

***

The 2019 Maserati MC20 purred heavily through the empty city streets as the sun slowly began to rise. Today was going to be a good day, Deborah was sure of it, or at least she was sure a positive mental attitude was the best approach to having a successful day. The upcoming light flicked to amber; she pressed her Italian leather shoe hard down on the chrome peddle and the car roared into life.

She was the first into the office, not surprisingly, given today's guest. While many of the team worked late to ensure the office was in an exemplary state, it was Deborah's job to give it the final check first thing.

She glanced at her watch. Mr Johansson would be landing shortly. *No doubt he'll be fast tracked through security.* She strolled around the office, straightening stray pieces of paper and folders, ensuring photographs were upright on desks, before heading into her office to give it a final once over. She hoped the day would go well, hoped she would be able to showcase the great stuff her teams had been doing, and, of course, hoped there would be an opportunity to discuss career progression.

Before long, people began to arrive, for most earlier than normal, fully aware of the magnitude of the day. Instructions to look their professional best had been clearly communicated and reinforced by Deborah the day before. Jonathan arrived at the Design hub in his brand new tailored light grey suit, juxtaposed with his strained brown church shoes, which unfortunately were the smartest pair he owned.

"And what do we have here?" Jess enquired. "Guys, it looks like we don't only have one special guest arriving today, but we also have a celebrity in our midst. Mr Washington, is it?" she joked, elbowing Freddy harder than intended and causing his large frame to double over. "Oh, get up, you're about fifteen stone," she said, rolling her eyes, while Freddy struggled for breath.

"You know the doctor said I have that thing…"

"What thing? You're just a pansy. Look at our new 007 over here."

Jonathan was growing more anxious by the minute.

Freddy regained normal breathing. "I see the perks to the world of D&I know no end. What is the budget for the programme now?" he said with a laugh that triggered a pain where Jess had previously connected.

"It's a work… gift, to look professional for special occasions like today," Jonathan replied as matter-of-factly as he could manage.

"You mean Deborah's dressed up her prize poodle to show off to the powers that be," Freddy fired, only to be met with another elbow from Jess.

"Be nice. Don't mind him, he's just jealous he hasn't got a nice suit like that."

"Well, the thing is Western Fashion designers don't cater to the robust gentleman, sadly. Did I tell you about the time I was in Milan and…"

Everyone turned back to their desks before he could continue with his latest tall tale.

Trish ran and rapped furiously on Deborah's door. Deborah was familiar with the impatient knock. "Come in."

"He's here, he's here. He's on his way up in the lift."

"Right," Deborah replied, composing herself., as she stood and straightened her skirt and matching suit jacket.

She waited outside the office with Trish in eager, yet nervous, anticipation, as if a head of state was about to arrive. The lift doors seemed to open more gingerly than usual, as if a celebrity singer was about to appear and take centre stage.

"Debby!" the loud voice said, as she approached for a firm handshake.

"Welcome, Mr. Johansson, how was your flight?" she asked with a beaming smile.

"Not too bad. Tried to sleep most of the way but ended up watching a couple of movies instead. You know I don't get much time to go to the cinema."

"Of course, I'm sure. This is my number two, Trish Cleaver."

"Hey, Trish, I've heard good things."

Trish swooned at the prospect he had heard of her at all.

"Come with me. We'll give you a quick tour of the office and then you can meet some of the team."

"Sounds perfect," he replied, using his long arm to hold the door open for the two women.

The trio paraded around the office while everyone did their best impressions of being hard at work; some opting for timely and intense phone calls, others in heated debates with one another about current projects. All finely prepared to immediately end their current engagement should they be one of the 'lucky' few called upon to say hello to the boss. After a coffee and meeting with the senior team, it was time to meet with the D&I squad; it was Jonathan's time to shine.

An instant message popped up as Jonathan anxiously watched the minutes disappear from the clock at the top of his screen. It was Jenna. The sight of her name alone calmed him. The message was a simple: 'You got this!?' with an emoji thumbs up. Typing dots appeared at the

bottom of the chat box. It was nearly time to head in –
he knew this wasn't a meeting to be late for – but he was
keen for any further encouragement. He stood as the
message arrived: 'Just be you. And don't be afraid to ask
the difficult questions,' it read, followed by a smile face.
The latter part of the message triggered a rise in nerves as
he headed into the meeting room. The group sat on
tenterhooks as they awaited the arrival of Mr Johansson
and Deborah. Rachel attempted to make some small talk
to ease the tension, but Jonathan was too distracted,
focusing on the messages he'd practised with Jenna and
Deborah. Rachel was relieved of duty by the chatty
entrance of Deborah and Mr Johansson, who were
seemingly locked into a discussion about something
important. Mr Johansson broke the conversation and
began to greet the room seamlessly, leaving Deborah
hanging mid-sentence and struggling to catch up with his
new focus.

"And you are?" he asked warmly. With a bright smile
and firm hand shake, he gave each person considered
attention, before smoothly moving to the next. Jonathan
received a particularly warm welcome: "So, this is our
guy?!" Johansson said rhetorically. Deborah nodded
proudly. "Looking sharp," he said with an 'ok' sign using
his thumb and index finger. Jonathan wondered if he
knew the origin of the suit.

The group headed for coffee. Deborah decided this
would be as good a time as any to broach her issue of
personal interest. "Mr Johansson, not to jump into a big
discussion now, but I wondered if you and the team have
had an opportunity to think any more about...
development openings."

He sipped his coffee. "Deb, you don't have to worry,
leave it with me. As long as you keep getting the guys to
deliver on the ground, you have my word you won't be

forgotten about. Relax, ok?"

"Great, just wanted to check. I know you have a lot on and of course you know I like to run a sturdy ship," she replied, trying to ignore the fact that he had once again failed to commit to anything.

He looked out across the office and saw Jonathan at his desk. "And you know what is a big part of it? Can we trust you to have a firm hand to guide this ship? To keep your crew," he laughed to himself, "to keep your people aligned and focused, on message. We need team players, we like team players at all levels. With all these requests, let's hope you have everyone on the right side."

She noticed his subtle shift in tone from amiable to directive. "Of course, sir, you can count on me, we're all on the same team here." She followed his gaze towards Jonathan.

"Good, good. You've got that big awards celebration coming up, right?" he said, refocussing her on the upcoming spectacle.

"We do. Should be a great night for the company."

"Exactly, and a little bird tells me our great company may be in for some recognition," he said, tapping his nose gently with his index finger. "Do you have any of those custard cookie – I mean 'biscuits'? Love those things!"

"We'll find some for you," she replied in defeat.

The group sat down and after some chit-chat the conversation moved to work-related matters. "Guys and gals, I wanted to start by giving my personal thanks for all the great work you've been doing. It's been really important and noticed by us all." He gave a not-so-subtle glance in Jonathan's direction. "As you know, the work you've been doing not only serves the company, but also helps *others* who greatly need it." The rhetoric was met with enthusiastic nods from around the room, many were checking to ensure Jonathan was following suit. "So, what I would ask from you all is to keep up the good work, keep delivering for all those who need you."

The comment felt targeted, a tailored trigger to join the conversation. Jonathan cleared his throat. "Mr. Johansson, I have a question."

"Of course, I want to hear from our Champion. You must be happy with how things are going," Johansson said with a wide smile and tented fingers to demonstrate his intent listening.

"We have done some great things, but I believe we can go further and try to... address some things that would really have an impact."

Jonathan's comment was enough for Deborah to intervene: "I think what young Jonathan means is, we could always do more, but he's delighted with what we've done so far, right?" She finished with a tone that suggested everyone should agree. Most of the room provided the expected nods of agreement.

Jonathan was less enthusiastic. "Not exactly," he said.

"Go on," Mr Johansson replied pensively, casting a critical eye in Deborah's direction.

"I think we have to be mindful," Jonathan struggled to find the appropriately deferential words, "we are doing work that truly benefits those we want to help and not only us as a company."

An awkward silence fell on the room. "Uh huh... important thought, Jonathan." Mr Johansson attempted to pick up the energy in the room. "And nothing less than I would expect from our Champion... keeping us honest!"

"Right, so what's next?" Deborah jumped in, in a desperate attempt to move things forward.

Trish sprang into action. "We have the highlights reel!"

"Yes, yes, the highlights reel, perfect, Trish."

The group sat back and basked in five minutes of self-congratulatory footage of the squad's achievements. Despite the impressive production value, Jonathan didn't feel much like celebrating.

***

Yami sat in front of her ring lit mobile phone and hit record. "Hey guys, welcome to another tutorial with your girl, Yam; remember to like, follow and subscribe, so I can keep bringing that good content to you! And, if you're really feeling like showing love, you can give a super-like and make a small donation. You know how they say, 'every little helps!'" She laughed before pausing the video and checking her notes for the next section of the tutorial. As she looked away from her notes to practise the next segment, she glanced at a picture of herself and Jenna as babies together on a fluffy white rug. Yami was hugging and leaning in to kiss her big sister. The picture was a perfect snap shot of Yami's love and admiration for her hero. Yami looked at the light and back to the picture. She wondered if she expressed often enough how much love and gratitude she had for her sister, how her hard work and protection always enabled her to pursue her dreams. She picked up her phone and sent Jenna a silly emoji, without any context, as she often would, knowing the running joke would make her sister smile.

***

The day was drawing to a close and Deborah headed to her office to check (again) if Mr Johansson had everything he needed before his *important* dinner. It had been a while since she'd played host to someone so influential in her career, and the strain was starting to catch up with her. "Everything ok, sir?"

"Yes, yes, just catching up with some e-mails."

"Great. We'll probably leave in about half an hour or so, if that's ok with you, sir?"

"That's fine, and you can stop the sir stuff."

"No problem–"

"Actually, there was one other thing."

"Yes?"

"Your man… our young Champ… are we sure everything is good there?"

Deborah was dreading this conversation, hoping the congratulatory video would have glossed over it. "I'm not entirely sure what you mean?" He tilted his head and gave her knowing look. "I think he's a bit high spirited, you know? Keen to make a difference."

"Right. But let's make sure he's keen to make a difference in the *right* way, especially with the awards do coming up," he said, pointedly.

"Understood Sir… boss." She exited the room before he could respond.

***

"How are you doing, old boy?" he said, slowly standing from his seat at the plush dinner table.

"Always the best. That's one thing I know I'll get from you," Johansson replied, impressed as ever by the standards set by his boss.

"Well, we have to try don't we? Not like we can give you decent weather, is it?" he chuckled.

Mr Johansson took a seat. A waiter materialised instantly. "A bottle of Krug 1928, please."

"Right away, Sir," the waiter replied before

performing a sharp military style about face turn and magically disappearing.

The usual family small talk was exchanged. Mr Johansson was careful to show the correct level of deference to one of the most powerful men in the Western Hemisphere, knowing full well this was never intended to be a three-course affair.

"How are things going over at Inertia?" he asked casually.

"Our numbers are firming up, sir. The Q scores, company reputation, and new business have shot through the roof in the last couple of quarters."

"You're seeing the benefit of the D&I work, then?"

"We are. You were right, it's really made an impact, although I'm not so sure about the political work. The profit margins in that sector are pretty thin," Johansson counselled openly.

"My boy, not everything is about profits," Bill said emphatically before taking a large bite out of a freshly buttered bread roll.

Chapter 19

Charitable Nights

The annual charity night was the highlight of the year for all the residents at Reedmore. It was an evening of wholesome entertainment; bingo, dancing, and live performances from the residents and staff. Everything from songs to comedy. Jonathan had been drafted in with some other family members to help set things up. He was teetering on a step ladder, struggling with the banner, when Dale approached to lend a hand. "You ok there?"

Jonathan looked down, slightly surprised to see the face of a person he didn't seem to vibe with. "Just trying to get this thing up."

Dale steadied the shaky ladder. "Anyway ... I wanted to say... I wanted to say thanks."

Jonathan was sure he had misheard. "Sorry?"

Dale cleared his throat. "I wanted to say thanks for what you did the other day, helping my nan like that, appreciate it," he managed to force out.

Jonathan's mind raced back. "Ah, no worries. You'd do it for my gran, I'm sure." There was a brief silence while they both considered if that was actually true. "So how long has your gran been here? My nan has mentioned her to me before."

"She's actually only been here for about a year. We had to transfer her from St Joseph's; she wasn't getting on with the people there."

The two carried on with small talk as the sign went up. Dale was surprised at how easy it was to talk to someone *like him*.

The talent on show ranged from a five-ball juggler to a comedian and impersonator, people who Jonathan didn't recognise, but still found funny. Harold, a wispy grey-haired man, crooned about a lost love. He was accompanied by one of the carers playing the piano. The emotion in the Sinatra-esque rendition had the audience in a trance. Jonathan's mind wandered to thoughts of Jenna.

Dale caught his new found acquaintance in a reminiscent gaze. "A lucky lady?"

Jonathan snapped back into the room. "Ha, something like that, just not the lucky guy."

"I wish I had someone like that, like the song, you know?" Dale said wistfully.

"Yeah, I know, but at least you don't have someone without having them, you know?"

"Right… right," Dale said, confused by the statement, but keen to show empathy.

"No, you don't," Jonathan said, bursting into laughter.

Dale quickly joined in. The pair were met with ardent calls for hush from the audience members trying to enjoy the show. Dale had flashbacks of being told off in primary school assembly for talking with Andy.

***

April and Doris were sat together, rocking back and forth in tranquil coordination with the rest of the audience.

Dale approached with two white plastic cups of lukewarm lager. "Thought we deserved something after all the work we put in today," he said with a laugh.

"Thanks," Jonathan replied, taking one of the cups.

They sipped slowly, watching the performance.

"Guess the budget didn't get much further than the banner and the disco lights," Dale joked in reference to the low-quality beverage.

Jonathan laughed along. "At least they're enjoying it," he said, gesturing to their happy grandparents.

"Guess that's what it's all about," Dale replied.

Dale's phone buzzed: it was Andy: 'Where the fuck are you? We need to meet!'

***

Meghan popped her head round the living room door. "Tea?"

Deborah was so deep in her book she almost missed the offer. "Yes, darling, thank you."

Meghan headed towards the kitchen before spinning back to the living room. "Wait. You're actually reading it."

"I am. Why is that surprising? I like to read."

"I mean, sometimes you do. I thought at best you'd watch the video," Meghan said, reluctantly revealing the low expectations she had for her mother's commitment.

"No, I'm very *woke* now, as you should know, and I am identifying the analogous struggles of not only my fellow women, but also other marginalised groups," she declared.

"Who are you and where is my mother?" Meghan joked before acknowledging her effort. "Well, I'm pleasantly surprised and very proud. You've earned yourself some biscuits with that tea," Meghan said,

213

kissing her mum on the forehead before heading to the kitchen for a second time.

***

"Mate, you have to clean up some of this shit," Freddy said as he examined Jonathan's crowded apartment, which was now even more crowded with all his books.

"That's not why you're here, Fred," Jonathan replied.

"And why am I here again?" Freddy double checked.

"You are here, good sir, to help make jollof and gari."

"Gary? I didn't know Gaz was coming, too," Freddy said, very satisfied as always with his own humour.

Jonathan ignored the joke. He pulled up the recipe on his laptop. Freddy grabbed the bag of tomatoes, and the pair went to work.

***

Deborah listened intently to the presentation before the Q&A began. She reflected on her moments of unconscious bias. The more she thought, the more came to mind, along with a queasy feeling in her stomach. *Am I that out of touch?* She thought about how Meghan would rate her level of Unconscious Bias and hoped she would be more forgiving in her judgement, given her efforts to try to learn more. The more she learned, the harder it became to turn a blind eye to the requests being made and the direction she was being given by the EC.

"Wait, so you mean to tell me, without me even knowing it, I could be acting in a discriminatory way?"

"Yep, exactly, based on biases and conditioning that we all build up over time."

"How can I be blamed for something I've not even intended to do?" Charlie asked belligerently.

Freddy nodded in agreement. "He has a point," he whispered to Jess, who shushed him.

"It's not straight forward, but these are very real things we need to be mindful of and try to address."

Jenna watched on, impressed at how much Jonathan had come on since their early sessions together. She watched how he controlled the conversations, clearly communicated his points, and moved the discussion along.

Deborah too was proud of how her Champion had grown. His level of command in the session prevented her from chipping in, almost. "I think what Jonathan is saying is that, if we maintain a high level of self-awareness, we can more easily pick up on any moments of potential unconscious bias, right?"

"Right," Jonathan affirmed.

"And remember, this is not a blame game," Deborah continued getting into her stride before Jonathan cut her off.

"Right. So any other questions before we close today's session?" he asked, openly but with authority. There was no response. "Ok, thanks. We'll see you at the next one."

Rachel threw a signal his way. "Oh, wait. One more thing. We have our International Women's Day celebrations coming up. The ask is to wear one item of pink clothing and bring some money for a donation. Thanks all, and remember we have some traditional Ghanaian food in the kitchen, prepared by yours truly."

"And me?" Freddy muffled loudly behind a pretend cough.

"And Freddy," Jonathan acknowledged with a roll of his eyes.

Everyone gathered in the kitchen and milled around the food, grabbing plates and helping themselves to the dishes. "Interesting smell," Charlie said, more loudly than necessary.

"And how exactly are we supposed to eat whatever that is?" Diane asked, pointing at the gari.

Jenna grazed on the jollof in the corner of the kitchen. For a first attempt, it wasn't too bad. She watched as people came up to congratulate Jonathan on a well delivered session. She could see he had a glow about him, exuding a confidence she'd never associated with him before.

"It's not *that* good!" Charlotte said, popping up next to her.

"Never said it was."

"You didn't have to, your dreamy stare across the room gave it away. But I'm guessing it's not just a certain student's culinary skills that have caught your attention."

Jenna was surprised to hear Charlotte use the word, 'culinary'. "Did you look that up?"

"What do you mean?" Charlotte said with guilt. "And don't change the subject. I can see it all over your face, you're starting to like this guy, aren't you?"

"Shh, it's always boys and men with you. I told you we're friends, and that's all it is."

"So you've not noticed the change in him? Practically everyone in the office has, but you expect me to believe the person who spends the most time with him hasn't?"

"He's the same guy."

"You might tell yourself that, and I'm sure he is the same in many ways, but I know how you and pretty much everyone else feels about confidence. Your list of exes would agree, so I think it's a safe bet to say he is very much on your radar."

Jenna tried her best to ignore her.

"You mean to tell me, if he told you tomorrow that he wanted to stop your little hook up sessions, I mean study sessions, you wouldn't be disappointed?"

"*Stop*! Go and try the rice."

"Ok, madam, I can see I've touched a nerve. And I'm on a no carb diet at the moment, have a date with a semi-professional footballer at the weekend, don't i? And I need to squeeze into my favourite jeans."

"The ones from 2012, your famous Olympic jeans."

"The very same," she said showing off her figure to Jenna.

Jenna laughed and rolled her eyes. "Anyway, by the way Diane is choking on the rice I'm guessing it's a bit too spicy for me," she disappeared as quickly as she'd arrived. Jenna tried to ignore Charlotte's teasing, *we're just friends*, she told herself repeatedly.

Chapter 20

J And C

Jenna's phone buzzed to life again; she glanced away from her laptop to the animated device without retrieving it. She'd developed a sixth sense for when he would message, or perhaps it was simply because it was so rare for anyone to text her after 10 at night. *I don't want to hear from him, I don't care what he has to say*, she told herself for the 1,000th time. There was some truth to her statement, but it was largely posturing, posturing for her own benefit. She laughed at how hard it was to be honest with oneself; even with no one around, even when all alone. As it always eventually did, her fortitude lapsed. She looked at the phone. The message preview showed three words – 'I miss you'.

She never felt better for reading his messages, usually worse on the occasions she would reply. Her moments of weakness that would lead to a tirade of back-and-forth, emotion, pain, love, and more spilling over. The perennial blame game that was ultimately destined for a dead end. 'A family man,' he would say. After the moments they'd shared, she was amazed he could utter those words. Jenna was so much smarter than this, or at least she was supposed to be. She was the mature one who her friends would come to with 'those' stories, and yet in some ironic twist of fate, she had become the tragically stereotypical heroine she pitied so often.

It was easier to blame him. She had an effect on him. From that first day at the project, she was different around him. Her usual clarity of judgement became misty, her firm exterior softer. He wasn't even her type physically, far too well-groomed and beautiful, not the more rugged look she typically went for, but he was charming - disarmingly so. He had a seductive way of being that felt innocent; he was easy to be around. She remembered taking his card, lying on her bed as she played with it in her hands. Suddenly she was a teenager again.

At that point of course it was not romantic, but there had been an air of excitement. The meeting of the local leaders was inspiring. It was great to meet so many 'normal' people who, like her, wanted to make a difference. CJ was a great speaker. His natural charisma came across when he spoke, he was naturally captivating. His apparent care and interest for the everyday person resonated with her. Though she was not someone who was ever particularly passionate about politics, he made her start to think differently, that maybe she could work within the system. It didn't feel strange that he was asking her out for dinner to hear more of her thoughts on issues, or that he never mentioned his personal life or his family. Perhaps what was worse was that she'd never enquired.

'The best times are unexpected': words from one of her favourite love songs, from one of her favourite artists. The words meant something to her even before she had the pleasure of experiencing the sentiment for herself; almost as if they were pre-ordained. That first evening up until that point had gone well. She'd been impressed by the behind-the-scenes look into local politics, being privy to discussions, negotiations, and tactics that took place at the upper-level council meeting. Of course, seeing CJ in his element was an electric sight; the way he controlled the momentum of the discussion, landing his points effectively and influencing his peers.

Seeing him in action was exhilarating, but it didn't stop there. Jenna also had the opportunity to interrogate him one on one, gaining precious insights into his thought process and how the game worked. Jenna fired question after question as they drove back from the meeting. She was riding high on a mix of adrenaline and the cheap wine provided for the attendees.

"Why did you wait to challenge the Lib Dem candidate on the housing topic?"

He laughed. "A lot of it is to do with timing. I knew the broader budget topic would come up at some point, and that would provide a fulcrum to wedge home the housing issue."

"Ahh, of course," she crooned in satisfaction.

"Did you have a good time?" he asked, looking deeply into her eyes.

"It was wonderful... I don't know where to start," she replied openly.

"It was nice to have you there."

She giggled. He made her feel childlike; a feeling she hadn't felt in so long. Her life was so serious, there was so much responsibility, so much to think about; with CJ things were easier.

"I'm sure it was annoying for you to have someone else to worry about."

"Not at all. I feel very comfortable with you." He readjusted himself in his seat as he caught himself starting to sweat.

Jenna was unsure how to respond but was also beginning to heat up. The pair looked for distractions as the tension and temperature rose, in what suddenly felt like a very small back seat.

CJ reached for his mobile; the screen was filled with messages and prompts. His mind was as far away from work as it could be, but some e-mail clearage might be just the thing he needed to decompress. He flicked through his screen, his fingers clammy with sweat. Jenna took inspiration and also pulled her phone out, absent mindedly scrolling.

Trying to reply to an email he was fairly sure he hadn't properly digested, he dropped his phone onto the floor of the car. "Fuck!" he shouted as he fished around under the seat. He couldn't get hold of it. In a rush, he stooped down to try and improve his reach. The car jogged as it turned, causing him, off balance, to fall on top of Jenna, his hands on the top of her bare legs underneath her mid-length skirt. She'd caught him, attempting to keep him propped up as she was locked in against the corner of the seat, their eyes fixed upon one another; he instinctively dived in. Lips, tongues, and saliva, Jenna seemed prepared for the embrace; heavy breathing and condensation filled the back seat. CJ's outstretched right arm fumbled around behind him for the divider switch, but the driver had already glanced into the rear-view mirror and raised the divider for his boss. CJ hadn't felt this out of control in so long, able to truly let go.

Jenna was dizzy, struggling to be content with the reality of the moment. His hands were everywhere. She could feel how wet she was, ashamedly so; she didn't want him to touch her and know how much she wanted him. She gained a footing in the situation and was able to slowly kiss back. They kissed passionately. CJ's hand travelled up her skirt, his fingers on her thighs made her tremble, he was so close. She attempted to push him back, but the energy used clearly suggested this was not a reflection of her true feelings. He kissed her again and pushed his hand further up, now feeling her dripping wet underwear for himself. He began to play with her through the soaking material before pushing two fingers inside. She screamed as quietly as she could, trying to maintain an element of control. As wet as she was, she was very tight, his fingers could not go deeper. He retreated and began to stroke her. He placed his hand gently over her mouth as she moaned. The pleasure was so intense, she bit down on the palm of his hand. As she did, sirens blared and blue flashing lights lit up the inside of their cabin. CJ jumped away as he was brought back to reality. The pair fixed their clothes as he lowered the windows to allow the cold night air to soothe the back seat. He hit the intercom switch. "How far away are we, Albert?"

"About two minutes, sir," the driver replied.

Jenna rushed to the bathroom as soon as she got in, not wanting to risk being seen by her sister. Her head was still spinning, it felt like she'd been in a whirlwind for a long time now. *What had just happened? This isn't me*, she thought. This was the first time, and as much as she knew it should have been, deeper down she knew it would not be the last.

***

"Just a second," Jonathan shouted from his bedroom, bringing Jenna back into the room from her daydream. She was feeling exhausted again, something she'd gotten used to over the years as the person who rarely said no and who wanted to achieve so much.

Jonathan was conflicted about the team attending the D&I awards given the fact they were still yet to deliver on

so many activities; nevertheless, sensing an opportunity
to spend time with Jenna, he had invited her over to hear
his potential speech for the event. He didn't want to
admit it, but he was also excited by what sounded like a
glitzy event, something he'd never experienced before,
and also the potential to win an award: another first.

Jenna had briefly tried to communicate her scepticism
around an awards ceremony for work that she considered
should have been happening anyway; her gut told her it
would quickly become a pageant for self-congratulation.

"A few of us from the team are going. I don't know,
it feels weird getting an award when all we've really done
is a couple of campaigns and an ad," Jonathan shouted.

"Still mad about the ad," she jabbed.

Although the message was in jest, it was well received
as it showed Jenna's growing relaxation and, dare he say
it?, flirtatiousness with him.

"I'm pro CJ for PM," he replied.

Jenna went back on track. "I hear you, you're a good
person. I get why this doesn't sit quite right with you…
what are you doing in there?"

Jonathan pondered how good of a person he really
was, thinking about what he might be willing to do for a
promotion, for some more money to help his gran.
'Thanks…' he said slowly. "I'm coming," he added.

"Just make sure, if you do win something, you get the
message out there about the work that really needs to
happen, what D&I should be about."

"I promise. Right, are you ready?"

"I've been ready for thirty minutes. You know I have
other things to do, right?"

Jonathan slowly entered the room in his new black
suit with waistcoat and bow tie, also from his boss
benefactor.

"Wow!" Jenna exclaimed automatically before she

223

had a chance to catch her own thoughts. The tailored suit hugged him in all the right areas. She could see a shape, a level of athleticism in him that she hadn't noticed before; he looked great.

"So, what do you think?" he asked with a mix of apprehension and confidence, already pleased with what he'd observed in the mirror.

"You look really good," she admitted, as her heart kicked up a beat.

"Phew. Thought it might be a bit too much. All this suit stuff is still new for me. Have you got time to hear the draft speech? Kinda dumb really, but Deborah said we should be prepared just in case."

"Sure, go for it."

Jonathan brought his phone out and had a quick look at his notes, before replacing it in his pocket. He went on to deliver a confident and eloquent speech.

"That was fantastic. Only make sure you strain those areas of focus messages," Jenna said, proud that she'd been rubbing off on him.

"I'll keep practising."

"I think you've pretty much got it. Wait, your tie is a little off, hold on." She proceeded to straighten his tie. *His after shave is amazing, this must be new.* She felt slightly lightheaded. His breath was warm and minty, like he'd just been chewing gum.

"Is it ok?" he asked, as she finished with the adjustment without taking a step back.

"I think it's ok. What do you think?"

"I hope so…"

An eternity seemed to pass before he plunged, his lips meeting hers with a spark of static; she didn't flinch. The kiss seemed to go on and on, before Jenna's phone sprang into life, shattering the moment. She turned quickly, practically diving for her phone on the sofa.

It was Yami. She answered in a fluster.

"Sis, where did you put my shaver? Tell me you didn't throw it out again? Where are you, anyway?"

Jenna struggled to follow the questions, her head still spinning. "What?"

"Shaver? Where is it? Where are you? When are you coming back?"

"There are shavers underneath the bathroom sink. I'm at Jonathan's, I'll be back soon."

"Ooo, more study time with *geek boy*!"

"Bye!" Jenna said, putting the phone down. "Sorry about that. I should go," she said in a rush, grabbing her bag and jacket and heading for the door.

"Wait!" he called.

"Chat tomorrow," she said without turning back.

It was Jonathan's turn to try and figure out what had just happened.

***

The office was filled with bright pink ribbons and streamers. Famous quotes and pictures were posted up on the walls, all in celebration of International Women's Day. Rachel diligently gave out ribbons to everyone, ensuring nobody was missed.

Jess wondered why the ribbons had to be pink, and Charlie's ribbon managed to accidentally fall off. "For me personally, I'm glad we're finally celebrating women properly. As a lover of the fairer sex, I can comfortably state this is long overdue!"

"You know there are no women interested in sleeping with you remotely with in earshot?" Jess said, sparking a laugh from Jonathan.

"So how much were you involved with this one, then? O should I say, how much time did you spend with

Professor Jenna setting it up?" she jabbed.

"I didn't have much involvement in this plan. Rachel was keen to take the lead. Not sure if she checked in with Jenna."

Jenna and Charlotte sipped their teas and studied the posters. "Didn't realise a woman invented that, or did that? Bloody hell, this is good," Charlotte declared.

"We're missing a few faces, I think."

Charlotte knew Jenna well enough to read the subtext. "Have you looked at all the posters? Maybe there is a bit more... variety... in the meeting rooms."

"I doubt it," Jenna replied.

Deborah strolled around the office perusing the posters of legendary, ground-breaking women. She wondered where her name would stack up in the annals of history; what had she contributed? Would the next promotion get her to a place of meaning? She studied a poster of Susan B. Anthony, one of the leading suffragettes.

Rachel walked past. "Inspiring, right? Imagine, if it wasn't for women like her pushing the barriers of oppression, we wouldn't have the fundamental right to vote."

Deborah nodded quietly as she processed the information. Jenna approached.

"Impressive stuff, right?" Deborah said to her.

"I supposed, but Susan B. Anthony didn't fight for the suffrage of all women. African-American women were isolated from the movement and didn't gain the right to vote until 1965 with the Voting Rights Act."

"We're trying, Jenna!" Deborah shouted in her direction as Jenna walked away.

"Always something," Deborah said to Rachel.

"She's not wrong," Rachel returned awkwardly.

The entire office piled into the meeting room for a

226

speech-and-cupcakes session. Rachel stood at the front while Trish handed out cupcakes. "Thanks for joining us today. Thanks to Deborah and the D&I team for allowing us to put this on. It's really important to recognise *all* the great women who have sacrificed in the search for the equality that most of us are fortunate enough to benefit from in the West." Rachel glanced towards Jenna, who calmly chewed her cupcake. "Women too suffer from instances of microaggressions and unconscious bias, and many of the personal and systemic challenges that impact people of colour. To recognise the struggles that are still with us today we will be donating £15,000 to a local women's refuge." The announcement was met with a round of applause.

Everyone made their way back to their desks. Jenna ran up behind Jonathan. "Did you know about that donation?"

"I didn't," he said, aware of what the next question would be.

"But there aren't any resources to help with the core activities? The community support?"

"Apparently not," he said, reinforcing the position they both knew to be true.

"And?" Jenna asked as she spun his around to face her. She folded her arms and tapped one foot, impatiently waiting for an answer.

"I know, I was already on it," he confessed, placing the palms of his hands together to signify a prayer for patience.

"Let me know if I can help?" she offered as he walked away. She tried not to stare at his behind, which she swore was becoming more shapely.

***

"Freddy!" Jess called to the lumbering giant as he played Minecraft while listening to Slipknot. Jess resorted to removing the headphones and shouting in his ears.

"What are you doing? Is that necessary?"

"Yes, because you couldn't hear me."

"What?"

"You think Jonathan is ok? With all the champion stuff?"

Freddy gave a split second of thought. "Do I think Jonathan is loving all the extra attention and time with the love of his life and the boss? Yeah, I think he's fine."

"Well yeah, I don't know, it could be a lot of pressure. Maybe it's affecting him…"

"You mean he's getting more cocky? I've seen that. And doing less of the day job? I've seen that too. I've been picking up his work for bloody weeks now!"

Jess rolled her eyes. "You're not doing his work now. Get back to your ruddy mining."

"Minecraft!" he fired back as he reaffixed his headphones and turned up the music.

Chapter 21

Comi-Co

Jonathan's world had changed a lot in recent months. Some things he was happy about, while other things he was still coming to terms with. Considering there was so much flux in his life, he was really happy with a milestone that remained constant: the annual UK Comic Convention, or Comi-Co to the initiated. The weekend event brought together comic, anime, and geek patrons from all over the country in a festival of fandom.

Jonathan met up with Tommy from his MediEvil Quest group to attend the event at the convention centre. Jonathan was dressed in a near-perfect replica of his favourite character Aarato from the show *Ninjita*, while Tommy wore an outfit from his favourite character in MediEvil quest, Eriganus.

Tommy was late as usual. It wasn't much of a problem on this occasion as it gave Jonathan an opportunity to take in all the amazing costumes, which was half the fun of the experience.

"Johnny", Tommy shouted as he waddled up a walk way; his plastic armour, while lighter than the real thing, made it difficult for him to walk. Even with all the noise of the event, Tommy's clattering outfit still managed to stand out. They embraced with an awkward hug, costumes and accessories clashing against one another.

"Good to see you," Jonathan said with an air of relief that surprised him. He'd needed today more than he realised.

"And you too, pal," Tommy replied.

Tommy was Jonathan's only 'Black' friend, a concept that hadn't landed for him before he was swept up with all things D&I. He wondered if he could even consider him to be 'Black' as he was technically mixed race. Either way, he was the closest he had.

"So are you ready for this?" Tommy asked.

"You know it!" he exclaimed, as they showed their entrance tickets and headed inside.

This was his eighth convention, but Jonathan was always amazed at the size of the event. "Is it bigger this year?"

"You say that every year," Tommy replied with a laugh. "Oh, look, there's the signatures for the original Pokémon!" he shouted as he headed off into the crowd without looking back. Jonathan tracked after him, realising the reality of chasing Tommy was what lay ahead for most of the day.

The pair walked into another large space, sipping large bright-blue ice slushies. Tommy was thrilled with Charizard's signatures and was keen to see what other prizes he could get his hands on before the afternoon was over. Jonathan was enjoying the day but couldn't shake a sense of paranoia that followed him around. He could swear people were staring at him and Tommy. The pair queued to get a signature from one of the lead characters in *Mask of Thrones*. "Hey, Tommy, random question."

Tommy was making eyes with some attractive-looking Elves. He shot them a wink and a kiss.

"Tommy?" Jonathan repeated.

"Huh? Sorry, I was… never mind, what's up?"

"Do you think people are looking at us?"

"How do you mean?"

"I mean staring at us… like, look at him over there." Jonathan pointed to a guy in a Yoda outfit, who was way too tall for the character. The guy turned away after being caught in the act. Jonathan stormed over to him. "Sorry, mate, everything ok?" he asked hotly.

The guy squirmed. Suddenly, one of his friends popped up out of nowhere. "Just never seen a… *Ninja…* like you before."

"What do you mean?"

"You know what I mean… Aarato isn't black, is he? Neither is Eriganus who your mate is trying to pose as."

At the back of his mind, he had thought that was the problem, that it was the source of attention, but why hadn't he picked up on it before? Had it always been this way?

Tommy attempted to drag Jonathan away. "It's not worth it, come on, we've got signatures to get."

"Did you hear what he said? It's all *fantasy*! It's fucking made up!" he shouted at the two guys as he was dragged away.

The incident had soured the mood of the afternoon, but there was still something to look forward to. His favourite comic book publishers would be announcing their next generation of movie adaptations. It was the only chance to get this information first-hand from the directors, and also an opportunity to ask the writers, directors, and actors questions. Tommy had gone to the bathroom again. The blue slushies went straight through him, but he couldn't get enough of them. Jonathan was tasked with saving seats for the pair of them. He was powerwalking in the hall entrance when he bumped into a well-made-up *Lord of the Rings* Orc.

"Watch it!" the Orc said.

"Excuse me," Jonathan spat out, fixing his now messy blonde wig.

"Jonathan, is that you?"

Jonathan recognised the voice but couldn't place the person, not under all the make-up.

The Orc could see he was struggling to recognise him. "It's me, Dale, from the home," he brushed the hair from his wig to one side.

"Dale? Ha, how are you doing?" The pair embraced each other.

"I'm good, didn't know you were a *Galactic* fan?"

"Yeah, I love it, all this stuff really."

"It's a bit of a secret love for me. The lads I hang around with wouldn't really get it. Have you had a chance to see *Redeemers 3*?"

"I did. Did you get the tattoo?"

"Of course!"

They simultaneously raised their sleeves to show off their impressive new wash off tattoos.

"Have you got anyone to sit with?"

"I'm actually here alone."

"Come and sit with me and my mate, he's just in the bathroom."

"Are you sure?"

"Of course, no problem," the pair headed in and found some seats. The entire auditorium of extravagantly clad fans was transfixed by the presentation of *Galactic* studio boss, Chris Benpine. The large, bearded studio head delivered an impassioned speech about the next wave of *Galactic* movies, complete with teasers for three of the movies due to be released in the next five years. Each teaser was met with wild celebrations, akin to die-hard fans cheering on a championship-winning team. Jonathan and Dale exchanged grins of glee, the collective shared jubilation in the room creating an ephemeral bond.

***

Deborah power-walked as best she could toward the large meeting room; being late was bad enough, but being late for a budget meeting was unacceptable. She hoped Dan would be unwittingly buying her time with one of his fishing stories. The rambling tales of his exploits along the estuaries of the south coast had taken up many precious minutes she would never get back. As her stride lengthened she caught frantically waving hands from the Chaucer meeting room. The dramatic actions caused her to pause and peer through the glass wall; it was Charlie, engaged in a passionate rant with three other men. Her gut told her this was worth checking in on. Charlie had become even more disgruntled than usual over the past few months.

"I'm telling you, Andrew Jackman is right. It is a global conspiracy and if we don't do something about it quickly we're going to be wiped out!" he declared, standing up in the heat of the moment. As he finished his point, the door opened and Deborah peered in.

"Charlie, is everything ok in here?" she asked gently so as not to further antagonise the already charged individual.

Charlie was caught completely off guard. "Huh, yes, of course... we're just having a meeting."

She looked at his compatriots, who shared the same look of childlike guilt. Deborah glanced at the YouTube video playing in the background, the titleofo which read 'The War Against White Men, The Global Stewards'.

"So, what are you watching?" she asked, nodding towards the screen.

"That... that... that's just a bit of educational material, a bit of 'content'," he said in air quotes, "to stimulate a creative discussion."

"And what's the discussion about, might I ask?"

"Well... it's about developing challenges that are likely... that may occur, given certain narratives," he replied innocently.

"Charlie–"

"It's an affinity group, ok? I thought we were all about inclusivity now? Inclusivity includes us all, right?" he spat petulantly.

Deborah took in a deep breath and checked her watch.

"It's not a problem, I checked in with HR. The guidelines state any definable demographic is entitled to form an affinity group of their peers, should they wish. And I'm sorry, if we have to sit through micro-this, unconscious-that, and all the women's stuff, then we can have our own space, too," he declared to murmurs of agreement from the rest of the boy's club.

"I have to go, but we will catch up on this." She raced towards the budget meeting. *Men are such babies. They have the world but still want more.*

Charlie rolled his eyes at her departure. "I'm telling you, we can't do anything anymore, not even have a civil discussion in private." His compatriots nodded along as he clicked play on the video.

Chapter 22

D&I Appreciation

The team piled into the black taxi. Jonathan had mixed feelings about his earlier conversation with Deborah. Despite her tacit acknowledgement of all the 'great work' Jenna had been doing in support of the D&I initiatives, Deborah felt it was inappropriate for her to attend the awards dinner, as she was not an official team member and they only had a limited number of tickets. In typical fashion, Jenna was gracious about not being invited, although he could tell she was masking some discomfort.

Deborah and Trish led the small talk as they usually did; Trish providing a one-person echo chamber for conversation and laughter. Jonathan briefly wondered why Trish had earned a ticket when she had contributed nothing to the initiatives. He watched as she chuckled away at Deborah's jokes. Even Charlie got a ticket; Charlie, the same person who made his disinterest and annoyance at all things D&I evident to everyone.

Deborah glanced across at Jonathan, noticing he was not engaged in the chit-chat and, more than that, he was disgruntled. She hoped he could be trusted to deliver the acceptance speech on message; after all, she had played her part by allowing the kids to come to the office.

Jonathan was impressed by the scale of the event.

He'd never been invited to an industry award show before. It was typically not something the design team qualified for. The black-tie dress code, large round tables, and white table cloths brought an element of prestige and glamour to what was the first-ever industry Diversity and Inclusion Awards. Jonathan took in the surroundings. The Gala ballroom was filled with people. He couldn't help but notice that, despite the theme of the awards, most of the guests were white. He was seated on Deborah's left-hand side, with Trish as ever on her right.

"Waiter, waiter!" Charlie shouted, already tipsy after downing three glasses of wine; the way he saw it he may as well get something out of this wasted evening.

Jonathan had to admit, there was something extraordinary about being at an event like this. Maybe Jenna was wrong, perhaps this was a sign of genuine change. After all, there had never been an event like this before, so surely it could be considered a sign of progress? He thought about what she had said to him when he broke the news about the award show: "I don't need to be there as long as our message gets out. You have the opportunity to say what needs to be said."

The evening rolled on, and various awards were given out. Jonathan noticed there only seemed to be one person of colour on each table, at most two, and the person of diversity was not usually the person who went up to collect the award. There was something off about largely middle-aged white people collecting awards on diversity in front of a largely white middle-aged audience; somewhat self-congratulatory.

Deborah leaned in to Jonathan. "Isn't this great?" The classic semi-rhetorical question that only required a response if it was in agreement with the assertion. In response, Jonathan smiled without showing any teeth.

"So many great projects and initiatives being

recognised," she declared in self-congratulatory fashion. "You must be really proud too... being able to celebrate with your peers," she said, gesturing around the room.

It was beginning to sink in: this was not a genuine attempt to recognise hard work in an important area, it was a narcissistic PR stunt performed by wannabe saviours. And he was complicit, he was one of the enablers crucial to allowing the facade to continue. He didn't feel proud but knew he could do something to get closer to the feeling.

"And the winner is INERTIA! For their Bentalago Reaffirmation campaign. Collecting the award we have Deborah Tate and Jonathan Archer."

Deborah strode proudly onto the stage. Jonathan slowly followed behind, feeling less celebratory by the moment. Deborah practically barged the attractive brunette announcer away from the podium, pulling her notes from her clutch bag. She failed to check if Jonathan was present before beginning her speech. "I would like to start by saying thank you to everyone, my entire team, for supporting me so much with these diverse and inclusive efforts. It wasn't easy, I had to fight hard. Many said we should be using our resources on other initiatives, but I pushed back and said 'No, no, we must persevere'."

Despite being familiar with Deborah's bombast and levels of self-appreciation, Jonathan was still taken aback by what he was hearing. This apparent angel of all things diverse and inclusive was the same person who did not want to have the kids at the office or to do any of the other more meaningful acts like the intern programme. The majority of the crowd seemed to be eating it up. Jonathan wondered if perhaps it was because it was late in the evening and everyone was sufficiently watered.

The attractive brunette pushed her way back across the podium. "Perhaps we can hear from your colleague?"

she suggested, inviting Jonathan to speak.

"I wasn't quite finished…"

"It's good to hear from a variety of team members, inclusivity and all," the lady said passive aggressively.

Jonathan seized the opportunity. "Thank you," he said to the host. "Yes, I would also like to thank everyone for the great work they've done, particularly around the Bentalago campaign. But, while we take a moment to recognise our achievements, it's important that we remember *a lot more* needs to be done. We are just at the beginning of our work." The sentiment seemed to take the air out of the room. This was not the positive upbeat message that Deborah was hoping for.

"We also need to make sure the work we do doesn't only serve the companies and institutions that we work for, but actually the people we intend to help." He made the comment while locking eyes with Deborah; his point was made. "I hope everyone enjoys the rest of the night!" He swiped the glass trophy and stormed off stage. Most of the audience was in a state of shock, but a smattering of applause began, led largely by the host.

***

Deborah pondered the e-mail. She knew it was inevitable. He wasn't just going to disappear after all the hype and promotion they'd placed around him. She also knew the EC was not going to allow any major activities to take place. The advertisers' guild D&I awards showcase was coming up and they had already promised Jonathan would attend. If he backed out, the company would look terrible. Perhaps a small concession to tide him over, but the longer term looked bleak. She had to keep the bosses happy if she was ever going to get her promotion. She'd worked her entire life for it; it was time to start the recruitment process. Deborah began to type the subject line for the e-mail to HR: 'MORE BLACK PEO...' 'WE NEED TO HIRE MORE BLACK...' She deleted and tried again.

PART 4

Chapter 23

Recruitment, recruitment, recruitment

Deborah had received sign off from Mr. Johansson and the rest of the executive committee to commence the targeted search for new, more *compliant* recruits. HR had been told to screen for candidates who were 'driven and ambitious,' code in this instance for those who would not let ethical concerns get in the way of career opportunities.

She had been instructed to move quickly, the board did not want to lose any of the momentum or goodwill that had been built up over the recent months. She would be seeing potential candidates for one-to-one interviews; instead of the usual multi-step, panel approach, Deborah would be making the call. Deborah sat with a round faced young gentleman, as with the others, his CV was strong; solid academic background and good prior experience.

"So what are your views on unconscious bias," she asked.

The candidate was taken by surprise. He fumbled around with his words. "Well, it's important, and important not to judge people too harshly…" unsure of what type of answer his potential employer was looking for. Deborah raised an unimpressed eyebrow in response.

The next candidate didn't fare much better. "Would you say there is a systemic problem of underrepresentation in the industry?"

"Um, right, well of course there are issues that need to be addressed, but these are difficult and will take time…" was the best the girl could come up with on the spot.

"Right, anything further?" Deborah asked, hoping to hear more specifics.

Deborah knew the remit wasn't necessarily strict expertise in this area, but she couldn't help herself. "What are your thoughts on the glass ceiling and how can we best overcome it in a way that is fair to everyone?" she challenged the next candidate.

"Hmm, I've always been told that if you work hard enough you will be rewarded and that you can achieve anything."

"Oh, so you believe women have been complaining needlessly about barriers to progression into senior management," she replied in testy fashion, the comment striking a personal chord.

After meeting with several bright candidates, the process had been whittled down to two leading contenders, Roger Smalls and Keisha Cunningham. Both were well educated, keen, and charming in their own ways. It could have gone either way, but something was nudging her towards Roger. He reminded her of someone, but she couldn't put her finger on it.

***

CJ realised early on in his political career that people, like life, were rarely Black and White. That most of us spent most of our time in the grey: a view he knew many of his peers used to justify their murky dealings, and a view he used to try and justify his affair with Jenna.

The morning Flo confronted him about the pair of underwear that were too small (and 'tacky') to be hers, which she'd found in his coat pocket as she searched for the car keys, was one he'd never forget. The pain in her eyes, the rage and anguish he'd caused the woman he loved, the mother of his children. She did the best she could to project a composed face, telling him she was leaving and didn't know if she would ever be back. How he was speechless for once in his life, no charming wit or one-liners to get him out of the tricky situation, just an overwhelming feeling of shame and guilt. How he began to drink heavily again, before Bill intervened and insisted he end things with Jenna, irrespective of how she made him feel seen, heard, or understood, or what he had promised to her. Running for office meant presenting an image of family, particularly for someone who was already *novel* in the eyes of most of the public. He wouldn't be afforded the luxury of infidelity some of his fairer peers enjoyed. Bill had even spoken with Flo, doing his best to talk her down and persuade her to give CJ one more chance. People being there for you in tough moments, helping you work your way out of the grey, was important, but at what cost? Was it worth it? How much would he need to concede to make history? A history he wasn't even sure he cared to make any longer.

***

An opportunity to meaningfully give back had finally arrived. Jenna was frantically running around the office, trying to ensure everything was ready for the kids. Charlotte was doing her best to assist with the setup, while also attempting to keep her friend calm. "It'll be fine, everything is sorted. Lunch is ready, the guys are prepared for the meet and greet, and your presentation will be great! Just relax," she stated.

Jenna took a deep breath and closed her eyes. It was unlike her to be so stressed out, especially when working with the kids, but she was desperate for things to go well; especially as Deborah and the team were so reluctant to do the activity in the first place. She also realised she had pushed Jonathan hard to achieve more meaningful milestones with the programme.

Deborah peered through her office blinds, tea in hand, as Jenna, Jonathan, Charlotte and the others busied themselves with the preparation. She took a sip and allowed herself to revel in a sense of grace; she hoped they would enjoy the moment; change was coming.

"Jonathan, can you double check all the food is out? They'll be here in a second," Jenna asked.

He nodded and headed to the kitchen. Jenna's phone buzzed with a message from Dotty, one of the project leaders bringing the kids to the office: they were in the lobby. Jenna rushed for the lift, heading to meet them. Some of the teenagers ran to Jenna as she stepped out of the lift. Of course there were a couple who were 'too cool' to show that emotion, but she could tell they were pleased to see her.

"Alright guys, remember what we discussed, everyone has to be on their best behaviour, right?" They nodded in agreement. "This is Jenna's place of work so, if you misbehave, there won't be any invitations back."

They took the stairs up because they were too big a group for the lift. They congregated again outside the double doors. The large Inertia sign was emblazoned next to the doors. Sherifa went over and traced his hand across. He and many of the other kids were in a state of awe. Kamal pushed through in excitement, some of the others following closely behind. Dotty called after them, "Slow down!"

Kamal's eyes were wide in amazement at all the people, desks, computer screens. "Wow, everyone is so… old," he muttered, to the laughter of his friends.

Jenna managed to catch up and get in front of the group. She led them towards the kitchen. "Keep your hands to yourself," she shouted over her shoulder. The group followed behind in line like lemmings. The kids waved happily at the employees who had stopped to observe their guests, many returning warm waves and smiles. Some, however, were not so happy with the adolescent visitors.

Charlie was perched against a corner wall with a friend. "What's next, a visit from prisoners?" he snorted sarcastically, taking a sip of coffee from a polystyrene cup.

The young visitors were wowed again once they set eyes on the lunch time spread. There seemed to be food from every corner of the world: sushi, pizza, salads, falafel, sandwiches, an assortment of crips and snacks. They ran over and began helping themselves.

"Wait until you're invited!" Dotty shouted as they piled their plates.

"It's ok, it's all for them," Jenna said, more calm now that they had arrived safely.

"How are we doing? All good?" Jonathan asked, appearing at Jenna's side.

"Looking good, I think," she said, watching the feast commence. She headed to the office floor, and cleared her throat: "Everyone, please make your way to the kitchen and join the guys. Remember, please make an effort to engage with them before the talk begins."

Charlie rolled his eyes as team members made their way into the kitchen.

Freddy made an assertive beeline for the food, bumping into a couple of kids along the way. "Welcome to adult life," he chuckled to himself.

Jonathan watched on happily as the teens ate, mixed with staff, chatted and laughed.

Sherifa spoke with Rachel. "So, Miss, what do you do?"

"You don't have to call me Miss. Rachel is fine."

"Oh, ok, Mrs Rachel, what do you do here?"

"Well, I'm in Ana–. I try to figure out why things work well or don't work so well," she replied, hoping her plain language translation hit the mark.

"But like, what things?"

"Things like campaigns and stuff."

"What's a campaign?"

Rachel was stumped.

Across the kitchen Edward had been cornered by a couple of boys. "Woah, that's a nice watch! How much is it?" Jamal asked.

"Well, it's about fifteen thou." He caught himself, before sliding his sleeve over his watch.

"Fifteen Racks!" Kamal said.

"The price isn't important, it was a gift," Edward tried to shuffle his sleeve.

"I bet you have a nice car and dat too, big yard?"

"Yard?"

"You know, crib…" They stared at one another as if they were speaking different languages.

"A home," Dotty said, sensing the man was struggling. "Kamal, why don't you go and grab some more pizza, give the man a break?"

Jonathan saw one of the kids standing all alone. He wore glasses and a jumper that was too long. He reminded him of himself. He approached carefully not to intimidate the shy looking student. "How's it going?" he

246

asked.

The kid looked either side of him, as if he were speaking to someone else.

"A lot of people here, right?"

He nodded in response.

"Kinda loud, too?"

He nodded again, this time with a smile.

"So, what's your favourite subject?

He thought carefully, "Maths or physics."

"Wow, you must be really clever, that's so cool."

The boy smiled in response to the compliment, but then his smile faded.

"What's up? Being smart is cool," Jonathan offered. The comment didn't seem to land. "I guess being smart isn't always the best thing when you're young."

He nodded and looked towards Jamal, who was holding court with four different adults.

"You know, we all have different talents. I was never good at maths I hated it but wished I was good at it. I liked to draw, and that wasn't the most popular thing, but I enjoyed it. Sometimes you have to do what makes you happy, even if it doesn't seem cool."

He nodded, seemingly accepting the argument put forward.

Jenna watched on in admiration, a warm feeling growing.

Charlotte popped up in typical fashion. "You like him!" she joked in a childish voice.

"What? Don't know what you mean," she said with a smile.

"Mmhmm, well, I'm going to get more pizza before these little bastards finish it all."

"Charlotte!"

***

After a satisfying lunch, it was time for the kids to hear about what the guys at Inertia did. Jenna gave an articulate presentation, breaking down the basics of the company.

"When you hear it like that, it's a wonder we make any money at all," Charlotte whispered to a friend.

Then it was time for some of the kids to speak about their mentoring project and some of their fund-raising activities. Kamal eagerly kicked off the impassioned, if under-rehearsed, speech about the 'pain gain' challenge the kids had conducted as part of their fund-raising efforts. In the challenge, the boys had their legs waxed by the girls, raising money for the pain endured during the process. Some amusing and viral footage was captured of the bravely naïve teenagers shrieking in pain at each unceremonious yank of a wax strip. Most of the office was captivated by the enthusiastic showcase from the youngsters. Even Charlie's typically icy façade seemed to melt ever so slightly from the energy of the adolescents.

***

Roger stooped to re-tie his brand new soft, Italian leather shoes. Catching a glimpse of his handsome reflection in the tip of his shoes, he smiled. He checked his watch as the lift began to rise: *right on time*.

Meanwhile, Deborah was keeping an eye on time, hoping Roger would buck the stereotype and be punctual. She had slipped out of the staff meeting early to meet the new recruit for the surprise introduction.

The ping of the elevator preceded the slow opening of the doors, almost as if a contestant was about to take the stage on a singing show. Roger was as immaculate as she remembered, strikingly handsome and piercingly professional. "Roger, so good to see you, how are you?" she asked with a wide smile.

"I'm great, thank you, Deborah, how are you?"

"Perfect, happier for seeing you. Ready to meet the team?" she asked, as she showed him into the office.

Rachel was finishing up the AOB section as Deborah entered the room. "If that's everything, I think we can let you guys get back to it," she said as she looked at Deborah for confirmation.

"Just one more thing," Deborah declared. The office was caught off guard by her sudden reappearance. "I have a lovely surprise for you all. As part of our strategic recruitment programme, I am delighted to introduce our newest team member, Roger Smalls!"

She stood to one side and ushered him in.

Roger calmly stepped into the room, unphased by the many pairs of eyes trained upon him, as if staring at him would only ever be the natural recourse. He didn't wait for any further invitation, instead took the initiative and introduced himself. His deep voice echoed around the room. "Hello. I'm really excited about joining the team and getting a chance to work with you all." He found Jenna and then Jonathan, both taken aback by their new team member.

Deborah began a round of applause that was quickly picked up by Trish and then the rest of the office. "Roger will be starting properly from tomorrow, but I thought this would be a great opportunity to introduce him to everyone. I'm sure Roger is looking forward to getting to work, and will also be involved with some of our extracurricular activities," she said, making eye contact with Jonathan.

Jenna and Jonathan looked at each other, a subconscious urge for reassurance. Neither was clear on how to take the newbie, nor Deborah's pointed remark about his willingness to participate in other programmes. New employees had never bothered Jonathan before; why should this be any different? Yet, for some reason, it was, in his gut he knew it was.

Jonathan tried to unwind with an episode of *Ninjita*, but he was restless. His phone buzzed to life. It was Jenna: *We should catch up about how we push Deborah and the team on next steps re. the core activities. What did you think of the new guy?... Ally?*

Messages from Jenna would always lift his spirit, but something was holding him back.

Jenna watched the reply bubble pop up and disappear as Jonathan seemingly struggled to craft a reply. *Yep, just tell me when you're free... I don't see why not.* The message finished with an awkward emoji face, a drop of sweat falling from the caricature's brow.

"Did you hear me?" Yami said, bringing Jenna back into the room.

"Sorry, what did you say?"

"I said, I'm going to order something. Do you want anything?"

"No, I'm ok."

"You've been on the phone so much lately. Texting your man friend again?"

***

CJ drew the palms of his hands up and down his face in a frustrated washing motion. "I don't understand. This is what you said you wanted. Pushed me for," he protested in astonishment, despite having had this conversation many times before.

"Don't start, CJ, you know it wasn't like that. Don't

piss me off," Flo replied with venom.

CJ hated to admit it, but he enjoyed the rare occasions his wife let down her manicured façade and showed some unfettered passion and authenticity. "I'm not trying to, I'm trying to do what I thought would make you happy, would make *us* happy, the kids included."

"Don't bring the damn kids into this! You know what the kids want? The kids want to spend more than half an hour a week with their father. They want to be able to see you when they're not about to go to bed, that's what they want."

CJ took a second to catch his breath and take a sip of his whisky. "We've worked so hard, come so far. We are *this* close." He held his thumb and index finger close together.

"There used to be a 'We,' an 'Us', now it's just 'You'. Your bloody events, trips, and fucking text messages." Flo immediately hated herself for bringing up the messages. She'd promised not to: the counsellor was clear on that.

CJ could see the pain in his wife's eyes. It brought everything rushing back; all the emotion, the heart ache and betrayal, Jenna. He attempted to reassure her. "Bill says it won't be much longer now. The truth is the backbenchers are unlikely to endorse me, anyway. Once I'm officially out of the race, I'll take some time and step back, I promise."

"Fuck Bill! Bill is not in this fucking marriage, not that you would know it, the amount his name comes up. CJ, you are good at many things, it's something I love about you but, no matter how much time you spend with Bill and those in leadership, you won't be able to lie like they do."

CJ was quiet, unsure of his next move, the next

251

sentence that would ameliorate her grievances.

Flo could see the consternation on his face; she'd figured he'd had enough for one day. "Oh, and CJ, we both know the chances of you losing are low. You never lose at anything." She grabbed the bottle of merlot from the counter and headed to the den before he had a chance to respond.

***

Roger was in early for his first day. Naturally the early riser, he would typically be in the gym before work on most days. Today, however, he decided to forego his ritual and instead use the extra time to ensure his outfit was spot on for his first day. He wore a pair of light chinos, finely pressed, a light blue oxford shirt, equally well pressed and tucked in securely, underneath a navy-blue jacket. More formal than the typical office attire, but he had been raised to believe those who dress smart get their mindset in a smart place.

The office was practically empty when he arrived. Deborah had told him the hot desk policy was first come first served, but he was still slightly wary about getting on the wrong side of people too soon. He was heading towards the kitchen in search of coffee when he saw a familiar face from the meeting. His mind shot back to one of the interview discussions with Deborah. *We are keen for our more diverse employees to participate in our D&I activities. Of course, you can provide valuable input*, she had said. *I know you understand the value of balance in business, it's critical in most things. Let's just say our current Champion is lacking balance from a business perspective. I hope you'll be able to help restore that … balance.*

Roger was experienced enough to receive the message as intended: 'This nigger has become too uppity

252

and needs to be put back in his place.' The way Roger saw it, someone would end up doing it, so why not him? Better another brother gets some benefit out of it, he thought. He gave Jonathan a subtle nod as he walked by.

Jonathan returned a wave, pretending not to feel the chill in his spine.

***

Peeved by another unproductive career progression meeting with Deborah, Charlie jostled with the crowd of commuters on the packed Northern line platform. He begrudgingly allowed a woman he considered entitled onto the Tube in front of him. He was not thanked for his chivalry. Squeezed into the sticky rush hour carriage, he was unable to move his body. He was left with the options of facing a woman who was giving him a judgmental look, suggesting that he was inappropriately pressed against a young lady, or looking up at the panel adverts. He decided the adverts were the lesser of two evils. Directly above him was a well-built ex-Olympic athlete advertising vitamins for men's health; the model had a broad smile as he cradled his attractive wife and two young children. Three busy and sweaty changes later he made it home.

At the end of the station, the crowd of commuters rushing for the open doors of the northbound Northern line train pushed Jenna, who was trying not to think about the latest unproductive promotion debate she'd had with Deborah, onto her carriage. She was squeezed into the metal container like tuna, with one enormous man in front of her and another smaller man behind who seemed to be caressing her bum and discreetly grinding on it. She attempted to turn her head to glare at the man but could barely move, so she was forced to endure until the next stop at least. Her field of vision was limited to adverts or, off to her left, a scowling older woman who had a look of contempt, as if she had somehow deliberately stationed herself in this uncomfortable and unsafe position on the packed train. She switched to the ads; the view wasn't much better. She was faced with a make-up ad: four beautiful white women and one racially ambiguous woman, all smiling brightly with perfect flawless skin. The strap line read, 'For all-natural beauty.' Jenna began to simmer. She closed her eyes and centred herself, patiently waiting for the journey to end. Some busy, invasive, and uncomfortable stops later, she was home.

Charlie slumped in front of the TV allowing himself a break before contemplating making a start on dinner. He had promised his wife he would try to help more around the house with her going back to work. He watched the news. The reporter had a milk chocolate hue. He reported on potential strike action because of strains on the healthcare system. Charlie tried his best to watch but struggled to stomach the journalism. He didn't recall the healthcare system ever being so strained when he was a kid. He flicked over only to be met with the party political announcement for Calvin James. He couldn't escape it, it was everywhere. He headed to the kitchen and made a start on dinner. Before long, his wife arrived back with Josh, his son, who had a broad smile on his face. His wife, as was becoming the case more often, did not have a smile on her face. She was still unhappy that Charlie had not hit the level of seniority that would allow her to be at home as preferred. "Good day, son?"

"Yes, Dad, I got an A on my report."

"You did? That's great, what was it on?"

"President Obama."

"Oh… great choice, son," he said with faded enthusiasm.

His wife cast a look of warning at Charlie, knowing what her husband would be thinking.

Jenna struggled with two shopping bags through her estate. She witnessed the usual congregation of teenage boys underneath a dim yellow street light, someone playing tinny drill music from a phone speaker. She ignored the childish cat calls from the adolescents, who were probably yet to sit their GCSEs, trying to maintain a level of grace and understanding in the knowledge that, following further cuts, there was nothing for *the youth* to do after school.

She stepped into the ancient, discoloured elevator that had the perpetual tang of urine, which on occasion would be more pungent. It creaked slowly up to her floor. She returned to the flat and collapsed onto the sofa. The place was dark. Yami was yet to arrive home. She fumbled around for the remote in the darkness, rather than turning on the light. She finally found it underneath a piece of her sister's underwear. She lobbed the underwear across the room in protest and put the TV on. She flicked around, struggling to find anything of interest between cooking contests, property-based reality shows, and evening news. All had a distinct lack of representation in her eyes. She settled on the property show, where a young middle-class couple were buying their second home, this time away from the city but on the commuter belt, so 'Richard' could easily get into the city for work. Jenna seethed at the apparent ease of life for the two who were unsure if they would be able to scrape together enough for the £750,000 property without dipping into Richard's pension pot. She looked

around at her cramped rented apartment, the damp
dripping from the corner of the room, and switched to
the cooking show. A low-level celebrity was choosing the
best toad-in-the-hole from the two options put forward.
She remarked about her days growing up and how this
was always one of her favourite dishes. Jenna wondered if
she had even tasted toad-in-the-hole as she tried to figure
out the contents of the misshapen dish. Jenna finally gave
up on TV and decided to give her eyes a rest before Yami
came back full of life, and before she would have to
embark on her work for the evening.

Chapter 24

Expensive Sins

No matter how glamourous or expensive they were, and they usually were both, hotels always made Jenna feel cheap. They were a constant reminder of the illegitimacy of what they had, not that it could even be given a credible title. Yet, despite it all, here she was, waiting patiently again for CJ to arrive. She perused the mini bar in search of a drink to help her relax a little. *This is going to be a discussion, nothing more*, she reassured herself. But then why had she worn so much make-up, the perfume he'd gifted her? The matching underwear? a small voice in the back of her head questioned provocatively; Jenna tried her best to ignore it.

She lay on the large soft bed, arms spread out, feet swinging off the edge, as the door handle turned. She sprang up.

"Excuse me," a voice called through the partially opened door. "I have a bottle of champagne on ice, courtesy of Mr James. May I come in?"

"Yes, of course."

"Madam, there is an accompanying message from Mr James, saying he will be running a bit late, but to have a drink while you wait."

"Thank you," Jenna replied, suppressing her

frustration.

"Anything else I can do for madam?" The porter awaited a tip.

"No, nothing," she replied, before realising the undertone of the request. "I'm sorry, I don't have any money on me right now," she admitted, embarrassed, having left her larger purse in her work rucksack. *The perils of getting dressed up*, she thought as she eyed her small clutch bag, which only had enough room for her phone and Oyster card.

At least I get champagne, that's what Charlotte and Yami would say.

She lay on the bed again and looked through some questions about Medical Apartheid Jonathan had sent her while she sipped her champagne. She was impressed by how thought provoking and incisive his lines of interrogation were getting. Before long, the door handle jostled again. This time a more familiar voice called, "I'm so sorry I'm late, J, I just couldn't get away."

Jenna shot up again, downing the rest of her champagne and quickly looking in the dresser mirror. "I guess I shouldn't be surprised. It's not your first time, and at least you had the sense to send champagne," she replied, giving him a hug, a tighter than she had planned.

"I promise, I'll make it up to you," he teased.

"It's fine, the champagne is enough, and we only came to talk, right, away from prying eyes?"

"How much of that champagne did you have?"

It was so good, and she wouldn't be able to drink like this at any other time, she'd lost count. "I don't know, how long have you kept me waiting?"

He pulled the bottle out of the melting icy water. There was about a quarter left. "A long time, apparently," he replied, pouring himself a glass and topping her up with the remainder. "So, what did you want to talk about?" he asked as he kicked off his shoes.

"All this campaign stuff, working more with Inertia: do we not need some ground rules or something?"

"Not happy to be seeing more of me?" he replied with his typical cheek.

"No!" she said as she tried not to smile.

"I don't know, your eyes say otherwise."

She turned away and took a big gulp. He matched her and set his glass on the table.

He stood behind her as she looked out of the large window with the fantastic view of the London skyline. CJ grabbed her by the waist and kissed the side of her neck. Jenna felt herself buckle; she wished it was the champagne, but knew it was the touch of his lips. "Stop, CJ, this isn't what this is about," she protested weakly.

"Is that why you wore my favourite perfume?"

She had no response.

He slid his finger underneath her bra strap. "And my favourite underwear?"

Still no answer. He took the silence as a signal to continue to kiss her neck and around the top of her shoulders. Then he raised the back of her dress, exposing her underwear. He slipped his fingers between her legs and felt how warm and wet she was.

"CJ," she pleaded softly as she moaned.

He spun her around and kissed her deeply before turning her back to face the window and bending her forward. Jenna had one hand pressed against the steaming glass and the other over her mouth to muffle her cries.

***

"Are you sure you have time for a bath?" she asked from the expansive luxury bathroom, as CJ lay on the bed drinking some water.

"For you, I always have time."

"If only that were true," she shot back.

Jenna's phone lay on the bedside table vibrating away. CJ picked it up. The contact's name was Jonathan and by the looks of it there were several messages. "J, looks like some guy is trying to get hold of you. Hope I don't have anything to worry about?" he said in a patronisingly sarcastic tone.

Jenna checked her phone. "Oh fuck."

"Who is it?" he asked, slightly more genuinely.

"It's nothing, I can sort it tomorrow."

"Right answer, because now it's bath time!" he said, slapping Jenna on her bare bottom and chasing her into the bathroom with a fresh bottle of champagne.

***

Jonathan sat quietly in his room, attempting to focus on the Quest, but constantly glancing at the dark screen of his phone, praying it would spring into life. He could swear they were connecting, vibing. It wasn't like her to go so long without replying. He hoped nothing was wrong.

***

William 'Bill' Fullop eased back into his favourite dark green leather seat in the Whitmore study. Cigar smoke wafted in the air as murmured discussions took place. This, he thought, was one of the last refuges of a civilisation on the brink of destruction. But even here, a bastion of institution and heritage, he could not escape the tenacity of change. This used to be a place of integrity and seniority, but now, so many different faces.

Bill had been around, he'd seen pretty much most things – the fall of the industrial era, the rise of city finance, terror threats from the IRA – but this new dawn was different. After years of control and domination, the tides of fate seemed to be turning. They would now have to make a concession, give something back. As unpalatable as the idea sounded, he was always taught that there is opportunity in every scenario, you just had to look hard enough.

Politics had never been a dream of Bill's. He was a businessman, just like his father, but he was more ambitious. Wealth was important. Everyone he knew had wealth. Of course, wealth came with a level of influence, but real power: that still resided to a degree with public office. He had gifts and many advantages in life, but he unfortunately lacked the patience for people and had sadly also inherited his father's looks; a combination which meant a run at office himself would always be challenging, even with his sizeable coffers. A few years back, it had dawned on him he didn't have to be directly in office to be in office. As if the realisation had been recognised by the universe, it was not long after that he met a talented young upstart called Calvin James.

An attractive young waitress approached with a carafe of his favourite whisky. "A little more, Sir?" she asked sweetly, fluttering her lashes.

"Yes," he replied, carefully studying the girl.

"Distracted, are we?" Henry said sarcastically, approaching from behind the waitress.

"I don't have any idea what you mean," Bill responded.

Henry took the seat next to him. "I'm sure you don't," he replied with a smirk. "So, how is our boy doing?"

"Well enough, I suppose. A little rattled by events."

"Yes, I suppose they are a little challenging. He's a strong boy, he'll survive it," Henry responded confidently as he lit his cigar.

"And you, how are your ventures doing?"

Henry took several deep puffs. "Yes, yes, we're definitely seeing some upturn. Moving more units, getting more exposure for some of the businesses."

"Well, guess you were right then," Bill conceded.

"I always am, old chap. Just because the winds are changing, it doesn't mean you lose control of the ship," Henry finished with a smile.

Chapter 25

The King Is Dead, Long Live The King!

Jonathan rushed to the meeting, frustrated his previous meeting on the Giphar account had run over. It was almost as if Patricia was being deliberately slow with her closing. He pushed the door open without knocking, the meeting well underway. Deborah was in the middle of a tirade as he entered. The entire room turned his way like a parliament of owls.

"Ah, you've finally decided to grace us with your presence," Deborah stated sarcastically. "Not the best example for our new recruit," she continued, looking at Roger, who smiled in response. "Take a seat, come on now," she finished in her school mistress tone.

Jonathan obliged, squeezing into the only available seat between Rachel and Edward.

"To bring our tardy team member up to speed. I was sharing the news that Roger has been gracious enough to agree to support you as a Co-Champion. We know there's a lot of pressure on your shoulders, so I'm sure you'll be happy with the help." The message was more of an instruction than anything else; not up for debate.

Jonathan was uncomfortable, not only because of his

awkward seat. This was once a space where he had dominion, was heard, respected. Suddenly he felt like his omissible old self. He looked over at Roger, who was focused on Deborah.

"Following guidance from the board and great success with the Bentalago campaign, we will be continuing to support clients who need assistance with any issues or reputation management. Similarly, with the well-received political activities, we will continue to offer services and consultation in that arena too. The board is keen that we prioritise these areas of focus. You should be happy with your work, Jonathan," she said somewhat ironically. She tried her best to deliver the message with the cold austerity of a senior leader, the senior leader she wanted to become, this is what it would take: a hardened heart and no space for compassion or sensitivity.

The strategic prioritisation left Jonathan in a state of mild shock. In his heart, he knew this was no real surprise; even with all the complaints, protestations, and challenges, the message was clear - core foundational activities would not be a focus for the group. Jonathan zoned out for the rest of the meeting, present but mentally vacant, pondering what his next move would be. His natural reaction was to check-in with Jenna, but another part of him told him he had to be more independent and assertive. That's what she wanted to see in him; more importantly, that's who he wanted to be.

***

"They want us to what?" Dale said, generally unsure if he'd heard correctly and knowing that misunderstandings were his forte.

"They want us to kill the geezer," Andy repeated.

Dale quietly pondered the request. "But, And, isn't

that a bit… a bit much?" he enquired softly.

Andy had thought the exact same thing when he was pulled into the solo meeting with Robbo. He knew from the very beginning meetings alone with Robbo usually ended with having to do something you didn't want to do, but this?

"I know, it's a lot, but they really see this guy as a threat to the country, to national security. They say we'll be heroes… I've never really seen Robbo like it… and they're trusting us… and there's ten large in it for each of us."

Dale knew which part of the sell he found most compelling, "Ten large? Are they trusting us, or throwin us to the lions?" Dale replied instinctively, almost surprising himself with his level of candour.

"Are you going to tell Robbo and the lads no?" Andy asked rhetorically

Dale thought for a second, he knew the answer. Dale wouldn't say no to making Robbo a cuppa, let alone something this big, they wouldn't see the light of day. He tried to think about the upside: being 'heroes' among the group. Maybe they'd get their pictures up at the clubhouse next to legends like Kirby Armstrong and The Bishop. Despite the thoughts of grandeur and success, something wasn't sitting right in his gut. He thought about Jonathan, Mr. Saj, and his nan with April. "I don't know, Andy, this feels like a step too far. A bit of intimidation is one thing… but murder? We'll go down for life."

"No, no, Robbo says he has cover. Our connections in the force and higher up have got our backs. They really don't want this guy to win. They say it will start a civil war, so by doing this we're actually going to be saving loads of people anyway." Andy was trying to convince himself as much as Dale. "I need you, mate. You know I always have your back. It's me and you to the end." He offered his arm to Dale for a Rocky style semi high-five.

Dale stared at the hand. He didn't like this at all, but what else could he do, leave his best mate hanging? That wasn't an option. He slammed his hand into Andy's, just like Apollo and Rocky.

***

Jonathan paced back and forth in front of the bathroom mirror. "Hey Roger... Roge... Roger!" He practised, adjusting his pitch and tone. "Roger, I wanted a moment of your time to discuss." No, too formal. "Roger, I wanted to grab you for a minute for a chat... Roge, got a sec?" He paced in growing agitation.

After his personal pep talk, Jonathan had decided to set a one-to-one meeting with Roger in the hopes of getting his support for the intern scheme. Despite various larger group meetings together, Roger seemed to avoid alone time with him, even declining a coffee catch up because he was 'busy' despite the time being clear in his calendar; perhaps it was all in his head. This meeting was supposed to be in alignment with the wider D&I squad, but he had separately told them it would not be going ahead.

Roger pushed the meeting room door open to be met with the surprise of an almost empty room. Jonathan looked up from his laptop. "Roger, good to see you. Glad you could make it."

Roger looked around. "I thought there would be more people... the rest of the squad?"

Jonathan paused. "They couldn't make it, it's just us." He could see the discomfort on his face. "I wanted to get your thoughts on something, as 'Co-Champion'," he said with air quotes.

Roger took his seat slowly. "So, what have you got for me?"

Jonathan cleared his throat. "I wanted to make sure I had your support on the internship programme. Basically, it's a key init–"

"I've heard about the programme."

Jonathan waited for him to continue, but there was nothing. "Then I'm hoping I can count on–"

"Let me stop you there, friend," Roger interjected. The assertion of friendship sounded disingenuous. "The 'core programme'," he stated with condescending air quotes, "is a… good… idea, but there are other more… pressing activities we need to focus on beforehand."

Jonathan wondered how, in such a short time, this man presumed to have such an in depth understanding of what was a priority to the programme. He decided to entertain the suggestion of his colleague. "For example?"

Roger was silent again, mind turning over. "For example, the new political campaigns. It's important we maintain a visible front on all of these issues."

"Right, that is important, but don't you think we need to focus on more impactful work? With the intern programme, we could–"

Jonathan was stopped in his tracks again, this time by Roger's raised hand. "Jonathan, you've been doing some great work, but I'm here to ensure that moving forward the squad's activities are *fully* aligned with the strategic priorities of the company."

"Fully aligned?" Jonathan tested.

"Fully." Tense silence spread across the room.

"Can I ask you something?"

"Sure, fire away," Roger replied assuredly.

"What is this about for you?"

"What is what about?" Roger responded, feigning ignorance.

"This work, what we're trying to do here?"

"Well, trying to help of course… within the confines of the company structure and vision."

"Is that it? Structure, vision, strategy?"

"This isn't a charity, Jonathan," Roger said in a patronising tone.

The statement made Jonathan laugh. He couldn't tell if it was more because of what he'd said or the way he'd said it. "Yes, I know, thanks for clearing that up." There was a pause in the back and forth, a chance for either side to gather their thoughts. "You know, I feel like I used to be like you."

"Really?" Roger responded with genuine surprise.

"Yep, I didn't have much of an interest, couldn't see how it was particularly relevant. Bad things happen every day, right, all over the world."

"But I do care, that's why I'm here," he said with a laugh.

"But, *do you*? How can you if you don't support the real work?"

"Real work? I know you and your girlfriend think you're Rosa Parks and Martin-Luther King, but I don't think your little lunch time school sessions and award shows count as real work? Or your face on the posters? I bet you didn't push too hard against that. You think any of this is going to make a real difference? You think Deborah or any of them will go home at the end of the day and think yeah you know what, they've got a point, maybe I shouldn't be so racist? Shouldn't be scared of the Black kid in the tracksuit bottoms on the way home, ha," he laughed for effect. "At least we can try and get something out of it while there's attention, before they move on to the next thing. So, if I'm benefiting a bit, so what? Don't I count, too? Wouldn't the 'ancestors' have wanted that for me?"

"It's not about you or me, it's about us doing what we can for others, people like us."

Unfortunately, his point didn't land as he hoped. Roger was focused on his mission. "I can't support this, sorry."

"Is that what you've been told to say by your boss?" Jonathan jabbed.

"*My* boss? Your boss, too. You might think you're better than me, but our pay comes from the exact same place." Roger had had enough of being chastised and spoken down to. He got out of his seat and left the meeting room.

"Fuck!" Jonathan shouted, hitting the table. He'd failed.

***

The bi-annual family dinner was something Deborah had long dreaded, and something that seemed to come around all too often. She had begun to think the title of family dinner was perhaps too grand, considering it was only her older brother and his wife and daughter. The dinner would alternate between their respective homes. It was Deborah's turn to host, so, in addition to the inevitable patronising lecture from big brother, she now had the hassle of preparing a meal that would be suitable for not only *his* highly discerning taste buds, but also her niece's vegan diet. With everything going on at work, this meal was something she did not need.

Deborah rushed around the kitchen, checking on the roast while trying to keep a close eye on Becca's gluten free pasta and vegan toad in the hole; she prayed the vegan toad in the hole and roast lamb would be ready at the same time. She shouted again for Meghan to come down: they would be arriving shortly. Meghan said she would attend on the condition she didn't have to help make dinner or clean up after. A hard bargain, but Deborah didn't want to think about trying to get through the dinner alone. She was draining the brussels sprouts when the doorbell rang.

"Fuck, they're early. He always does this." She cursed as she burned her hand trying to check her watch while finishing the draining. "Meghan, can you get the door, *please*!" she shouted.

"Ok, ok, you don't have to shout," Meghan replied as she descended the stairs, over-ear headphones hanging around her neck. "Hi, Uncle Peter," she said sweetly, as she opened the door.

"Hello, truffle," he replied, giving her a big hug and handing her an expensive bottle of champagne. "Brought something we could actually drink. God knows what your mother likes isn't up to scratch. Where is my little sister?"

"She's in the kitchen; I think she's nearly done."

"I hope you helped her this time, truffle. Her meals are much more satisfactory when you lend a hand. Cooking was never one of your mother's strong points; not that she has many. Probably part of the reason your dad left," he muttered as he walked towards the kitchen.

"Hi, Aunty Emerald," Meghan said to the retiring and often inebriated woman who had the striking beauty of a faded 1920s movie star, with the post fame depression to match. "Becca," she said flatly, sticking her tongue out as they always did to greet one another as kids. The pair were very different, despite being only a year apart. Meghan had always followed a progressive alternative path, while Becca was the archetypal princess. Meghan knew that, as a feminist, she needed to accept and be supportive of all women, irrespective of how they chose to live their lives, but her cousin's perpetual damsel in distress routine was hard even for her to take. Becca returned the tongue and rolled her eyes.

"How are you, Petey?" Deborah said as she brought the meal through to the dining room. "Good, good, things at work are a bit of a mess with all the election stuff going on. Interest rate keeps bouncing up and down. In honesty, I hope that coloured fellow doesn't get in. The markets won't react well to it," he said openly.

The comment caused Meghan and Deborah to look at one another. Meghan's facial expression suggested that her mother should say something. Without words, Deborah communicated now was not the time. The meal would be hard enough without having to challenge her brother on issues of race.

"I hope the lamb's not too well done. You know there should be a spot of blood on the plate, right?"

"I remember how you like it," Deborah replied. She attempted a change of direction. "And how are you, Emeral? Still–?" She stopped in her own tracks. After all these years, she didn't actually know what her sister-in-law did every day, aside from doing her makeup and drinking.

Emerald replied with a vacant nod, suggesting she acknowledged that Deborah had done her due diligence as a host by attempting to show an interest.

"She's fine. What has she got to complain about? Woman hasn't done a day's work in her life," Peter lamented as he took a deep swig of his champagne. "Have you got any port, Debbie? I only brought one bottle of the good stuff and I doubt it's going to last the entire meal."

"Not if you keep drinking like that," Emerald said under her breath.

"She speaks! What was that, dear wife? I didn't quite hear you."

Meghan took the opportunity to jump in and steer

the conversation a different way. "How is college, Becca?"

Peter jumped in before Becca had a chance to reply. "That bloody school, hell on earth, they get an arm and a leg in tuition fees, and they're filling their heads with nonsense. It's gay this and lesbian that. Black oppression. They can barely touch a history book anymore," he moaned while he chewed on a fatty piece of lamb.

Becca knew better than to antagonise her father, especially when he'd had a drink.

But Meghan had almost lost patience with her uncle and was ready to fight back. "I think it's good we're taught about different types of people. Helps build a more cohesive and supportive society, don't you think, Mum?" she said, trying to bring her into the conversation.

"Huh?" Deborah replied, as if she hadn't heard the question, not wanting to be involved.

"Mum is actually doing some great stuff at work with Diversity and Inclusion, and she's been helping out with the James campaign," Meghan continued proudly.

"Well, not exactly. We were asked to support with a small ad, and there was a directive to do some D&I work," she confessed.

"D&I, Diversity, this is exactly what I mean. It's everywhere. You can't walk three feet before some PC liberal bashes you over the head with the latest buzz word. It's a conspiracy, a travesty, I tell you. God willing, Monroe will win. The country is utterly doomed with a *nigger* at the helm."

The word caused everyone to stop. Emerald had her mouth open, baby boiled potatoes suspended in mid-air. Everyone was aware of Peter's more archaic views, but the vitriol and candour of that word had shocked them all.

"Peter, we don't use that word in this house."

He realised he'd overstepped the mark. Even Becca had a look of disappointment cast across her face. "What? Ok, I'm the old fogey, I guess. The 'coloured gentleman': is that better for everyone's sensibilities?"

"I think I've lost my appetite," Meghan said. She excused herself from the table and headed back upstairs.

"What?" Peter said defensively to the remainder of the group. "You'd think I killed someone." The group continued to eat in silence. Peter, feeling the tiniest amount of guilt, attempted to redeem himself. "So, Debbie, are you on for that promotion yet? Want me to see if I can pull some strings?"

The suggestion she needed her brother's help to get something she'd worked hard for and, in her eyes, had rightfully earned made her blood boil. She thought about the lessons of the patriarchy she'd picked up in her reading. "I will get that promotion on my own, thank you. We don't all have an old boys' network to help us get on in the world," she said pointedly.

"Bah, it's the way of the world," he said defiantly. "Any more Yorkshires?" he asked innocently.

***

How has it come to this? Charlie thought as he looked around the sophisticated waiting room. He separated the stack of magazines on the coffee table in front of him. He didn't recognise any of the titles. From the covers of a couple, he could tell they were pop culture publications. One called *Splurge* seemed to be focused on luxury living. To him it was just more evidence, that he didn't need, to prove the world was going down the pan.

Charlie glanced up at the young, attractive receptionist as she tapped away at her computer. He hoped to subtly get her attention. In his younger days, he had no issue getting the attention of women; fitting a description that white people would regard as 'tall, dark and handsome', he had his pick. He couldn't tell if declining interest in him was to do with him getting older, global narratives changing, or a combination of both. Either way, it was another sore spot to add to his increasingly aching ego. Being 'strongly encouraged' by Deborah to attend careers guidance with Mr Whitmore might have been the final straw. Still, he could not afford to risk his job, especially with things so rocky at home – unemployed or between roles would not look good to the judge in any potential custody hearing.

A call from the receptionist snapped him out of thought. "Mr Whitmore will see you now," she said sweetly.

Charlie stood up and headed towards the office. *Fuck it, why not try?* "So, how long have you been working here?" he asked with a suggestive smile.

The receptionist returned an embarrassed laugh, more for him than for herself. "Sorry, we can't engage in personal discussion with service users."

Her pitiful tone of voice and use of the term 'service user' castrated Charlie with an abruptness he'd not thought possible. "Right," he replied as he attempted to scrape his ego off the floor and head into the office.

He was hit with a subtle lavender scent when he entered the room. Mr Whitmore was busy scribbling something down on a note pad. "If you take a seat on the sofa, I'll be over in a second."

The size of the room surprised him: *clearly, I picked the wrong field of work.* The sofa was plush. He felt his back slowly get consumed by the soft padding.

"Right, so, I'm Mr. Whitmore, careers and guidance counsellor, and you are…" he looked through his notes as he took a seat opposite Charlie. "You are… dum dum dum," he hummed to himself.

Charlie was taken aback by Mr. Whitmore's youthful look. He didn't look much older than his eldest who was just about to sit his GCSEs. "Sorry, did you say counsellor?"

Mr. Whitmore, ignored him. "You are, Charlie Huntsworth, correct?" He could see Charlie looking his way blankly. "Sorry, did you say something? It's been a busy week, you know how it is, right?"

Charlie attempted to hide his growing annoyance. "I asked if you were a counsellor?"

"Yes, that's right. I provide career's guidance and counselling services for employees struggling with change," he said confidently as he perused Charlie's file, "and it looks like you're having some trouble with change, is that right?" he asked with a broad smile, which was intended to be welcoming, but was received as patronising.

"I don't know if I would say I'm struggling so much as I'm not convinced all change is good change."

"Uh huh… uh huh," he said as he scribbled some notes.

This unsettled Charlie. "What are you writing?"

"Oh nothing, don't worry, just relax. We're going to have a simple discussion and see if we can't get to the bottom of your… concerns."

"Honestly, this has all been blown out of proportion. I don't even have any major concerns," he backpeddled. "It's just…"

"Just what?" he asked earnestly as he recrossed his legs

"Listen, I don't need to be here. I don't need guidance or counselling or whatever it is they think I need. I was fine before all of this… everything was fine before all of this."

"All of what, Mr. Huntsworth?"

Charlie looked at him as if he knew full well what he meant. "All of this," he said, gesturing to the pictures around the room. "Mandela and Obama, in particular."

"Mmhmm," Whitmore continued to scribble.

"What are you writing?"

"It's nothing. So, what do you think is bringing you most... angst?"

"It's not only me, you know, I'm not the oddball. I even made a–" he stopped himself.

"Continue... do you feel like you're not being heard?"

He thought for a second. "I guess you could put it that way."

"Right... right, not being heard..." Whitmore said as he wrote.

"I simply want things to be fair."

"Would you say the notion of unfairness is new to you?"

"No, don't try that angle with me. It's not only Blacks and gays and women who have it tough. I've never had anything given to me. My dad had two jobs, and my mum worked part-time. I didn't have much growing up. I got a scholarship to go to a grammar school and busted my ass to get into a good university. The idea that, as a white man, I've had it all is ridiculous – that is what I have concern about," he declared.

Chapter 26

Margate Rock

Young Roger would run to his room and slam the door before his mum could see his tears or his bruises. From a young age, he learned to protect his mum at all costs, even in situations where he was the victim. There were of course times when he was unable to hide the daily signs of bullying, when his only pair of trousers was ripped, and he tried to pretend it happened during a game of football. His mum would see the angst on his face as he made up the latest story, the best comfort she could provide being words of fortitude and encouragement: "Just stick with it". So sticking with it was what he learned how to do, as best he could. When he was knocked down, he would get back u. Insults of 'mud face' and 'nig-nog' he would try to ignore, try to not let them affect him. He learned in time how to fit in, the things to say that made his time at Harmaton's least stressful and most smooth. Assimilation tactics ranged from being silent and flying under the radar, to complimenting the popular, and on occasion providing entertainment. Slowly but surely the bullying subsided. He even began to make what he considered to be friends. By the time he arrived at college, he didn't really see much difference between himself and his peers. It had become second nature to quell any potential difference that arose between them.

***

Maybe it won't be so bad… there's absolutely no way this won't be bad, Deborah thought as she joined the meeting. Mr Johansson and the team were already waiting for her on the line: not a good sign.

"Deb, baby, talk to me, what's going on over there?"

"Sir, as you will see from the numbers, the overall programme is doing really well," she replied, in her best attempt to distract from the elephant in the room.

"Ha, well that maybe so, but it seems our in-house issue has become one for the world." Deborah waited, unsure of what to say. "You know, I hate social media, I really do. Stupid kids glued to their phones all day, kinda makes me a bit sick, you know? But one of the great things about this whole digital connectiveness thing is that news travels fast, super-fast, and it feels like you can be in places without actually being places. So, it didn't take very long for Margorie, my PA, to pull together a selection of Twitter and Instagram posts about your boy's performance at the D&I awards. I mean, the nerve of these guys! It's all take, take, take. Not only do we acknowledge them as contributors and provide them a safe space for blah, blah, blah, we go even further and give them an award show… and it *still* isn't enough. Fucking ungrateful." He finished his mini rant with "Well, that's it. Your boy is out. No more being cordial and gentle. He goes. Bring the *other one* in fully."

"But, sir, if you'll allow me, I know Jonathan has been a bit… out of character recently, but I believe, given time, we can bring him back on side."

"This is not a discussion, Deb, it's a directive. He's

had his chance, and he doesn't know how to play ball. Time to go with the guy who does." He ended the call before giving Deborah a chance to respond.

She sat silently in her dimly lit office. Despite the meeting going exactly as she'd expected, she was no closer to working out how she would break the news to Jonathan.

***

Dale had not been able to sleep since the acceptance of the final mission with Andy. He was unable to work out whether it was the task at hand, or his changing world view, that was giving him the most trouble. He'd been spending less time with Andy, something his mate had picked up on. He was craving more time alone for reflection, something he'd never experienced before. The Reedmore beach trip might provide the perfect opportunity to get some space from everything; even if they were only going to Margate.

Jonathan linked arms with his gran as she walked gingerly, still managing to hold her ice cream. Jonathan, too, was enjoying an ice cream, despite the weather not being strictly warm enough to eat one. It was something that came with the seaside: you kinda had to do it. The group of elderly folk, with supporting carers, friends, and family, made their way onto the reserved area on the beach. Jonathan was slightly concerned about how some of the older people would make it up out of the chairs.

Greta began an announcement once everyone had found a seat. "Right, everyone, listen up. I'm going to keep this short and sweet, because I'm sure you want to get on with enjoying the…" she looked up for the sun and found only pale grey clouds, "…the beach. Make sure one of the care team knows where you are if you're going to leave the seating area."

Jonathan wondered how far any one of the residents could actually get, even if they really wanted to.

Just as Greta finished her safety speech, Jonathan's gran dropped her ice cream. "To ras," she uttered in annoyance.

"Sorry Gran, I'll get you another."

"No, no, it's too sweet for mi anyway."

"Come on, it's your day at the beach. You need an ice cream," he said as he headed off towards the ice cream van. As he walked, he caught Dale's eye. He hadn't seen him since the convention. He gave him a wave and gestured to the van, offering him an ice cream. Dale initially shook his head, and then whispered something to his nan before heading towards Jonathan.

"Long time no see. How are you doing?" Jonathan asked.

"Not too bad," Dale replied heavily, the weight of his words suggesting otherwise.

"You sure? Everything ok? Your nan ok?"

"She's fine. I've just got a lot on at the minute, you know?"

"Want to talk about it?" Jonathan offered as he paid for the ice cream.

Dale paused, considering the suggestion.

Jonathan could tell he had a lot on his mind. "Give me a second. I'll drop this off with my gran, and then we can have a walk. I think Old Gill wants to show his swimsuit off to the ladies anyway," he said with a laugh.

"Yeah, don't want to be around for that," Dale conceded.

They strolled down the promenade. The dilapidated shop fronts and wind-swept litter reminded Dale of his neighbourhood. He wondered how much of the rest of the country was in this shape.

"Talk to me, what's up? You were on better form at the convention," Jonathan noted.

"I don't know, I'm starting to look at life a bit differently, I guess. I've always been a bit of a… follower… Not sure I can do it anymore," Dale admitted to Jonathan and, for the first time, to himself.

"Looking at things differently is probably a good thing. Guess that's how you learn and grow. I've begun looking at things differently, too."

They walked in silence for a while.

"But it's not easy, right?" Dale finally said. "I don't get why it can't be easier?"

"It's life, I guess. My gran always says, 'Life it nah gon be easy'."

Dale tried his best to interpret the patois. "Hmm. Have you ever been asked to do something you knew wasn't right?"

The question threw Jonathan slightly. There was a darkness to it. "How do you mean?"

"Like I said, something you know is probably a step too far," Dale broached softly.

Jonathan wasn't sure how to respond but could tell Dale needed something more than his silence. "Yeah, kind of. People have asked me to do things I don't believe in." He thought about some of the requests Deborah had made of him.

"And what did you do?" Dale asked, with an air of desperation, hoping he was close to some direction for his moral compass.

"I pushed back, but it wasn't easy… I needed help from a friend." He thought about Jenna.

Dale looked at Jonathan. "I'm not like you. I'm not the hero that goes around saving people's nan's."

Jonathan blushed at the compliment, a brief moment

of positive affirmation that was quickly washed away by a feeling of guilt about his own gran's condition and the precarious financial situation they found themselves in.

"I don't think I'm strong enough to push back," Dale continued.

"What do you mean? You're more like me than you think. We both love comics and the Galactic universe. We both look after our grans. And, like I said, I needed a bit of support… I'm around if you need some of that," he offered sincerely.

Dale pondered. He really didn't like the amount of thinking he was doing these days.

Jonathan checked his watch. "We better head back. Old Gill has probably caused a riot by now."

Chapter 27

Bombs Away

"Just do it. Let's get it over with," Dale said hurriedly, as they crouched behind a beige Saloon parked across the road from their target's home.

"You do it. I thought you wanted to do it," Andy replied in annoyance, as he fiddled with the settings on the device, which were becoming slippery as his fingers dripped with sweat.

"I wanted to do it, and you said no, I'd mess it up," Dale replied testily.

"I said I'd mess *you* up if you did it wrong!" Andy replied sternly. "I've done everything. I got the explosive, I got the address, I convinced Robbo to let you come along. Now it's the least you could do," he finished, exasperated.

Dale begrudgingly conceded he was in this now, so what difference did it make? He moved slowly from his crouched position to the edge of the target car, only to trip on his shoelace and drop the explosive, scraping his arm on the pavement. "Fuck!" he screamed.

"Fuckin ell, Dale. You'll wake the whole neighbourhood. *And* blow us up."

As Dale looked sheepishly Andy's way for sympathy that was not forthcoming, he gathered himself, picked up the device and continued. Andy looked at his watch: five minutes to. CJ would be leaving any moment. They had to hurry.

The sun was starting to rise, increasing their chances of being seen. Andy silently willed Dale to finish the task as quickly as he could. He peered over the bonnet of the car to check on Dale, who was taking longer than desired, seemingly struggling to attach the IED to the undercarriage of the car. "Come on!" he whispered as loudly as he could without attracting attention, urging his compatriot to finish so they could prepare their exit. Not for the first time, Andy regretted that his often-interrogated sense of duty had led him to choose Dale as his partner.

Dale fiddled away with the straps for what felt like an eternity. His heart was in his mouth the entire time. He was trying his best to focus on the task and ignore the feeling of guilt that repeatedly stabbed him in the pit of his stomach. 'Click' went the harness, secured in place. He stopped for moments that felt like decades as his internal conflict continued. His mind bounced back and forth between the £10,000, images of his nan, conversations with Jonathan, and thoughts of Andy. As if the pressure in this situation wasn't high enough without everything else on his mind. *Why did I have to grow a conscience now?* he lamented. *Focus*, he thought, *you're here now. What was the order of activation?* He struggled to remember the sequence needed to arm the device. "Green for three, and then yellow and red together," he whispered, trying to remember the mnemonic he'd come up with to ensure he wouldn't forget. "Three green trees, and yellow and red, the home and away strips for Carlton United." Yeah that was it. Or was it? Was his subconscious deliberately messing with his memory to sabotage the mission? But no, the Carlton strips were that order. It would be armed. He could hear distant whispers that sounded almost cat-like but he realised they were more likely Andy beckoning him to hurry up. *Ok, this is it, it's done, time to go*, he thought, as he checked the device one last time. He felt like he was frozen in time as he had what he could only describe as an out of body experience where he watched himself detach one of the wires. He quickly shimmied out from under the car and re-joined Andy across the street.

"Are we set?" Andy asked.

Dale nodded in response, at peace with his performance of the task.

Andy checked his watch again. It was two minutes to. *Any time now.*

They waited patiently, time moving slowly as the pressure built.

"Andy…" Dale began, wanting to share his action with his compatriot.

"Shh!" Andy replied. "Not now."

The seconds slowly passed until they heard a latch on the door from across the street, followed by some mumbled conversation which sounded like a disagreement between CJ and his wife.

This was it, their moment. CJ opened the gate at the end of a short path and approached his car, briefcase in hand. He stopped as he arrived at his car, patting down his suit jacket, searching in his pockets for something.

"Probably forgotten his keys," Dale said, more loudly than necessary.

"Shhh! You're gonna get us pinched," Andy hissed.

CJ made his way back to the front door to retrieve his lost item. Before long, he was back and getting into his car.

"We can't get this wrong," Andy said to himself as much as Dale, as he readied his thumb over the trigger, waiting for the engine to start.

CJ fiddled around inside the car, appearing to be sorting out his radio station and adjusting the mirror and seat as if someone else had been recently driving the car. Then a rumble as the engine rolled over and came to life. That was the signal. Andy hit the trigger.

An odd hissing sound and smoke came from underneath the car, but not the loud explosion they were expecting. The MP had not picked up on either as he prepared to set off, until he seemed to realise he couldn't see out of his back window because of the fog.

"What's happening, Andy?" Dale asked with faux ignorance.

"Fuck, you tell me. Why isn't the car in a thousand fucking pieces, Dale?" He already assumed the mess up was linked to his partner. He clicked the trigger a few more times. Nothing, just more smoke. At that point the MP exited his car to explore the mysterious situation.

They'd blown their chance.

"Fuck it, let's get out of here before the pigs get here," he told Dale, practically dragging him away from the scene by his collar.

Jenna was busy at her desk when the news alert flashed up on her phone: PRIME MINISTERIAL CANDIDATE SURVIVES BOMB ATTACK. Her heart dropped to the bottom of her stomach. *Is he ok?* She quickly checked her messages, opening their chat; the series of unanswered messages amplified the feeling of guilt. *He was worried. He needed someone and I wasn't there.* She stood and headed for a quiet space while trying to call him, but it went straight to voicemail. She sent a series of messages, all receiving a solitary tick. *Fuck, I need to know if he's ok.* Her head was spinning. She rushed for the door. Charlotte and Jonathan were watching her unusually erratic moves from a distance. They exchanged confused looks and shrugged shoulders.

Flo, Colleen, and the rest of CJ's team insisted that he go in for a check-up, despite his protests that it was unnecessary and he was totally fine. "Can't I even look at my phone? What if something important comes through? The election is only a couple of days away."

"You'll be fine without your phone for a second," Flo said as she affectionately dabbed his brow for sweat that wasn't there.

"Close call," Bill said. "But it will take more than a cowardly bomb scare to keep our man down." He sounded so convincing that he believed his own words. "How are you feeling?"

"I'm fine, honestly. I appreciate everyone being here, but nothing happened to me. If we let them derail the last leg of the campaign, they win. Let me up out of here," CJ protested.

"Give it a little time. We'll have you out in no time. The media are keen to speak with you, make sure you keep that spirit for the interviews."

Bill insisted CJ wear the small head bandage, if not for safety, for effect. Streams of journalists were lined up at the hospital gate waiting for CJ's exit. "Mr. James, Mr. James, how are you doing? Have you fully recovered?"

"I'm fine, thank you, just a bit shaken up, but we have an election to win, right?"

Cheers went up from a group of supporters in the crowd.

"Mr. James, is it safe for you to continue on the campaign? Do you have a message for NBF?"

"I can't predict the future, but I know that one of the values this great country was built upon is bravery, and this is the time to be brave and not let cowards bully us.

We have a chance to make history!" he declared emphatically, triggering another round of cheers from the growing crowd. "Yep, Reece, go on," he said to one of the more familiar journalists.

"What do you say to those who suggest these attacks prove the country is not ready for the level of change you would bring forward?"

"I would say those people are in the distinct minority. I believe the majority of the country wants positive change. The country wants to feel included again in the social contract and that is what I'm offering."

Colleen stepped in. "Okay, that's enough for now. Mr. James needs to rest if he's going to be ready for the final few days of the campaign. I think you can all understand that." The crowd begrudgingly agreed and parted ways so CJ and Flo could make their way to the car.

The car ride was filled with a surprising level of tension. "What's wrong, not happy that I made it through?"

"Don't, CJ," she said, brushing his hand away from her thigh. "They could have killed you," she said, guilt washing over her for encouraging her husband to pursue office. She shot daggers at Bill for attempting to influence her. The reality hit. She nearly lost the love of her life over an election. An outpouring of tears and emotions engulfed her. "What's it going to take? Are you going to actually have to die, or me, or one of the kids?" She sobbed, as she brought him to her chest.

"Hun, baby, can't breathe," he muttered through her damp shirt as she held him awkwardly but tightly. "Come on, Flo, that's not fair. You can't put this on me. You wanted this remember? I had to be strategic to make history." He spoke with more resentment than he'd planned for.

"I know, I was wrong… I got swept up in the hype… lost track of what's most important for my family," she admitted, cutting her eyes again at Bill. "Is it really worth it, CJ?"

"Can I answer after I've won, at least?" he said in jest, trying to lighten the mood. "Too soon?"

She turned away to stare out of the tinted window, CJ sighed deeply. She threw his phone at him. "This wouldn't stop buzzing and beeping, as always." He looked at the hundreds of concerned messages and missed calls. Several from one name in particular that always made him feel better.

***

Can we meet? the message read.

Jenna's instincts screamed no, but her body said the opposite. *Quickly, just to check you're ok*, she replied, swiftly following up with, *No funny business.*

I have no idea what you mean, he replied with a smiling emoji.

***

Jonathan called and texted Jenna, but nothing: no answer. It was really unlike her to leave in the middle of the day without saying a word. He was worried; he presumed it was some kind of family emergency. He wouldn't be able to relax until he knew she was ok.

Jenna hated that she instinctively cared so much. After everything they had been through this was much more than he deserved. Yet in the head of the moment her mind ceded control to her heart.

Jonathan decided to head to Jenna's flat. *I won't stay long, just make sure everything is fine.* His phone buzzed frantically with news alerts. He briefly registered something about Calvin James, but now was not the time for political updates, it was time to be there for Jenna. As he approached her building, he saw a figure that resembled Jenna leaving the main doors in a rush, almost panicked. He decided to trail behind, unsure if it was her, and now more uncertain if she'd want to see him. He followed her to the high street and watched her enter what could have been a café but was hard to make out. He was waiting a few shops down unsure whether to follow, when a tall man in dark clothing approached the door. There was something about him that looked familiar. After a few minutes, Jonathan decided to make a pass by without being seen. *She's probably seeing a friend. But then why the panic?*

Chapter 28

Opportunity In Loss

"It's tight, Mr. Fullop, really tight. Too close to call, even with the bomb incident. It seems people are even more divided. Some are scared about what other attacks could take place if he wins."

"These stupid people. You line everything up and they still can't do what they're supposed to, mindless idiots."

"I would suggest something to push things over the top."

"Mmhmm, understood." He reached for his mobile and began typing a message.

***

They met at a small café near Jenna's volunteer academy, it was hard to meet anywhere in public where CJ would not attract attention, and meeting in private was not something Jenna trusted herself to do. CJ wore his most non-descript outfit: navy blue trousers, black shoes, and navy jacket, with a dark beanie to cover some of his face. He arrived first and ordered a tea for them both, remembering the way Jenna liked it from their pillow talks at the hotel. He yearned for those days again. Jenna rushed through the door to escape the shower she'd been caught in. Her mack was dripping wet, but to CJ she looked even more beautiful. *Focus*, he thought, *don't want to scare her off.* He stood to embrace her, giving her a tight hug. "Good to see you, J,"

"And you, safe and well," she replied as she slid into the booth.

"Told you, I'm in one piece. Not that easy to get rid of me."

"As if anyone would want to do that," she replied before she had a chance to catch her words. "I mean…"

"It's ok, I know what you mean. To be honest, if it's near-death experiences I need to get your attention, I would happily gamble with a few more."

She'd missed his sense of humour. She missed the way his eyes would smile when he found himself particularly funny.

"So, I heard they might delay the election, to make sure things are safe?"

"There was talk of it, but my team thinks it's best if we try to capitalise on the momentum from the incident."

She wasn't surprised by his team's appraisal of the situation: *what's the risk to a Black man's life when an election win is at stake?* "What do you think?" she asked.

"I think we all have to die one day, but we don't all get a shot at being PM."

Jenna hated and loved his blasé, care free approach to life; whether it be spilling coffee on his shirt or an attempt on his life. His refusal to be impeded by fear somehow translated into a sense of great control of his world. Despite her admiration she was concerned, "Promise you'll be careful."

He reached out to touch her hand. "I promise."

His phone began to ring. He tried to ignore it. "Probably the security detail. They were surprisingly hard to shake after everything."

"I don't want to get you in trouble," she said as the phone rang again.

"Let me quickly check it." His pupils automatically dilated at the name on the screen. He quickly answered, knowing the calls were likely to continue. "Yeah, I've just stepped out for a bit of fresh air… uh huh… no, I won't be long… Sure, I'll grab some on the way back. Gotta go now." He put the phone down and saw the look on Jenna's face. The look which said she knew who was on the line, the look that said she'd heard him lie like that before.

"Listen, I should go," she said.

"No, can't you stay a bit longer?"

"No, I should get back. I'm glad you're ok. Good luck for Thursday. I'll be cheering you on." She was gone in an instant.

CJ slammed his fists on the table.

Jonathan power-walked away from the café, heavy rain soaking him. *How could I have been so blind?* The firm slap of reality hit him: *our conversations about CJ, the way they were together during the ad, how did I miss it?*

***

The coffee machine whirred into life after Charlotte had deposited her pod and hit the large coffee option. She had read caffeine can suppress hunger, so she felt this could be a life hack to support her new calorie control efforts. She flexed her hand, examining her nails absent mindedly, when she was approached from behind.

"Charlotte, is it?"

She spun in surprise to be met with Roger's broad smile, a smile and face she found attractive, but that were firmly off limits based on reports from Jenna. She replied with the minimal level of workplace civility: "It is." She picked up her coffee.

"I've been meaning to say hello," he said, thrown off by her frosty reception.

"Hello," she replied with a sarcastic wave as she swanned back into the main office area.

Ok, he said to himself, deciding to dust off his bruised ego with a coffee of his own. The machine whirred into life again as Charlie walked in with a colleague Roger hadn't met.

"This is what I and *many* others have been saying, we can't have a PM who is this divisive. It simply won't work," Charlie proclaimed, relaying an article from his phone to his friend and loudly enough to capture anyone else in the immediate vicinity.

"Is this the bomb attack?" Roger asked, attempting to join the conversation.

Charlie gave him a full body examination, as if deciding whether or not to allow him to partake. "I suppose you think he would be great for the country?"

Roger read the tone. He'd played this game many times before, and in fact shared Charlie's disdain for the candidate. "I don't. I think he's smug. He rubs me up the wrong way."

"Finally, someone like you... someone *else* is saying what is so clear," Charlie said, almost congratulating Roger on his wise assessment.

Roger sipped his coffee, satisfied with the validation received.

***

"The 'Stand with Us' campaign. Debby, this is it, this is the moment we've been waiting for to kick it up into fith gear!" Mr Johansson said enthusiastically.

"But, sir, while I understand it is important to show our support during such difficult periods, perhaps it would be more appropriate to wait until things die down a little, as a sign of sensitivity... after all, it was a man's life at risk," Deborah said, shocking herself at her level of candour, but questioning if she had lost all rational control. This was not the best route to promotion.

Mr. Johansson received a whisper in his ear, He mumbled inaudibly in agreement. "Deb, I love your spirit, your energy, that's how you've become the fine people leader that you are. Can't knock it, right?" he asked the other committee members on the call. "But this isn't a request. I'm sure I don't need to remind you that review time isn't far away, so make sure you have your priorities in order. It would be a real shame if you were to miss out on what was due through *misplaced loyalties,*" he said with a dark conviction that left no ambiguities as to the intent of the message.

"Understood, sir," she replied automatically, pulling down her blazer to signify acquiescence. She closed the call, sighed in frustration and saw a message on her phone: it was Meghan. Deborah knew her daughter was a large driving factor behind her growing conscience and looming guilt. The last thing she needed now was a dressing down about her unethical behaviour.

She opened her computer and looked at the proposal for the campaign again. Clicking through slides, she tried to convince herself it wasn't so bad. Even if the timing was less than subtle, they were doing a good thing. "Stand with us," she said out loud. The campaign would position Bentalago active wear to the forefront of all media outlets. The mood boards and imagery were aggressive, or maybe it was because she was out of touch. This after all was what the kids wanted to wear; according to the focus groups, at least. Did it send the right message? Perhaps not, but if they didn't run it, Jump would find another firm that would. Deborah knew she should run it past the D&I squad; that's partly what they were there for, to pressure-test these types of ideas. At least then she could share some of the accountability.

***

Deborah strutted into the meeting room and closed the door firmly behind her. "Right, listen up! Shhhhh!" she said loudly, trying to get focus in the room. "We don't have long and election day is nearly here. We need to get the campaign up and running like yesterday."

"Deborah, do you not think that now is not the best time? Perhaps we should wait until things die down and let the election pass?" Rachel said.

"Thanks for the suggestion, but that's not an option. We want to make an impact and capitalise on the momentum," she declared as convincingly as she could, as if these were her own genuine thoughts.

Jonathan hadn't been able to think straight since seeing Jenna and CJ together. Like a grizzled detective working his last case, he tried his best to cobble the pieces together. *Why were they alone? So soon after he'd been attacked? Her panic. Their familiarity on the ad shoot, her boy trouble.* He was desperate for any explanation other than the one he kept landing on: Occam's Razor. *Focus, be present.* His mind had been only broadly processing the conversation in the room. Directing his full attention to the matter at hand, he could not believe what he was hearing. A man nearly died and they wanted to launch a campaign off the back of it, the week of the election. He felt waves of anxiety wash over him. He tried to centre himself, to focus like Aarato, the way Jenna had shown him. He stood up, "We can't do this!"

"I'm sorry some of you feel that way, but it's not up for discussion. This is what we've been directed to do."

"Even if it's wrong?" he asked.

"That may be your opinion, but we don't all see it that way. If you're not comfortable with this, perhaps it's time for you to step down."

"Happily," he said as he stormed out of the meeting room.

Rachel felt uncomfortable. Even Roger was slightly uneasy.

"Now that bit of drama is over with, we can continue with the plan. Roger, I know you can adequately step in for our less committed colleague."

Roger nodded.

Jonathan had never felt rage like this. He left the building in search of fresh air and a plan; he knew there was only one person to speak to, but things felt awkward since seeing her in the cafe. He began to second guess himself. *Were things actually off? Or was this just more anxiety and paranoia, insecurity triggered by seeing the woman he loved so comfortable with another man?* He tried his best to rationalise: *it was only ego, they were just having a coffee, was there anything to even be upset about?* But the churn in his gut said differently, his intuition was inflamed.

***

Jenna had been downcast since her meeting with CJ; annoyed she'd let herself be vulnerable again with him, even if it was only for a split second. *You won't miss what's not meant for you*, she reassured herself. She looked at her phone, there were lots of messages from Jonathan. She cupped her face with her hands and inhaled deeply: *ok, back to business, shake it off.*

***

They were to meet at his place, agreeing that work no longer was a safe space for sensitive discussions, and the prospect of some much-needed air on the way to Jonathan's greatly appealed.

Despite being in a place of mixed feelings, Jonathan jumped at the suggestion before thinking it through. His haste meant he spent the next couple of hours trying his best to make his vividly child-like apartment look as grown up as possible. Posters were removed, action figures and game controllers hidden. He'd never actually had a woman over who he was attracted to. *This isn't a date, it's about the programme. Focus on that.* But his mind wandered to the café scene as the doorbell rang.

He took a second to compose himself, checking his breath on the palm of his hand, before searching for a mint. "Hey, you, how are… I'm sorry, that was stupid," he said awkwardly as he answered the door.

Jenna laughed. Only two seconds had passed, but he'd already made her feel better. "Can I come in?"

"Ha sure, that's probably a good idea, right?"

"I think so," she replied as she walked past him. "So, do I get the tour? Or are certain rooms off limits, just for the ladies."

"Of course not, it's all for you." He felt himself blushing. "I mean you can see it all, follow me," he said as he hurried ahead to show off his compact apartment.

"You've got a nice place. I'd like to live alone sometimes or, you know, with someone who isn't family."

"Yeah, being alone has its upsides. Can go to bed whenever I like," he said, realising it probably sounded more juvenile than intended. "But can get a bit lonely too," he said honestly.

"Sometimes you can feel alone even with people around you," she answered wistfully.

"Are you ok? It's just you seemed a bit distant and the other day… you left in a hurry."

"I'm fine… I think." In typical Jenna fashion she deflected the attention away from herself. "Anyway, what's all this with the programme? They want to do what?"

Jonathan took her through the details of the campaign to leverage the bomb attempt on CJ. He watched closely to see if mention of his name would illicit a reaction. He swore he picked up a twinge of an eye flicker but couldn't be sure. "And if that wasn't bad enough, there's was still no sign of progress on the foundational activities the company signed up to. I just left. Deborah basically kicked me out. Honestly, I think I'm done with it now. I can't keep being the marionette. They've got Roger now anyway."

Jenna tried to not let her personal history with CJ cloud her judgement. She knew this would have pissed her off, even if she never knew who CJ was. "These lot, man, they never change, do they? It's always exploitation."

Jonathan could read the dejection in her body language. He felt bad for adding to whatever weight she was already carrying. "There must be something we can do?"

"I don't know, we tried, we pushed. We're just not on the same page." Jenna was surprised at her own lack of enthusiasm, but she took it as proof that some things just needed to happen within the community.

"I'm going to quit!" he declared triumphantly.

"Is that the best thing, really? At least while you're involved, you can try to influence things."

"Like I've done so far?"

"You've done some good things. The kids wouldn't have been able to come in if it wasn't for you. You've helped to educate people in the office."

"*You* helped to educate people in the office. I merely repeated the words."

"It was a team effort," she said warmly.

"Guess we do make a good team," he said, hoping the idea would plant in her mind.

They were sitting on the floor together. She leaned on his shoulder. His heart began to thud. He'd waited so long for this moment, *don't spoil it*. "Hey, have you ever seen *Ninjata*?"

"No, what's that?"

"Let me show you." The pair chilled and enjoyed the anime show together. Jonathan brought out a selection of popcorn, plantain chips, and mixed nuts. He enthusiastically described the plot and character back stories in detail. Jenna couldn't help but get swept up in his energy. They both needed some time to switch off for an evening. The problems of diversity, inclusion, equity, and elections could wait.

***

Jenna was unsure how much time had passed when she woke. Her mind foggy, she tried to get her bearings. It was unlike her to nap, even less so in an unfamiliar environment. She looked across the sofa. Jonathan was passed out, mouth open, snoring gently; the TV was still playing the anime show. They really must have been tired to sleep with that volume. She quietly gathered her things, not wanting to disturb him from his deep slumber. She attempted to close the door gently, but the crash of the locks made more noise than planned; she hoped she hadn't woken him as she made her way home.

The crash of the door brought Jonathan back to reality with a bang. He'd been having an amazing dream where he and Aarato were attempting to free Jenna from the clutches of Emperor Mantu. His mouth was dry and vision blurry as he looked around the dark room, lit only by the glare of his loud television. It hit him: Jenna was here. "Jenna?" he called out. No response. He plodded around his flat, realising she must have left. He checked his phone to see if she had left a message. There were seventeen missed calls.

***

Jenna attempted to open her own door with as much care as she's closed Jonathan's, in the hope of not alerting her sister. The door made less noise, but she failed the mission, nonetheless.

"Sis!" Yami called from the sitting room. "Come here, did you see this?"

Jenna entered the living room for what she hoped would be a short conversation. "See what?"

"They're at it again. They tried to kill CJ with a bomb or something. I don't get how people can be so evil."

It was nice to see such compassion from her sister, but she really didn't have it in her to have another conversation about him. "I know, it's crazy," she said blandly.

"I mean, the man is *sooo* fine, how could anyone be upset with that?"

Jenna laughed at her sister's true motivations. "I'm going to my room."

"You ok, sis?" Yami shouted after her, worried she'd said something. "I'm sure he's a great politician too," she called "He's got my vote."

***

"Why didn't you try my landline?" Jonathan demanded. "What do you mean you don't use landline numbers anymore. What are they there for then? You should have found a way to get hold of me."

"I'm sorry sir, but we use the mobile number provided in cases of emergency. We also sent several texts," the nurse said directly, trying to be mindful of his heightened emotions.

"When can I go in and see her?"

"The doctors will let you in shortly, but remember she needs her rest," the nurse said, gently placing her hand on his shoulder for reassurance. Reassurance that did nothing to assuage the huge guilt he felt for missing the calls from the hospital. He looked skyward and considered the twisted joke that was being played on him the one day he'd managed to share time with the love of his life at his place.

He pulled out his phone and fired up his farming role-play game to pass the time. He tapped and fidgeted, but he couldn't focus. He was aimlessly hitting icons and logos, issuing instructions to his digital farm hands at random. A doctor opened the door, clipboard in hand. "How is she? Can I go in?" Jonathan asked in desperation.

"Mr. Archer, a second, please. I understand this is a difficult time, but your grandmother is in a delicate place and we have to be careful now. You can go in, but please, only a few minutes. She needs rest."

Jonathan tried to listen, but he wanted to get to his gran as quickly as possible. The doctor stepped to one side and Jonathan tried his best not to push past.

The room felt quiet and cold when he stepped in,

with devices he hadn't seen before beeping and murmuring at a low level. The sight of his gran attached to the various machines caused him to slow down, as if the prospect of getting closer would make the situation more real.

"Son, is that you?" a stifled voice whispered, unable to turn her face towards him.

"Yes, it's me," he replied softly, placing a hand on her arm, not yet ready to make contact.

"Good, I knew you would come," she said with a cough.

He held her arm tighter. "I'm sorry I didn't come sooner, I…"

"Stop, you na affi explain to me. You hav bin there for mi always." She began to cough again, the fit longer this time. Jonathan rocked her arm reassuringly, imploring her not to strain. "It for mi to say sorry to you, not supporting you more."

Jonathan's eyes moistened. He sniffled to hold his tears back, not wanting to let her hear him cry. He wanted to speak, to say something to make it all better, but found no words.

"Yet, you grow into a good man, someone I am very proud of. And you continue to grow and do good tings; dem look to you fi lead and show people a better path. I thank di lord for that." She suffered another spate of coughing, this time more aggressive. "You must promise me to continue."

Tears were in full flow now. "I promise"

His gran took his hand and squeezed it. They sat in silence, holding each other until her grip gradually loosened. Jonathan's tears continued to fall for the rest of the evening. He never let her hand go.

Chapter 29

Enough.

The hapless duo was sequestered up in Dale's bedroom, having precious few options of refuge.

"We are fucked, totally fucked!" Andy shouted as he paced back and forth, desperately trying to figure out their next move.

"Sorry, And, I don't know what happened."

"Tea, boys?" Dale's mum shouted upstairs, unhappy that they hadn't taken a moment to come down and properly say hello.

"No, Mum, we're fine," Dale called back.

Andy seethed with frustration and fear. "You fucking bottled it is what happened. Fuck! This was it, our big chance, Fuck!"

"It'll be alright, And. We'll figure something out, we always do."

"We? *We?* What have *we* ever figured out? You mean I will figure something out, or at least try to, and you know what, I don't fuckin know if I will – that was our 9th fuckin life!"

Dale could feel the genuine fear emanating from his friend. He felt bad for not sharing the exact feeling, but in truth he was relieved, very relieved. But he had to be careful not to show it.

Andy looked at him. "Well, say something then? You got us into the mess, what are we gonna do?"

Dale thought about his conversation with Jonathan at the beach. "Maybe we say we had a change of heart, that it wasn't the right thing to do?"

"You what?"

"Yeah, I mean, have you ever had a think about some of the stuff they're asking us to do? Is it even worth it? I mean, what are we getting out of any of this?"

"Oh, now you're thinking. Now you're a fuckin philosopher or summin? You needed to put your thought into executing the fuckin task at hand. That was the only thought you needed."

"I'm serious, And. Look at us, hurting people, for what? To impress Robbo and the lads? I don't know anything about this James fella. What's he done that's so bad?"

"Why the fuck are you worried about him? What's he done for you? You think he's worried about you when he's taking millions back to his mansion and fucking his model wife?"

"Is she a model?" Dale replied innocently.

Andy rolled his eyes. "He is part of the problem. We can't even keep a job, and Blacks like him are able to run the country. That shows how fucked things are."

"Yeah, but is that his fault?"

"Of course it fucking is. He's taken the job from a White man, just like our jobs were taken from us."

Dale pondered the proposition, but it didn't sit right with him.

"Anyway, save the questions for Jeremy Kyle. We gotta figure out what to tell Robbo."

***

Jonathan never thought he'd see the day when he wouldn't want to respond to messages from Jenna. To him, the past few days were not real, they couldn't be; missed calls and messages asking if she'd done anything wrong only added to the façade he wished he was living. After a couple days of complete radio silence, Jonathan realised he had to let the world know he was still alive. Short messages to Deborah, Jenna, and Freddy staved off panicked enquiries about his whereabouts.

Lying flat on his back in a dark room was how most of his days were spent since the passing of his gran. He was forced to move a couple of times a day to eat something or use the bathroom, although his appetite had dropped to practically nothing. Alone in his room, his time was spent mainly stuck in his head, blaming himself for not being there, blaming himself for not being able to provide better care, blaming himself for putting Jenna first. He continued to play over the final moments with the woman who cared for him most in his life: the words she'd said, to the very end supporting him. He thought about the promise he had made, everything that had been going on, how he was bending to appease against what he knew deep down wasn't right. He missed her so much the pain was relentless. He knew she would be watching over him and he knew what he had to do to make her proud.

***

Deborah tried her best to steel herself. *Life is hard. Nobody said it was supposed to be fair. You can't please everyone and some people will never be happy.*

"Listen, Jonathan," she began, although she could tell he was in no mood to listen, to be spoken down to or controlled. "I think we've been more than reasonable. I tried to be there for you. Didn't I give you support? Sometimes it's a game of give and take and, lately, you've not been giving."

"Support that only began when I was designated as your champion. I don't think you said two words to me before then, probably didn't even know my name."

She attempted to hide the guilt on her face at this accurate assertion. "No, come on, you've always been one of my guys, my Champ! Look, it may feel like that at times because I'm having to look after everyone. It can be hard to give everyone the personal attention they would like. I'm no superwoman," she finished self-deprecatingly.

"I can't do it, anymore. I can't sit back and be your puppet while you fail to deliver on anything meaningful."

"Jonathan, Champ, where is this all coming from? Is it Jenna? What has Jenna done to help out with the programme?"

Mention of Jenna's name made his blood boil. "Don't speak about Jenna, you don't know anything about her. Without her…"

"Without her, what?"

"Without her, I wouldn't be the man I am."

"Psshh, it's just a crush. I've seen it a thousand times before. If you stick it out, you can achieve big things with the company. Look how well Roger is doing."

Another name that raised emotions. "I don't want to be like Roger," he said definitely.

"So, you want to live in a fairy tale world where you and your girlfriend take down racism single-handed? I'm sorry to tell you, but that's not how things work," she said, trying to assuage her own guilt as much as anything else. "Do you think I got where I am by only doing what I wanted? No, I had to play the game, wait my turn. That's the problem with you people–," she caught herself, "That's the problem with some people, they want the world yesterday and that's not how things work. Things take time."

"That may be so, it may be time you have, but I don't. Here is my resignation letter. Thank you for all the ... opportunities." He dropped the letter on her desk and strode out. He'd never felt so free, so alive and empowered.

Deborah was alone with her thoughts again, more time to try to convince herself that what she was doing was right. *Even if it's not, what choice do I have? I have a boss too, they forget that.*

Jonathan's heart was pounding ferociously, his breath short and rapid. He found a quiet space down one of the corridors to compose himself. He closed his eyes and tried to clear his thoughts. He focused on his gran, began to take slow deep breaths and gradually felt calmer – *this it, no turning back.*

He said his goodbyes to Freddy and the gang.

"I can't believe you're doing this, mate. Isn't there another way?" Freddy said openly.

"It's gone too far. This is the right thing to do. I've wanted to start my own shop. Guess now I have no excuse not to."

"Was getting sick of you, anyway," Freddy replied, wiping a tear from his eye with his bear-like paw of a hand.

Jonathan collected his cardboard box full of design folders and a few models he had on his desk, and made his way to the lift.

Jenna chased behind. "Jonathan!" she called.

He'd hoped to escape without her seeing him in this emotional state. "I did it," he said with a smile of accomplishment.

She didn't know how to reply. She didn't want to see

him go but was proud of his commitment. "I'm going to miss you."

"I'm hoping it isn't the last time we'll see each other," he said, managing a laugh.

"Of course not. I mean at the office. I'll message you later." She kissed him on his cheek. A kiss that practically made it all worth it.

Things were moving so fast, there was so much Jenna wanted to say, needed to; she hadn't even had an opportunity to properly console him. She was heading back to her desk when she passed a flustered-looking Deborah. "Deborah, have you got a second?"

Really? Now? Better get it all over and done with, I guess. "What can I do for you?" she said with exaggerated grace

"Perhaps we should go in here." Jenna gestured to one of the vacant meeting rooms.

Deborah sighed, rolled her eyes and gestured for Jenna to lead the way with a flurry of her hand. "After you."

Deborah leaned against the meeting room table as Jenna positioned herself opposite. Charlotte had seen the two talking outside the meeting room and decided to try and get a closer look.

"So, what is it?" *As if I don't know.*

"I know you spoke with Jonathan, that he's left…"

"Let me stop you there before you get on your high racial horse. I tried to get him to stay," she interjected.

"That's not the point. The point is you failed to deliver on promises that were made and continued to exploit difficult circumstances for the benefit of the company and others."

"I'd say that's a pretty one-sided assessment."

"It's an accurate one. Jonathan felt he had no choice. You'd left him no other option."

"Well, as I said, I'm sorry about that, but it was really

on him. We work for a company, and the priorities of the company come before any individual. It's not personal. Now, if you'd excuse me, someone around here needs to actually do some work to try keep these lights on and your wages coming in."

"No. Are you actually sorry? Does any of this mean anything to you at all? I mean, come on, I get that you're White and doing well, but can't you see the injustice in any of this? Has that ever pierced your reality even for a second?"

"Listen, young lady, I've been very patient, and frankly I'm getting sick of everyone's sob story. I had it rough too. Just because you're black, it doesn't give you a monopoly on trauma and oppression, and yes, as a women I've had to fight my own battles too. Believe it or not, battles that helped give you the opportunities you have today, but you don't hear me crying about it or expecting an award."

"Nobody is expecting an award. We are asking for fairness, commitment to actual goals that could genuinely help people."

Deborah paused, in exhaustion as much as anything else.

"Do you have a problem with me?" Jenna asked frankly.

The sheer directness caught Deborah off guard. "What?"

"You heard. Do you have a problem with me? You've never so much as cast a genuine look my way, and I've been here for years. You didn't even consider me for the D&I squad."

"What? Hear me, lady: like I said to Jonathan, I look after an entire business. I don't have the time to be best friends with every employee. It doesn't mean I don't like you or have a special agenda against you." Deborah believed this to be true. She never had any conscious negative thoughts about Jenna. "I did all I could. I am sorry it's not worked out how you would have liked, but that's the end of it." She pushed past Jenna, heading out into the corridor. In her core she knew things weren't perfect, or perhaps even fair, but when was the world ever fair? Who said this world was going to be fair?

Jenna stayed in the meeting room, as frustrated she was before. Meanwhile, Charlotte, sensing something was about to go down, had positioned herself strategically in the corridor. It didn't take Deborah long to realise she was pretending not to eavesdrop while she played with her phone. Deborah did her best to ignore her as she headed to her office for refuge.

Charlotte gently knocked on the meeting room door. "Room for one more?" she said, sensing the tension in the air.

Jenna loved her friend, but she wasn't ready for a conversation. She nodded regardless, knowing she was unlikely to be left alone.

Charlotte could tell her girl was under it and, instead of her usual verbal tsunami, she simply put her arm around her.

***

An eerie tension had fallen across the office: no small talk, gossip, or laughter. It was almost as if there was a state of mourning or, at least, one of shock. Even Charlie seemed to have taken the news badly. Jenna attempted to concentrate on her work. She knew Jonathan would be ok, or at least she hoped he would. She checked her phone again: nothing from him. This state of limbo was torturous; she couldn't handle it any longer. Grabbing her coat, she headed for the door.

"What is up with everyone today? Trish asked no one in particular in sheer ignorance.

***

Jenna rushed through the library entrance and passed Violet on the counter, who barely raised her head from her book. She headed towards their desk, but he was nowhere to be seen. She'd been sure he'd be there, she knew it in her core.

"What are you doing here?" the voice said from behind. "You've not left too?"

"Thank god. I thought you might come here, but then I couldn't find you." She was tripping over her words.

"I went to the loo," Jonathan said as she hugged him. "I really should have left sooner," he added, as she wiped a tear from her cheek.

"I was worried about you. You didn't answer your phone."

"I didn't want to risk you calling me back... I'm kinda freestyling here, emotions running high, not sure how much discipline I had to see it through."

"You didn't have to leave."

"It's the new me, right: forthright, decisive, all that good shit." Jenna chuckled. "All the things you wanted me to be," he said, almost on autopilot.

She was unsure how to respond. "I didn't want anything from you. I mean, I didn't want you to be anything." She struggled to articulate herself, "I mean, you didn't need to do anything for me. You're fine the way you are."

"Jenna, I love you," he declared, a phenomenal weight lifting off his chest.

"Don't say that."

312

"I've always loved you, from day one," he pressed, the love tap now flowing freely.

"Look, I know a lot has happened today, emotions are high," she rationalised.

"Stop. This has nothing to do with any of that. This is about me and you, feelings I've had for longer than I remember. Feelings I've had to carry and hide for fear…" he trailed off as reality hit. "It's him, isn't it? CJ…"

"It's not that simple."

"I just realised: this isn't the fairy tale. This isn't me vanquishing the dragon and riding off with you into the distance… I'm sorry." Adrenaline running low and deflated, he was ready to concede.

"You don't have to be sorry, you're just being honest." She wished she could say more, give him something more positive, some grain of hope, but she didn't want to lie; to him, to herself. She'd seen too many lies.

He turned away. He couldn't face her. His heart was pounding. She put her arms around him from behind. He froze. This embrace was long desired, but not like this. *Don't let her see you cry*, he told himself.

Chapter 30

Pride and Shame

Meghan had tried to impart so much knowledge onto her mother from such a young age, at times Deborah would wonder who was mother and who was the daughter. While initially this would lead to friction and conflict, in time Deborah learned to 'lean in' and embrace her daughter's bright and active mind. She was still very much playing catch-up, with every other day bringing a new revelation or philosophy her way. Spirituality was one of her daughters many core values. Deborah could not pretend she'd absorbed much of her daughter's teachings, but one thing she did remember Meghan saying was, "Mum, you know nothing happens by accident, there's no such thing as coincidence." Deborah hadn't been able to grasp that concept until today.

The subject line simply read: *Deborah Tate*. She'd seen many appraisals before, usually from the assessor's perspective, but even with her own feedback assessments she'd not seen anything quite like this; it was clear immediately that it was not meant for her eyes. She quickly took some screen shots with her phone and then proceeded to expunge the email from her inbox.

She sat quietly in her study and studied the images

over and over again. Particular phrases seemed to leap off the screen: *adequate manager, performance aptitude reached. Progression potential limited. Inadequate for higher level strategic decisiveness.* The corporate jargon was as clear as it was vaguely verbose. Wordplay aside, the message was clear: after all her years of service, Deborah was not deemed promotion material. "Fucking bastards!" she shouted as she threw her phone across the room. "After everything I've done for them, given up my life, my marriage, my youth, and for what? To be deemed adequate but having limited progression potential." The assessment was brutal. Alone in her large house, empty and dark, all she could do was sob.

***

"Do I really have to wear the t-shirt?" CJ asked wearily, not dissimilar to a child being forced to wear their winter jacket.

Colleen gave him a telling look, a wordless answer to his question.

"Ok, give me the shirt. An XL, I guess, if it has to go over the shirt and tie. I thought the wrist bands would be enough."

"CJ, people have to know you're behind the campaign. You're the entire reason it was started."

"I know, I know, so people keep telling me. And, as Bill keeps saying, this is what's going to get us over the line."

"Right, exactly, so keep that in mind ahead of the debate – focus on the goal."

"I guess so, focus on the goal, focus on the goal."

***

"I didn't hear you come in," Deborah said as she nestled next to her daughter.

"Mum! Personal space!" Meghan exclaimed in protest of her mother's snuggles.

"Oh behave, we would sit like this all the time when you used to watch your Disney movies."

"Yeah, that stopped when I was eight, Mum."

"Guess you're right," she said despondently.

Meghan picked up on the sorrowful tone of her voice, and took the time to actually look at her mum.

"Are you ok?"

"What, me? Yes, I suppose so."

Meghan had seen her mum in many states, but rarely so timid. As much as she hated to admit it, she was proud of the strength her mum exhibited every day, even more so since her father left. "Mum, I've been able to tell when you're lying since I was eight!"

"I'm ok, I promise, just a tough day. What are you watching?"

"It's the final cross-party debate."

CJ looked pristine in a finely tailored royal-blue Italian suit. "I think what the honourable gentleman forgets is that, when his party took over, the national debt was a mere quarter of what it stands at today. I don't see how that is evidence of sound financial planning," he stated smoothly.

Deborah had to admit he was impressive, almost better on camera. His authenticity and passion were clear; *maybe he really is one of the few politicians who actually want to make a change*, she thought. She looked down at her daughter, who had silently managed to snuggle up to her mum, not unlike when she was eight. That little girl who was her world, the person she'd worked so hard for. *Can I really give up like this? Is this how my story ends?* She managed to retrieve her phone without disturbing

Meghan. She began to type an email: she would need some help.

Chapter 31

Deadline day

Only twenty-four hours until the election, and among the million and one things CJ had to fit into his day, he now had to do a Presser for the 'Stand with Us' campaign. "I wore the bloody t-shirt at the debate, isn't that enough?" he lamented.

"No, CJ, we've been over this. The debate went well, but we don't want to leave anything to chance. This will get us over the line for sure."

"For sure?" CJ asked.

"For sure."

CJ was unable to disclose the other reason why he was apprehensive about the event. There was a strong chance Jenna would be there. Not only was it her agency running the campaign, but some genius had decided to host it at their office because of 'short notice'. The last thing he needed was Flo getting suspicions about him spending more time with Jenna; that would be an ideal way to calm any election celebrations.

"Will it be quick, at least? It's the day before election day!"

"I know what day it is, CJ, but this has come down as a mandate from Bill. Take it up with him."

He considered the suggestion and decided to let it lie.

***

Jenna couldn't remember the last time she'd felt so much pressure. *What have I signed up to? Perhaps I can go back... no, this was the right thing.* If she needed a sign, her unlikely accomplice was a big one. The video was short but damning; even the most exclusive publicist would be hard pressed to explain away the vitriol. Jenna would have to switch the USB video files at the last moment after the technical run had taken place. Deborah would be preoccupied with CJ and his team but would provide cover for the change-over.

***

CJ checked his phone again. Jenna had returned to ignoring his messages. *Not even a 'good luck', or 'don't worry, I won't be around'.* He wanted to get the next twenty-four hours over with. The campaign trail had taken it out of him completely; a part of him wanted to lose if only so he could rest. Trying to work through all the policy reforms promised in the manifesto would be more complicated than campaigning.

Deborah had finished her introduction speech and welcomed CJ onstage complete with his arm in a decorative sling, which he considered to be overkill. He tried his best not to confuse the bullet points from this speech with the dozens he'd given in the past weeks. "And with that, I would like to share this video, which does a better job than I ever could of explaining the campaign initiatives." The crowd chuckled along to his self-deprecating humour. He fumbled with the remote as he attempted to start the video. "Where's the Netflix button?" he said with a laugh, entertaining the crowd to the last.

Finally, the screen sprang to life. The video showed a recording from an online meeting. Murmurs of confusion began in the crowd; people could not work out what they were looking at, but it was clear that this was not a video about a Diversity and Inclusion political campaign.

The audio boomed: "You see, Deborah, this is not about the people, it is about us and the company. The priorities of the company always come first: we're not a charity. Those D&I initiatives, the internship, local community funds and scholarships do not serve us, so why would we do it?" said Mr Johansson's voice.

Deborah feigned shock. CJ was genuinely surprised, even with his quick wit, unsure what to say or where to look. "I think we have some technical difficulties here, guys," he chuckled awkwardly. The video continued to play on loop, over and over, until one of the aides rushed to pull a series of cables in the hope of cutting power.

Jonathan could not believe what he had just witnessed. They'd been exposed, finally.

"What the fuck is going on here?" CJ whispered to Colleen.

"I don't know, sir."

"Let's get the fuck out of here." He apologised to the press and said they were already late for their next meeting, as they hurried towards the exit.

CJ thought he had experienced the limits of stress humanly possible through the trials and tribulations of the campaign, but there always seemed to be another level. He was on the phone to Colleen as he made it back home, barely stopping to give Flo a kiss on the cheek as he grabbed a breadstick, bottle of whisky, and headed to his study.

"What do you mean there was a problem with the device?" he asked in confusion. He was no engineer, but her explanation made little sense.

"The experts say, not only was a wire removed, but that it was 'inert'. It couldn't have actually blown in any case," Colleen told him.

"But the CCTV showed a guy under my car and then him and another man fleeing. It doesn't make sense?"

"I know, boss, but this is what they're saying. I'll let you know if I hear anything more."

"And on the video from today?" he asked.

"We're working on it, boss. We think we can do something with it," she said with restrained optimism.

"I'm counting on you. We can't fuck this up in the eleventh hour," CJ said, pouring himself a drink.

"It'll be fine, boss," she said.

He clicked off and crunched his breadstick.

He sat taking large gulps of whisky and re-read the text message, still unable to make sense of it: 'Sorry it had to come out like that. We ran out of options, J x'. CJ dialled the number for the fourth time in the last hour, desperately hoping this time he would get through.

The phone rang as Flo entered. "CJ, can you take it easy with the drink? You've been through half a bottle. The last thing you need heading into election day is a nasty hangover."

CJ knew she was right, but continued to sip nonetheless.

"Have you heard anything?" she asked.

He cupped the ringing phone as it rang out. "Colleen said they're working on it. She's hoping to spin it as another attempt from the NBF to sabotage the race," CJ replied, listening to the line. Flo was about to offer some further reassurance when the call connected. "Bill, give me some good news!" CJ demanded, caught up in the stress of the moment.

"My boy, it's all in hand. I've spoken to my contacts

in the media, and they assure me this sabotage attempt will be reported on accurately. The polls show the public is still impressed you haven't dropped out of the race given the bomb attack; people see you as a fearless leader." CJ listened intently, Bill's words alleviating his tension. "Just relax and leave it with me and the team. Try to enjoy this evening with Flo and the kids. There's a good chance that tomorrow things will change forever." Bill clicked off before CJ could respond.

He threw his mobile across his desk and exhaled deeply. He poured himself another whisky.

"Flo, hun, where are you?"

He was alone.

***

The town hall/party headquarters was buzzing with supporters, staff, and reporters; the energy was high and rising despite the early hour of the morning. Only a few constituencies were yet to call and the numbers were looking good. CJ was afforded a couple of hours of reprieve between the late-night rallying and the potential early morning celebrations; it had been a tough road, but he'd made it to the finish line. He sat in a back-room office and watched videos of his kids making a mess as they attempted to make banana bread in the kitchen. Flour, butter, and smashed banana were everywhere as Flo directed proceedings from a safe distance. The joy in their faces warmed his heart. Seeing his family in the kitchen at home brought him peace; he was more than ready to get back to them irrespective of the result.

He heard a calm knock on the door. "Come in," he called without turning around, knowing that only close team members knew where to find him.

"CJ, my boy, congratulations."

He quickly pocketed his phone, and spun around at the familiar voice. "Are we there? Have we crossed the line?"

"It's not official, but my sources tell me it's just a matter of counting the remaining votes now. You are about to become one of the most powerful men in the world. How does it feel - *Prime Minister James?*"

"To be honest, still sounds weird... but I guess I'll have to get used to it," he said with a smile.

"Yes, you will, and a lot more, my young friend, a lot more. Send Flo the good news. Undo your tie, man, you can celebrate now, you did it!"

"It doesn't feel real."

"It is. Oh, and how's everything at home? Still good?"

"Better recently, although I don't know how much Flo is going to love being *First Lady*, at least not the moving part. She's just about got things how she likes them at home."

"She'll love it, trust me."

"I can trust you, right?" CJ asked, far too late.

Bill headed down the corridor to his commandeered office. He checked his phone. The e-mail had arrived with the preliminary breakdown. He opened the door, made his way to his desk and fired up his laptop; as predicted the Conservatives had lost fifteen percent of their vote to the NBF, a significant enough decrease to swing the vote.

***

"Come on, how long am I going to get the silent treatment for, And?" Dale said, walking closely behind his friend. Despite Dale purchasing him a 'sorry' kebab, Andy was still pissed off at Dale. Not only had they messed up a huge job and probably put their lives on the line, they'd also messed up a huge payday.

"And?"

"What?!" Andy replied as they plodded down the quiet side street. "I'm eatin the fuckin kebab, ain't I? What more do you want from me?"

Dale cast his head down. "Just wanna talk again, mate. I'll make it up to you somehow."

"Ten large, Dale, ten fucking large! How are you going to make that up to me? Fuck!" he shouted before throwing the kebab into the street.

"Fuck sake, And, that was a tenner."

"A tenner, a fuckin tenner. Do you not realise what you cost us?"

"Looks like these boys don't know how to keep the neighbourhood clean," a voice called from the darkness, followed by group laughter.

Andy and Dale squinted to try and make out where the noise was coming from. A group of men stepped forward, faces they recognised, guys from the club.

"Alright, Boz, what are you guys up to? Heading over the club?"

"No, actually, we were after a couple of fuck-ups. You know any?" The group laughed again.

"Ha, none of that round here, lads," Dale said, attempting to join in with the laughter, but instead only bringing silence.

Andy noticed a couple of the guys in the back were carrying bats. One other had a pair of brass knuckles, another a glass bottle.

"Robbo sends his best wishes," Boz said as he advanced on them.

"Wait, wait, can't we talk about this?"

"What's to talk about? You fucked up and now you gotta pay the price, good talk?"

"Fuck, we tried."

"Well, Robbo did give you a choice. He said the dumb one can take it all as it was mainly him, or, if you're still feeling like saving the retard, you can have it all yourself? I personally tried to talk him out of it, said you both should get it, him for fucking up and you for always sticking with him."

"Alright, alright, fuck sake, give me a sec."

"Andy, no. It's alright, this was me."

"No, it was me. I forced you along."

"We're in this together, you and me. Like Rocky, right?"

"Look at these two lovers. Time's up!" Boz said.

"Fuck it, just me then," Andy said, walking towards the mob.

"You heard the man," Boz said as the guys stepped forward to meet Andy with a barrage of fists, wood, and glass.

Dale attempted to dive into the mele but was held back by two guys. All he could do was watch his friend get annihilated. "And! And! Stop, fuckin Stop! It's enough, it's enough, he's not fuckin moving," Dale yelled and spat as he was held up off the ground.

After what felt like an eternity, he was released. He ran over to his bloody brother, who was curled up and barely breathing. "You cunts!" he shouted as they wandered off back down the street laughing. He fumbled for his phone, his hand shaking, and struggled to make the emergency call. "Hello! Hello!" his voice trembled. "Emergency, I need an ambulance. There's an emergency on Cauper Street. My friend– my friend is hurt," he stuttered, one arm cradling his friend as he rocked him back and forth. "It'll be ok, And. the ambulance is coming. We've been through worse, right? Haven't we? I promise from now on, no more stupidity from me, no more letting you down, it stops from now, you hear me?" he cried as he spoke.

There was no response.

***

CJ laboured out of the car, his motor skills impaired by a cocktail of happiness, fatigue, and adrenaline.

"We'll be back for you in ninety minutes, Mr. Prime Minister. Shower, get some breakfast in you and then we'll head over to party HQ for the press event," Colleen shouted from the passenger seat.

"Uh huh," he replied as he stooped to pick up a letter. At first glance, it appeared to be a normal piece of post, but he could see it was hand written and without an address, just his name.

"Congratulations, CJ!" Miss Wilbur, his neighbour from three doors down, shouted as she walked her two Spaniels.

"Thanks, Miss Wilbur," he returned as he opened the letter. Again, handwritten, but the paper had jagged edges, as if it had been ripped from a pad or book. He began to read:

CJ, or maybe Prime Minister will be more accurate by the time you get to read this, if you ever do. To be honest, I don't know why I'm even writing this, it won't change anything, but I feel like I have to say something, for her, if not me. The past few months have changed me a lot, I've learned so many things, perhaps the most important being that the world isn't fair, you don't always get what you want, no matter how much you might want it, or how much you try. But, for some, for people like you, it all comes so easy; you get it all, the looks, the humour, the attention, the love. You have an amazing family, a wife that loves you and you're probably now the most powerful man in the country. But it's not enough, you had to have her too. I don't get it. Why? Why do people like you get to have it all and more, and people like me, well...

Ramblings aside, what I want to say, man to man, is I've seen what you do to her, how you hurt her, and it has to stop. If you want her in your life, do it the right way, honourably, not in secret or behind closed doors. She deserves so much more. Love her the way she should be loved.

Jonathan

CJ was dumbfounded by the letter, by what had he just read. *Jonathan, Jonathan:* the name was spinning in his head. He knew it from somewhere, but where? The hotel! Her phone, the advert: it must have been him. He sat on his doorstep, letter loosely held in his limp hand. He knew Jonathan was right; he'd always known that, but he was greedy. CJ knew things had to change, properly this time. The first day as leader of the country was as good a day as any to make the change.

PART 5

Chapter 32

Podding Deb

Following the fallout from the public exposure of Inertia, an unlikely friendship was starting to blossom between Deborah and Jenna, the basis of which was mutual respect and growing understanding of one another. A fruit of this budding connection was Jenna using one of Yami's social media contacts to get Deborah a slot on a popular cultural podcast.

Deborah jostled on a deceptively tight plastic chair as the portable standing lights of the rented studio space shone brightly over the minimal set. She was proud of herself for getting her version of events out there, even if she needed a push from Meghan to come on the show.

Podcast. What a funny word. With all the Tik-toking and Insta-booking, I guess podcasting followed suit.

Tonight, she was a guest on *North and South with Maya and Kiki*, two young Black girls from opposite ends of the city, Tottenham and Croydon. They were delighted to have her on for her behind the scenes expose on all the secrets of the now national Inertia Diversity and Inclusion scandal.

"Deb, girl, I can call you Deb, can't I?" Kiki said energetically

"Um." Had this person, who was young enough to be her daughter, just called her a girl?

Maya didn't wait for a response. "Great, so lovely to have you here with us."

"To talk about the Inertia incident," Kiki seamlessly joined in.

"Or the triple I, the Inertia inclusion incident," Maya quickly followed naturally.

"So, Deb, girl, give us the tea! What went down?"

Deb blushed a little under the spotlight of attention; she was surprised by this reaction as she'd been in the spotlight in one way or another for most of her career. Maybe it was the unfamiliar discussion format, or perhaps it was its salacious nature, but she found herself unusually hesitant. "Well, where do I start?" she opened.

"Start with the good bit," Kiki said.

"No, give us the background, a build up to that, for those in the know."

She began to lay the scenes of a colourful fiction, where she was the shining heroine. "It wasn't easy, as I'm sure you ladies know, being women in business."

"Mmhmm, mmhmm," they agreed.

"Constantly catering to the judgement of men."

"Preach and tell it!" Maya shouted.

"I... *we*," she quickly corrected, "came to the acknowledgement that more needed to be done to serve under-represented communities. You know I've *always* tried to do my bit to support."

"Ah, that's so cool you're sticking up for others."

"It's the right thing to do," she stated matter-of-factly, as if it was clearly the most natural thing in the world.

Meghan rolled her eyes as she watched the live stream on her phone. "Ever the performer, aren't you, Mother."

Deborah began to warm up. "We agreed it was a

330

priority and then I said, even though I'm well-read in matters of diversity, you can always learn more, right?"

The girls nodded in response.

"Why not get in an 'expert'," she said with air quotes and a sarcastic flick of her eyes, "who can give me a little tune up and educate the rest of the team."

"Right, right, good idea," Kiki said.

"And then, working closely with our expert, I led the development of the strategy and appointed a Champion, a person of colour, of course, to help lead our efforts. But, not long after that, we started to run into issues. While I and our Champion were passionate about making meaningful and impactful change, the board – the old White men," she clarified, "were determined to block me at every attempt. They wanted to use the initiatives only to serve the interests of the company. They had no interest in genuinely serving the communities we had promised to help."

Jenna almost choked on her plantain crisps. This was not how she remembered things.

"And this is where it got really challenging. I was heavily pressured to follow the company direction, meaning I had to go against my natural instinct and focus on the more self-serving campaigns and actions. I even tried to bring in more diversity to help balance things," she said emphatically.

Roger shook his head as he sipped his red wine.

"But then it went too far. It was the 'Stand with Us' campaign, initiated after the attempt on Prime Minister CJ's life, and that was the limit for me. I couldn't do it anymore. So, I decided to facilitate the exposé."

"Oh, so you were the mastermind behind that, too?" Maya asked.

"I was indeed."

Jenna snorted in derision.

"Someone had to make a stand. I'm not saying I'm a hero, but."

"Well, let me say it for you," Kiki chimed in, "You are!"

A beaming smile appeared across Deborah's face: this podcast wasn't so difficult after all.

***

"So, you didn't want to meet in the room?" he began in cheeky fashion. She gave him a testy look. "I'm joking, J, I'm joking. I know this isn't that... it's not that, is it?"

"CJ," she replied, rolling her eyes.

"Ok, I get it, turns out being PM doesn't change you that much."

"I wanted to meet here as a reminder... It doesn't matter, I just wanted to say congratulations and... and... draw a line."

Two middle aged women bustled passed the security detail. "Prime Minister James, we thought that was you. We wanted to come over and say congratulations personally. Of course, we both voted for you."

CJ switched into his public-facing mode, shooting his Hollywood smile. "Why thank you, it's amazing to have the support of two young ladies like yourselves."

They cooed in glee at the compliment as they toddled off. Jenna experienced a mix of cringe and awe at his ability to *handle* people, and how easily he could switch it on; she tried not to think he could have been anything other than genuine with her, but deep down she knew it was unlikely.

CJ switched his focus back to Jenna. "It's ok, J, I get it, and actually I wanted to say something too, but didn't know how. Things have been really good with Flo and the kids, plus I won't be able to slip away as easily," he stopped himself. "Listen, I need to apologise. I wasn't very statesmanlike in my handling of things."

She agreed.

"But it was… it was real for me."

This was candour for CJ, something Jenna had rarely seen in him. If she could have seen this vulnerability before, maybe things could have been different. *No*, she told herself, *stay focused*. The objective of the meeting was to end things.

"It means a lot to hear you say that," she admitted.

"So, do you have time for one last drink with the PM?"

"Just one," said Jenna, trying her best not to smile.

***

Across town, Roger arrived back from work, opening the door of his compact two-bedroom family home. He was met with the enthusiastic embrace of his young daughter, Stephanie, who as usual had a picture ready to share with him.

"What have we got today?" he asked warmly.

"Today we have safari!" she declared proudly, showcasing the selection of wild animals, including elephants, giraffes, and zebras, the picture full of vibrant colours.

"It's beautiful," he said, giving her a kiss. "Is there room on the fridge?" he asked, knowing the fridge was covered. She shook her head innocently. "Well, we're going to have to start a scrapbook," he declared.

"What's a scrapbook?" she asked.

"I'm going to show you. I used to have one, too."

They headed into the kitchen. His mum was sitting by the stove stirring a pot, her mobility getting increasingly worse with time. "Good day, son?" she asked.

"Yes, Mum," he replied, getting a drink from the fridge.

"Good. Hope you're settling in better now. I know you will do well there," she said confidently.

He poured himself some water and surveyed the small kitchen. There was barely enough room for the three of them. They needed somewhere bigger, especially with his mum getting older. "I *am* going to do well there." *I have to*.

Chapter 33

A Change of Climate

"Alright, relax, it's only a minor setback. We already have the tabloids spinning it as an alt-left attack against the company. Social media is taking a bit longer to tame," Oscar Jones, the CFO and current acting CEO, said to the Executive Committee.

"I think people are sick of all this race stuff. The mainstream public, the average man on the street, is sick of being made to feel bad for being White. It's mad when you think about it. So, ideas, people, ideas: a diversion, a new approach. How do we make this a win?"

"An apology?" a member of the Committee said.

"No, not an apology. We can't appear to be on the back foot here."

"How about we change the conversation? Change the focus?"

"Go on," Oscar encouraged.

"There's something that's been gaining traction. It has a wider reach than the whole Diversity and Inclusion stuff, and the beauty of it is even less tangible."

"I'm listening, I'm listening."

"The environment... hear me out. We focus on sustainability, the 'climate crisis', saving the world for all!"

"It's perfect. Why help only minorities when we can

help everyone, without helping anyone!"

"Exactly, totally intangible. How can anyone complain when it's impossible to measure the impact we're having? Full commitment, zero risk."

***

"So, can I move some of this... stuff?" Jenna asked gingerly as she examined Jonathan's messy desk.

"What do you mean?"

She cast her hand across the desk. "Exhibit A." She pointed to a model of a man with a staff, large hat and cloak.

"What? No, that's Wizard of Illumindor. That definitely stays."

"You'll need space to set up the office somewhere in this massive apartment," she joked.

"I know, but he stays."

"And this?" she pointed to another figurine.

"Maybe leave that job to me," Jonathan said defensively.

"Excited about the new venture, fresh start? Nervous?" she asked.

"Nervous," he confessed.

"You're going to do great now you'll have full creative freedom, no more Deborah or Roger holding you back."

"And you're going to help with the admin stuff?"

"Of course, all of that and the marketing. And Freddy said he was going to push some clients your way?"

"Yep, a couple of side projects off the books. They're happy with the rates and genuinely interested in supplier diversity. And I have a little something for you," Jonathan said with a mischievous smile on his face.

336

"What's that?" she replied with curiosity.

"Don't worry, it's good. Close your eyes."

"Come on, I'm not big on surprises." She closed her eyes.

Jonathan pulled a folder from underneath his desk, and flicked through carefully, trying to not make too much noise that might ruin the surprise. He pulled a sheet from the folder. "Ok, open your eyes."

Jenna wasn't quite sure what she was looking at initially, but then she saw the tagline below the intricate design. "You didn't? That is beautiful." She looked for more superlatives but was speechless. "You did this for me?"

Jonathan nodded, more than satisfied with her response. "You gotta start your first fair off right. I can send you the artwork and you can add it to the banners and flyers."

She jumped across the room and embraced him in a tight squeeze.

"Easy, easy," he said as a tear dropped down her cheek.

***

"We fully regret the incident that took place at the time of Prime Minister James' important electoral speech. The footage played in no way reflects the views of Inertia, our parent organisation, partners, or clients. We reject racism in all forms and are tirelessly committed to D&I efforts in all areas of work we do. Mr. Johansson has been suspended pending further investigation." Mr Jones the acting CEO read. "We have time for a couple of questions. Yes, you."

"What about Deborah Tate?"

"Miss Tate is a valued member of the organisation.

We've made a very generous offer to keep her, including progression, which we truly hope she accepts. Next question?"

"Is suspension enough? Should he not be terminated with immediate effect? I can imagine if another marginalised group was impacted in this way, the punishment would be more severe?"

Mr. Jones was stumped by the question. He removed his glasses and cleaned the bottle-shaped lens as he bought some time. "As I said, we stand against all forms of racism. Time is needed to properly assess the incident and make a fair adjudication about our next steps. Apologies, that's all I have time for." He quickly made his way off stage among yells from the audience with more questions about follow-up actions.

***

Jenna had never seen the academy hall quite like this. The space, usually filled with adrenaline-fuelled teenagers being chased and corralled by tired adult mentors, had transformed. It was a bit like a cool and culturally attuned Christmas fair. The different stalls showcasing wares and services from various Black businesses warmed her spirit. She was desperate to take a beat to enjoy the manifestation of her first ever Black Business Fair. After all the planning, hard work and dreaming, it was here, it was real. But the reality of creating something like this was the amount of hard work it took, and the hard work didn't stop on the day, With this being the first fair, she had to be meticulously hands-on. Even with the help of Yami, Jonathan, and Kwame, there was still so much to do to ensure everyone was set up and needs were met.

"Any more extension leads?" the owner of a shea butter stall asked Yami.

Yami shouted, "Sis, any more extension leads?"

"I might have a couple spare in the back there. Everyone was told to bring their own extension leads," Jenna said to nobody and everybody.

Slowly but surely, people began to wander into the hall. It seemed that Yami's social media marketing campaign, and some more traditional local flyering, had paid off. It probably didn't hurt that CJ had mentioned the event on the party website as a great example of local economic empowerment. However, he wouldn't have time to attend the inaugural event, kept away by a Middle-Eastern peace conference.

Jonathan studied Kwame, the 'new guy', carefully as he helped a shorter lady put up her stall sign.

"Thank you, that looks great," she said, but Jonathan was entranced in his observation.

"You good?" Yami asked, watching the voyeur.

"Huh? Yeah, no problem."

"Guess it's a bit awkward, following the whole library love affair?"

"I'm sure he's a good guy. She seems happy at least."

"She is. I've not seen her like this since... since, well, anyway."

Jonathan knew all too well. "Yeah, at least she's happy," he repeated slowly.

***

Jonathan was helping Jenna with some final registration numbers: she had ended up setting up extra stalls due to some last-minute additions.

"Who's selling the kenkey then?" a voice called from behind them.

They spun around.

Yami was surprised to see a person of colour with

such a well-spoken accent, and she was confused as to why he was asking for kenkey.

Jonathan smiled, pleasantly surprised to see the unexpected guest. "How did you even find out about this place?" he asked.

"And how did you find out about kenkey?" Jenna asked.

"Just because I read *The Times*, it doesn't mean I don't have social media, and I came across this flyer on my way to a friend's house."

"You have friends around here?" Jenna said, almost unable to deal with this string of shocking revelations.

Roger returned a smug look, exceedingly satisfied with Jenna's surprise. "I wanted to come and give my people some support. Anything wrong with that?"

"Not at all, happy to have you here. We don't have any kenkey, but I think we have some gari over here. Come with me," Jenna said, leading Roger to a stall at the end of the hall.

***

"You're doing the right thing, Prime Minister," several cabinet ministers offered as they left him alone with his thoughts, the budget paper and a pen in his hand poised for signature. *This is it*, he thought, *the reality of being in charge*. He laid the pen down on the desk, before thumbing through the heavy budget document; the action more for effect than anything else. He'd spent weeks going back and forth with MPs from both sides of the aisle, his cabinet ministers and experts. The budget that appeased the largest number of people didn't satisfy his own wants, nor the change he hoped to bring through public services. The first Black Prime Minister didn't come to be the saviour of the underserved, but instead perpetuated the chronic dynamic of disproportionate resourcing. He could hear Bill's voice in his head: 'this is what's needed to make history'. What history would he make? He signed the document with a quick flurry of his pen, as if he were ripping off a plaster. He threw the pen on the table and poured himself a large whisky. He sipped slowly and did what he liked to do most of all - think of Jenna.

Epilogue

'Beep, beep' went the sound of the fork lift truck as Dale tried to see over the stack of solar panels.

"Watch it!" yelled Andy from the factory floor as Dale whizzed by, barely in control of the vehicle.

CJ stood with scissors ready to open the new solar panel factory, one of the leading examples of the new administration's efforts to revitalise the domestic economy through upskilling workers in areas of new industrial development. "It's with great pride that I open this brand-new state of the art manufacturing facility here in the heart of Essex. This site is particularly important because, it is not only testament to the new era of British manufacturing, it is also an example of rejuvenation of our previous manufacturing heritage, with this being a former Jaguar production site. We have been able to help many in the area develop new skills and new careers. This initiative also supports our 2030 sustainability targets."

Dale and Andy were fortunate recipients of the programme, having secured not only training but full-time roles.

"What else have we got on today?" CJ asked as he and his entourage strode at pace to the car.

"You have a meeting with the Belgian prime minister after lunch, then you have a budget review with the OBR, and then the dinner with the commonwealth leaders,"

Colleen replied.

"Any chance I get to have dinner with my wife and family this week?" CJ asked in slight jest.

"Hm, I could maybe try and move a few things around, but it's a tough week," she confessed.

"Another tough week."

***

One of the challenges of having a home office was getting out, so Jonathan appreciated Tuesdays when he had to leave to leave his house and be social. Tuesdays were his days at the mentor programme. While he was fast falling in love with giving back and helping others, there was the added benefit of getting to see Jenna. Even though things were platonic, they'd grown to become good friends, important in one another lives.

***

Dale and Andy headed to The Swan, a new watering hole not too far from the factory. The pair were satisfied with a hard day's work and looking forward to a well-earned pint, when a faded pale blue transit van screeched to a halt next to them.

The side door crashed open. "Alright fellas, long time no see, the gaffer wants a word. In, now!" Andy and Dale shared an uneasy look. "I said in! Now!"

They acquiesced and climbed into the van, before it screeched away down the street. They arrived at an abandoned warehouse, where they were pushed through large double doors. The space was filled with crates of different sizes. In the corner was a make-shift office with Robbo sat at a desk, cigarette in mouth, scrawling ferociously on a notepad. They sat in silence in the fold out chairs opposite his desk and waited. Dale's palms began to sweat.

Robbo slowly lifted his head. "Alright lads, got a job for you."

Afterword

More To Do

As always, my first hope is that the book has been an entertaining, enjoyable, and enlightening read. Beyond that, the goal of highlighting challenges of superficial engagement with Diversity and Inclusion (or Diversity, Equity and Inclusion) are at the core of this story. I believe it's possible to commit to principles of D&I in an authentic and meaningful way, which includes supporting these efforts with significant resources. Building a better, fairer society is not an easy task, and was never going to be achieved in the short period of furore generated by George Floyd's death and the subsequent BLM movement.

Things we need to consider in the hope of doing better and effecting change:

Embedding D&I in your company's core values – D&I becoming mission critical, not peripheral

D&I activities and initiatives are often conducted as an adjunct to traditional business functions. The peripheral nature of this kind of positioning means it is easier to turn a blind eye, and not follow through on any commitments in the space because there will be no impact on day-to-day operations or the success or failure of the business. By embedding D&I practices, goals, and achievements into the core strategy of the business, investment, engagement, and commitment naturally increase, instead of being an elective afterthought.

Genuine resourcing

Another important approach is genuine and committed resourcing. D&I work is often left to well-meaning, but usually overworked employees who take on ambassador roles in addition to their already stressful day jobs. The organisation's lack of willingness to commit to proper resourcing in the area means that staff members have to become self-trained experts, as well as finding time to conduct activities on top of their daily roles. Ironically, many companies see this as some form of benevolence – the grace of allowing employees to take on extra work that will add value to the company, for free.

Behaviour Based Training

Ensuring training includes behaviour-based modelling, particularly from senior leaders, is important. Informative learning sessions without real-world changed behaviours is not impactful. Are Senior Leaders and others in the organisation truly modelling?

The Long Haul

The type of change and positive impact that meaningful D&I initiatives are trying to achieve should be large in scale and as such will take a lot of time and effort to achieve. This work is typically about attempting to readdress centuries of societal imbalance, not something that will be achieved overnight. The duration of commitment long past the relatively brief spotlight created by George Floyd was always going to be indicative, and was always going to be a simple way to differentiate the superficial from the truly committed.

Multi-tasking all the world's ills

Towards the end of the book the company make a switch of their superficial virtue-signalling attempts towards the environment. For clarity, this is by no means to undervalue the importance of the environment and sustainability initiatives; on the contrary, these issues are of huge importance. However, we need to be able to tackle multiple issues of importance, and not neglect one in favour of another – we need to avoid scenarios of the 'new favourite toy', avoid transient engagement.

More Black People

Through the story I attempted to take a satirical look at the issues of D&I, the lack of understanding, lack of care, and darker side of self-serving opportunism. To a degree it is tongue-in-cheek, but also, very close to things I've witnessed first-hand and further afield. I also wanted to showcase the complexity of people. None of us is perfect and things are rarely Black and White. I believe the average person wants to do *good* things, they want to help, but are often too busy and stressed, or, worse, disincentivised to do so. When looking at making meaningful large-scale change, I think part of the challenge is how we connect, relate, and subsequently bring people along. Through my writing I try to show the breadth of people within the Black community, not just to showcase the reality, but to challenge the stereotypical tropes that are often projected in mainstream media. This diversity naturally includes a diversity of thought and experience, varied from the monolithic view that is often placed upon the community. Jonathan, for example, doesn't fit the classic western Black male persona: he has to go on his own journey of enlightenment.

In closing

In 2020, when all the furore, hype, and attention was on issues of D&I, I and many others were painfully aware of the potential for this to be a short fuse and flash in the pan, if nothing more than because history had shown us there never had been a significant level of interest in the representation or inclusion of people of colour in a broad scale meaningful way; so the supposition that the world had suddenly transformed to a place of post-racial morality was surprising and unlikely. To unpick and repair the pain and injustice of the past was always going to take time, commitment, and patience; again difficult things to ask of anyone, particularly those in power, who were additionally being asked to share some of what they had. The result almost three years on is one of some progress, but there is a long way to go. Sadly, but unsurprisingly, the intense anti-racism flame that once ignited the world has faded to an ember. Many companies have failed to fulfil promises in the space, with D&I work left to well-intentioned employees to figure out in addition to their day jobs, with small budgets and little support from senior leaders. Perhaps to be expected, along with the fading enthusiasm from those in power to hold themselves accountable and steer organisations to a place of 'doing better', is the shift to a shiny new goal of virtue-signalling which, while well deserving, shouldn't come at the cost of the important societal issue of D&I.

Acknowledgements

I would like to thank my friends and family for their continued support during my writing process. Your encouragement has been critical to me reaching this point. As always, this book is for you all as much as it is for me.

I would like to thank Stuart Debar and SRL Publishing for taking a chance with me and this story. This issue could be considered niche, only impacting a small group of those in the West; yet Stuart recognised the importance of the topic and the value of the story to an undeserved community – for that I am grateful.

A special mention to those who showed so much belief in me, this story, and beyond. Those who wanted me to succeed, perhaps even more than I wanted it; that love and energy is truly appreciated.

SRL Publishing don't just publish books, we also do our best in keeping this world sustainable. In the UK alone, over 77 million books are destroyed each year, unsold and unread, due to overproduction and bigger profit margins.

Our business model is inherently sustainable by only printing what we sell. While this means our cost price is much higher, it means we have minimum waste and zero returns. We made a public promise in 2020 to never overprint our books for the sake of profit.

We give back to our planet by calculating the number of trees used for our products so we can then replace them. We also calculate our carbon emissions and support projects which reduce CO_2. These same projects also support the United Nations Sustainable Development Goals.

The way we operate means we knowingly waive our profit margins for the sake of the environment. Every book sold via the SRL website plants at least one tree.

To find out more, please visit
<u>*www.srlpublishing.co.uk/responsibility*</u>